Ian stared at Moida.

Her head barely reached his shoulder and yet she had set herself in combat with him. She was very pretty, and usually he could handle women, pretty or otherwise.

He wondered, with a sudden quirk of humor, what would happen if he kissed her and told her not to be a fool. He had solved diplomatic problems in that way before, and the idea of kissing Moida was by no means unpleasant. Her lips were sweetly curved—her looks grew on one, Ian thought. She was nearly as lovely in her own unmade-up way as his fiancée, Lynette. He felt almost guilty at the idea. How could this intrusive stranger compare with adorable Lynette?

Only later did Ian realize that she didn't compare with Lynette at all. She was different and lovely and he wanted her desperately!

Also in Pyramid Books
by
BARBARA CARTLAND

BLUE
HEATHER

Barbara Cartland

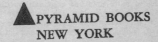
PYRAMID BOOKS
NEW YORK

BLUE HEATHER

A PYRAMID BOOK

First printing, September 1973

ISBN 0-515-03162-3

Pyramid Books are published by Pyramid Communications., Inc. Its trademarks, consisting of the word "Pyramid" and the portrayal of a pyramid, are registered in the United States Patent Office.

Pyramid Communications., Inc., 919 Third Avenue, New York, New York 10022

CONDITIONS OF SALE

1

The car rounded the corner and the coast line lay ahead stretching away into a grey horizon.

The long stretch of deserted sands was gold against the deep blue and emerald of the changing sea and in contrast the moors, rising high against the cloud-flecked sky, were solid and stalwart in their purple splendour.

It was so beautiful that Ian drew a deep breath.

He had forgotten how lovely the Highlands of Scotland could be—the Highlands in August with the grouse flighting low over the heather.

It was fifteen years since he had been here, and now that he was back again, he had all the thrill and rapture of a homecoming. He accelerated without realising it, impatient to reach his destination.

Fifteen years—it was a long time and he himself had been fifteen at the time.

He remembered driving to Skaig along this road with his mother. He could remember, too, returning from Skaig with her voice high and shrill beside him as she reiterated over and over again that she had been insulted.

He had been frightened of his great-uncle—indeed Duncan McCraggan had been an extremely frightening old man—but he had not felt insulted by his brusqueness and he had found it hard to sympathise with his mother then in what she was sure now had been her quite reasonable indignation.

He was sorry that he had never seen Great-Uncle Duncan again. The old man had been impressive with his white hair, beak-like nose and the sharply-etched lines of his face, which had given him a patriarchal expression.

Ian had found it difficult to talk to him and even more difficult to answer the sharp, inquisitive questions that his great-uncle had barked at him, but at the same time he had admired his relative.

Indeed Great-Uncle Duncan had been exactly what might have been expected of a Scottish Laird, Chieftain of his Clan, living in a half-ruined ancestral castle.

And now the castle was his!

For the first time since he had heard that his uncle was dead, Ian felt a sense of responsibility. He had been told the news when he was in Malaya. The letter had reached him three weeks late and there was nothing he could do about it.

He had not fully realised then what his great-uncle's death meant to him personally.

He had been so busy these past years that he had almost forgotten about Great-Uncle Duncan sitting in the fastness of his Highland eyrie like some forgotten eagle on a mountain crag.

It was months later that a letter from his mother told him what he should have remembered himself.

"I ran into your Cousin Isabel in Harrods a few days ago," she wrote: *"She looked more like a scatty hen than usual but she gushed a lot about you and said how wonderful it was that you were now Chieftain of the Clan, which reminded me that there is a letter here for you about Skaig Castle. I suppose sometime you will have to go up there and see what your uncle has left you beside the ruins!"*

Ian had smiled at the letter at the time. He sensed beneath the casual words that his mother still smarted with indignation against Great-Uncle Duncan.

Years might have passed, his great-uncle might be dead, but Beatrice McCraggan was not a woman to forgive or forget an insult.

She had been spoiled all her life. The daughter of an American railroad millionaire, the fairies had laid down a red carpet for her from the moment she was born and had stuffed her mouth not with one silver spoon but with a whole canteen of them.

She was pretty, she was intelligent, and she had so much money that Ian had long ago given up trying to keep count of her many possessions and investments.

Wherever his mother went, she had a fleet of secretaries, lawyers and factotums of all sorts and conditions who dealt with her and her affairs.

What was more, she was perfectly capable of commanding and keeping in subjection her private army, so why should her son worry about anything but his own career?

Beatrice, if she had known of Ian's private thoughts, would have applauded them. It was the sort of good, sound horse sense which she found commendable in theory and extremely irritating in practice.

They certainly would not have surprised her, because she had long ago given up being surprised at anything Ian thought or did.

The only battle she had ever lost was that of not being allowed to bring up her only child in what she considered was a sensible, modern manner.

Ian's father, a mild, easy-going man, very much infatuated with his pretty wife, had given in to her on everything but this.

Ian, he had said, should be given a conventional English education, and he was not going to have any son of his imbued with American ideas.

Beatrice had argued, but she might as well have had a controversy with the Sphinx; and eventually she was clever—and feminine—enough to know when to accept the inevitable.

Ian was sent to a preparatory school when he was

7

eight and to Eton, where his father had been educated, just before he was fourteen. His mother made periodic departures for America, but Ian did not accompany her.

Instead he spent his holidays in the English countryside, riding, shooting and fishing with his father, and only vaguely aware in his infancy that all the comforts and sport which he enjoyed were paid for by American dollars.

It was only when he grew up that he realised how bitterly his mother resented his independence of her, and then it was too late.

He had already settled in his own mind what he wished to make of his life and the fact that he had a great deal of money behind him was entirely incidental to his ambitions.

The last years of the war had given him the opportunity to show both his intelligence and his bravery, and when peace came he was already spoken of as a brilliant young man.

The following years saw him travelling all over the world from conference to conference, from trouble area to troubled area, being consulted and his advice listened to by men far older than himself and often far more experienced.

Officially he was attached to the War Office, but his powers extended far beyond those which were granted to him by rank and badge.

In Mayfair it was whispered that he was in a very secret part of the Secret Service. In the Foreign Office his name was mentioned frequently when there was an extra difficult piece of diplomacy to be attempted.

It was not surprising, therefore, that a few weeks after his thirtieth birthday Ian McCraggan suddenly felt very tired.

He had been rushed from one hemisphere to another in fast, specially-charted aeroplanes, trains, ships and armoured cars.

He had once, he reckoned, talked no less than six languages in an afternoon and finished up with a three-hour session with interpreters, which invariably made him feel frustrated and irritated because they were such slow and cumbersome mouthpieces for what he had to convey.

Even then he would not have applied for his long-delayed leave if he had not made a quite elementary and extremely foolish mistake in a report he sent in on his last mission.

His Chief pointed it out to him and laughed, but to Ian it was no laughing matter.

"Good God, Sir! Did I really write that?" he asked.

"Don't look so tragic about it," the Chief had answered, "there's no damage done."

"It might have caused an international incident," Ian said.

His Chief looked at him reflectively.

"When did you last have a holiday?" he asked. "No, don't tell me, I know the answer. It's time you took some time off. I know the Powers-That-Be want you to go to Japan, but it can wait. Take a month, or better still, two months; and while you are away, remember that you are young. Get drunk, get married, do any damn' thing that you like, but forget to look so serious about things."

Ian thought that his Chief must have been drinking; but when he got home to his flat and sat down in his chair, he realised that he was indeed very tired.

He had not had a moment for relaxation, to think of himself or even to enjoy himself for weeks, months, or was it years?

He began to ask himself when it was that he had last taken a girl out to dinner; and then, when he tried to think back, he began to laugh and picked up the telephone to speak to his mother.

They had long ago decided that they should not live together, but only as near as possible.

Beatrice had taken two super-luxury flats in Grosvenor Square, in the same building but on different floors. They could meet as often as they wished, but their

9

domestic arrangements did not clash one with the other.

It was at the moment that Ian spoke to his mother that things began to happen. He told her that he had got a holiday and she gave a cry of delight.

"How wonderful, darling! And it could not be at a better time. It has been the most amusing Season there has been since the war."

"Season for what?" Ian asked.

"Don't be so ridiculous. You know quite well what I mean by 'the Season'."

"You don't mean debs, the Eton and Harrow, and Henley?" Ian asked in tones of horror.

His mother laughed.

"Come to dinner and I will tell you what I mean."

Ian had gone to dinner and had met Lynette. There had been a crowd of other people there too. His mother's ideas of entertaining were always on a lavish scale; but afterwards he could only remember Lynette, with her wide, blue eyes and soft, ash-blonde hair which framed the loveliness of her oval face.

"I began to think you were a legend," she told him softly in a voice which somehow seemed to vibrate and gave a curious emphasis, an almost breathless poignancy to everything she said.

"Why?" he asked.

"Because one always heard about you and yet you never appeared. Your mother gives the most marvellous parties, everybody comes to them—everybody except you."

"I am here now," he suggested.

"Yes, I know."

Her eyes said strange things to him. He had looked into many women's eyes in his time, usually with some reason behind his interest other than because she was a woman.

He had learned very early that the intrigues of a foreign country may be disclosed in a soft whisper or learnt when one rested one's head on the same pillow.

10

There had been women—yes, many women—in Ian's life; but now he could think only of himself and not what else a woman had to offer him besides the invitation of two soft red lips.

"Let's go and dance somewhere," he suggested to Lynette, and was surprised at himself because he thought he was too tired to do anything but go to bed.

"Will your mother mind?" Lynette asked.

It was a purely conventional question. They both knew they could do what they wanted to, and yet there was something exciting in the thought that they were playing truant.

It seemed quite an adventure to a man whose life had been one long, desperate adventure for the past five years, to slip out into the warm darkness of Grosvenor Square, to search for a taxi to take them to a night club.

At a table lit with a rose-shaded light, Ian laid his hand on Lynette's.

"Tell me about yourself," he commanded her, and then felt that words were unnecessary.

Lynette's eyes meeting his were eloquent. Lynette's lips, full and crimson, were a silent invitation. He wanted to kiss her without further preliminaries. He wanted to hold her soft, sweetly-curved body in his arms.

"I've always wanted to meet you," Lynette was speaking very softly.

"And now you have. . . ."

He waited for her answer.

"I'm glad . . . and you?"

He paused before answering and her eyes fell before his.

"I'm afraid to say how glad I am."

"Afraid?"

She was surprised at the word.

"In case I say too much—and frighten you . . . or, worse still, make you angry with me!"

Lynette drew a deep breath.

"I don't think I should be . . . angry."

11

The band was playing an underlying harmony to their rising emotions, the fragrance of her hair, their nearness as they danced.

It was a magical, enchanted evening.

Ian, motoring along the coast road in the extreme north of the County of Sutherland, wished now that Lynette was with him.

He suddenly wanted to show her this part of the country, show it to her with all the pride of a man revealing to someone he loves the place to which he belongs.

This was where his roots were, this was the stock from which he had sprung. It was funny, he thought, that for so many years he had hardly given a thought to Skaig Castle or to his great-uncle and yet now he was acutely conscious of coming home.

If Lynette had been with him, he thought, he would have told her the names of the mountains whose tops could just be seen in the distance rising high over the moorlands.

He passed over the grey stone bridge which spanned the River Brora; another few miles and he would see the silver water of the Skaig flowing into the sea.

At the top of a narrow strath stook Skaig Castle, built on the side of the loch in a strategic position from which to view the approach of the enemy.

There the Clan McCraggan, once strong and powerful, had for centuries defended its possessions and defied the envy and hatred of its less-fortunate neighbours.

Defeated and laid low by treachery of the most outrageous sort in the sixteenth century, only a handful of McCraggans remained today. But their story was to be found in the history of Scotland; and with a glow of warmth Ian thought of the position which awaited him as Chieftain of the Clan.

Yes, Lynette should have been with him, he felt. He would like to have driven up to the castle with her, to have let her share with him the pride of being able to say,

"This is mine, my very own by tradition and right."

How proud his father would have been, he added as an afterthought. Ian had never underestimated the advantages which his mother's money had brought him, and yet he was insular enough to feel glad that this inheritance was owed entirely to his father.

He had often sensed beneath his father's innate reserve a feeling of discomfort and even embarrassment that he must live on his wife's money. He had a small income of his own, but as Beatrice had once said in a temper, it was not really enough to keep him in cigarettes.

Euan McCraggan had never complained. He had married Beatrice Stevenson because he loved her, and had refused to regret it; but Ian had known that the humiliating feeling of dependence had been there and he rejoiced now that Skaig and all that the possession of it meant was coming to him from his father's blood.

It was, however, typical of his mother that she should have discovered that there was a barony in abeyance which went with the Lairdship of Skaig.

After Great-Uncle Duncan's death she turned up the family papers which Ian's father kept unlisted, bundled together in a despatch box. From these Beatrice deduced that the arms had not been registered for two centuries and that the barony could be revived if application were made to the proper quarter.

"Lynette would like a title, darling," she said to Ian, and Ian could not resist replying: "And so would you!"

"If only I had known about it when your poor father was alive!" Beatrice sighed. "But it would have been no use, of course, because your great-uncle was entitled to it, as head of the family. If he had married and had children, it could not have been yours."

"I haven't got it yet," Ian said. "These things take time and there may be all sorts of snags we don't know about."

13

"It is quite definitely there in the family tree, and in the family papers," Beatrice said positively. "I have discovered that the right person to apply to is the Lord Lyon King of Arms in Edinburgh. We will consult him on our way up."

When Beatrice made up her mind to do a thing, it was seldom any use arguing with her; and Ian, occupied with Lynette, was content to let his mother do what she wished.

They had all motored to Edinburgh and there Ian had left them and come on ahead to prepare the castle for them.

"I want you to love Skaig, darling," Ian had said to Lynette before he left.

"I'm sure I shall love it—if you do." she answered, but he felt her reply was said too lightly.

He would not admit, even to himself, that he was afraid in case Lynette did not like Scotland and wanted only to live in London.

"I'll make you love it," Ian said fiercely.

Lynette looked at him in surprise, but anything she might have said was lost against the eagerness of his lips.

They were hard and possessive, and his kisses were those of a man determined to be master.

"Ian! Don't, darling!"

Lynette was trying to push him away from her, but he laughed at her efforts.

"I'll make you do what I want," he teased her, and weakly she capitulated to his insistence.

Ian had reached the point where he turned off the coast road up the Skaig strath before he remembered that there might be some difficulty in getting into the castle.

"I can't think what has happened at Skaig," his mother had said to him. "My last letter to the Factor, Mr. Scott, was returned marked 'Gone away'."

"Who is Mr. Scott? Should I know about him?" Ian enquired.

"It was he who wrote to tell us of your uncle's death," Beatrice replied. "At least, he wrote to you and your secretary brought it to me as you were in the East and no one could be quite certain where at that particular moment.

"I sent a wreath, of course, and then I wrote to Mr. Scott and told him to let us know exactly what arrangements were being made about the castle. I informed him that you would be away for some time and asked if there were any servants to be paid and what money he required for this."

"Surely Great-Uncle Duncan's solicitors were seeing to such things?" Ian enquired.

"No, your uncle's solicitor had been Mr. Scott's father, a legal man who was qualified. When he died, young Scott carried on as Factor to the Estate. No other solicitor was appointed."

"Then everything is in this man Scott's hands?"

"I gather so. That is what worried me. He wrote asking for some money for the keepers' wages. I sent him a thousand pounds. I had an acknowledgment, but no other information. After two months had gone by, I wrote again and that was when my letter was returned with 'Gone away' on it."

"I suppose there is a caretaker at the castle?" Ian suggested.

"I really have no idea," his mother replied. "I waited for you to come home and see to it for yourself. After all, I had rather a lot of things to see to. You couldn't expect me to go all that way could you?"

"Of course not," Ian replied.

If he had been in England, he would of course have gone to his great-uncle's funeral. As it was, it was nobody's fault that he could not be represented. It was only worrying to wonder what had happened between his uncle's death in January and August—seven months later.

The road up the strath was twisting and had a rough surface and he was obliged to go more slowly.

There was plenty of water in the river, he noticed, an unusual amount for this time of the year, and he thought that the prospects of catching a salmon looked good.

He remembered his great-uncle's obstinacy in that he would never let the fishing on the River Skaig, even when he himself had grown too old to fish.

Autocratic and obstinate as a mule when it suited him, Duncan McCraggan had sworn that he would have no damned Sassenach fishing in his river; and if there were any Scots rich enough to pay the rent that he would ask for the privilege, he was damned if he wanted to meet them.

So the Laird of Skaig had fished his own river with his friends. The poachers must have had a good time with it these past months, Ian thought, remembering some of the reports he had seen in the newspapers about poaching in the Highlands and the questions that had been asked in Parliament.

Today, the long reaches of the river were empty of fishermen; and as the road wound beside him, climbing higher and higher up the strath, Ian had his first view of the castle.

Gaunt and blackened with age, it stood on the edge of the loch, the moors stretching away behind it and a small wood of dark firs protecting it from the north winds.

Only the ruins could be seen from the roadway. Part of the castle had been rebuilt at the end of the eighteenth century, but this was round the other side.

The few scattered houses which constituted the village of Skaig were at the foot of a long steep incline which was the driveway up to the castle. Three shops, a manse, a school, a number of ugly grey houses and stone crofts, and a pompous villa, which Ian remembered housed the doctor, constituted the village.

There were also half a dozen new bungalows, he

16

noticed, which had been built since he was last here, but otherwise the place was unchanged.

He hesitated for a moment, wondering whether to stop and ask questions as to who was at the castle and what had happened to Mr. Scott, and then decided against it. He would go first to the castle.

He had a sudden longing to see it again. It had seemed romantic and magnificent to him as a schoolboy and he had been half-afraid it would have lost some of its magic.

The waters of the loch were very blue and in contrast the castle looked dark and foreboding.

The iron gates to the drive were rusty and sadly in need of a coat of paint; one of them was off its hinges, and the stone newel from one of the gate posts lay shattered in pieces on the ground.

Ian turned in at the gates; and then, as he manœuvred his big car, he saw something which made him put his foot on the brake—a notice.

It was printed in block capitals by hand, neatly done in red crayon on a piece of white paper and attached to a board which was tied with string to the iron gates.

It said, "Skaig Castle—Open to the Public from 2 p.m. to 6 p.m. daily. Admission 6d."

Ian stared at it for a moment, reading it as carefully as if it were a Foreign Office despatch; then with a frown between his eyes he drove up the pot-holed drive towards the castle.

As he reached the top of the drive and drove into the wide sweep before the Gothic-arched door of the ruins, he saw there were three cars parked neatly to one side.

He drew up his own on the opposite side almost with an air of defiance and, getting out, stood looking to see what had happened to the occupants.

The private part of the castle lay away to the west, as Ian well remembered; but the three empty cars were parked by the ruins and had contained, he was sure, sightseers who had paid sixpence to view his inheritance.

17

He lit a cigarette as if to give himself time to think and then, as he moved across towards the building, he saw in the doorway a table and beside it a small figure.

He had to draw nearer to see clearly that the table was pulled under the archway under cover from the wind which was blowing sharply across the loch.

It was a stall, Ian saw as he approached. Neatly laid out on a white tablecloth were a few lettuces, two cucumbers and some very green cooking apples. Beside them were half a dozen bunches of white heather tied together with ribbon, and in front on a large white dish was a salmon.

It had been neatly cut into small pieces and a piece of paper propped against it read, "Fresh salmon—5/-a pound."

While he was staring at the contents of the stall, there was the sound of a voice and three or four women appeared through the doorway.

"White heather!" one exclaimed. "Must have a bit of that for luck."

"Do you think it'll help me with me Pools?" one of the others asked.

"Don't be so soft, Alice. I'm going to take a bit of salmon home to Mother. She always did like salmon with her tea."

"Five shillings!" the third woman exclaimed. "It's quite a lot, isn't it? But I'll buy a piece for Aunt Dora. Can we have it cheaper if we have two pounds, I wonder?"

She turned, as she spoke, to the small figure standing beside the stall; and now Ian saw that it was a boy—a small, red-haired, freckled-faced boy, wearing a faded kilt and a green pullover.

"Nine and six if you take two pounds," he said slowly.

"That's only sixpence off," one of the ladies said.

"You won't get a salmon like that in any of the shops," the boy replied. "It was fresh out of the river this morning."

18

"Out of this river?" one of the ladies queried.

"That's right. Six pounds it weighed."

"It certainly looks nice," the woman admitted. "Oh! come on Gladys, cough up your four and nine and I'll do the same. We'll have two pounds, laddie, you can put it in the same piece of paper."

The small boy produced newspaper from behind the chair, wrapped up the salmon with what seemed an experienced hand and taking the money from the two women, counted it carefully.

"That's right," he said without a smile. "Do you want some white heather?"

"Regular little salesman, isn't he?" one of the women laughed. "Yes, I'll 'ave a bit."

The boy handed her a bunch, took her sixpence and put all the money into an old cigarette tin. Then, as the women walked away to the car, he looked up at Ian who was standing watching.

"Do you want to go into the castle?" he asked.

"I understand I pay sixpence for that privilege."

"That's right," the boy said. "You can give the money to me."

"Is there anyone to show me around?"

"My . . . my . . . there's a guide inside," the boy said. "She's got two parties with her now, but she will show you what you've missed."

"Thank you," Ian said.

He paid over his sixpence and walked into the castle. It was open to the sky, but the walls stood on four sides.

It was easy to see where the floors had once rested, there were the remains of a twisted staircase in one corner, the remains of a blackened fireplace, and many windows and doorways, empty and gaping now, but showing that it had once been a building of great size.

At the far end, across the broken, weed-covered floor, Ian saw a party of people—two men wearing tweed caps and smoking pipes, four women and a number of children, all engrossed in sucking or chewing sweetmeats of some sort.

One child dropped a brightly-coloured lollipop on a stick, and yelled. His mother picked it up, wiped it with a gloved hand and thrust it into the child's mouth again.

They were all listening to the girl who stood in the centre of them—the guide he had heard about, Ian decided—and he sauntered across to see what she was like.

She was small and dark, and her voice, he noted, was low and deep for a woman. There was a hint of laughter in it and despite his rising indignation, he found himself listening.

"It was from this room, in 1437, that Malcolm, Chieftain of the McCraggans, saw the Vikings approaching," she said. "They had come across the North Sea in their carved and painted ships to pillage the land, to take away the younger women and lay waste that which they could not steal.

"Malcolm McCraggan was determined to defy them. He called all of the clan whom he could muster into the castle. They drove in the cattle and the sheep, they barricaded the doors and defied the Vikings to do their worst.

"The McCraggans shot at them from the battlements and after a siege lasting for over a month, when the Vikings three times set fire to the castle, Malcolm McCraggan won and the Vikings returned to their own country, taking with them the cattle, sheep and young women belonging to many other clans, but nothing belonging to the Clan McCraggan."

"Fancy that now," said one of the listeners.

"What he wanted was an atomic bomb against that lot," one of the men remarked comically.

There was a squeal of laughter.

"I think you've seen everything now," the girl with the dark hair said. "I hope you have enjoyed it and will come again and tell your friends about it."

"We will that," one of the women said, and turned to walk towards the cars.

The guide stood for a minute watching the little crowd go; then, seeing Ian watching her, she walked across to him.

She was pretty, he decided as he watched her coming; her skin was very white and he saw that she had the dark, gold-flecked eyes which go with high cheek bones, and a proud carriage of body which comes from a long line of Scottish ancestry.

Yes, she was pretty, he thought to himself and wondered who the devil she was. She was wearing a tartan skirt, white blouse and green cardigan.

She was not fashionably dressed and yet it seemed to him that she fitted in perfectly with the grey walls, the struggling grass trying to grow between the broken stones, and the white clouds chasing themselves across the blue sky above.

She was part of Scotland, as much a part as the Skaig itself, and yet she had no right to be here.

If her appearance had for the moment softened him, now he felt his anger rising again. He waited until she came quite close to him.

"Do you want to see over the castle?" she asked.

"No!"

The monosyllable was sharp and he saw her eyebrows rise a little at his tone. She did not speak, but waited with a look of enquiry in her eyes.

"My name is Ian McCraggan," he said.

He saw her eyes widen and then very slowly a wave of crimson crept from the proud line of her chin into her cheeks.

"Ian McCraggan!" she repeated.

"Of Skaig Castle," he added.

He thought for a moment that she would begin to explain; her lips parted as though she would speak, and then almost sharply she seemed to change her mind. She glanced at her wrist watch.

21

"It is just six o'clock," she said. "I will close the castle and then we must talk."

"I think that is a good idea," Ian said grimly.

She turned away from him and called: "Cathy! Cathy!"

A small girl came running. She was about six years old, Ian guessed, and her hair, deep Titian red, was bright and dancing as she ran.

"Tell Hamish to put out the notice that we are closed now," the girl said to her.

"Is it time?" the child asked.

"Yes, it is nearly six o'clock."

"I'll go and tell Hamish," Cathy said.

She ran across to the stall. The girl looked up at Ian.

"Will you come this way?" she said.

He knew where she was leading him.

"Into the castle?" he asked.

"We can talk there," she said.

"So you have the keys!" he remarked.

"Yes, I have the keys."

She led the way, walking a few paces ahead. She was small-boned and he noticed the delicacy of her hands and the exquisite neatness of her ankles. She was a lady, he knew that, but who was she and where could she have come from?

He found his mind whirling with questions as he followed her through the ruins out on to the drive which bordered the lake.

The castle had been joined neatly on to the ruins, use had been made of one wall of the old building, and the new castle was in its own way almost as romantic.

It had turrets and tiny arrow-slit windows; on one side was a great clock tower and in the centre wide grey stone steps which led up to a huge iron-studded front door.

It was imposing and, as Ian well remembered, a schoolboy's idea of what a Scottish baronial castle should be.

22

In front of the house there were a few flower beds which were sadly in need of weeding. Ivy had grown over the upper windows and creeper straggled over the lower storey.

They walked in silence, the wind blowing the girl's dark hair against her cheeks which were as pale again now as they had been crimson before. The gulls were swirling overhead and on the far side of the loch Ian could see a gaggle of geese coming in on their evening flight.

He felt a sudden impulse to cry out aloud that this was his—his castle, his home, a place to which he would always return, do what else he might in his life.

The girl was walking ahead of him up the steps. She opened the door, which was not locked, and walked first into the big, square hall.

The walls were covered with stags' head, a stuffed badger stood on his hind legs and held an ash-tray in its paws, the rugs were made from the skins of wild cats.

The place was clean and dusted, Ian noticed, and it came to his mind that the explanation was, of course, that this girl and the children were caretaking here until such time as he arrived. Scott must have arranged it, he thought, and instead of being annoyed he should be grateful.

Perhaps they had not been paid and that was why they were collecting money as best they might from the tourists who wished to see the castle. There was a smile on his lips as the girl turned to face him.

She was about to speak, but Ian forestalled her.

"Before we go any further, won't you tell me your name? I've told you mine."

"It isn't really necessary," she answered, "but it is Moida MacDonald."

"Of course, that's the MacDonald tartan you are wearing!" Ian said. "It was puzzling me."

"I am afraid a great many things are going to puzzle you, Brigadier McCraggan," Moida said quietly.

23

"Indeed?" Ian replied. "Well, perhaps I had better ask the most obvious question first. What are you doing here?"

For a moment she hesitated, then quietly she answered him:

"We are squatters," she said.

2

Even the stags' heads on the walls seemed to open their mouths in astonishment.

For the moment Ian could only stare at the girl in front of him, and to his surprise he saw that there was an expression of hostility in her face.

He was not used to young women looking at him with what might almost be termed a glint of hatred in their eyes.

Yet the girl facing him proudly was undoubtedly at enmity with him, even though he had no idea what was the reason for it.

"Squatters!" he managed to stammer at length. "What exactly do you mean by that?"

"It is the usual description, I believe," Moida replied quietly, "for people who, having no home of their own, move into an unoccupied house."

"But the house is occupied. At least it was, and it will be again," Ian replied. "Are there no servants or caretakers here?"

"There's old Mrs. Mackay," she replied, "and her husband. They have lived here for sixty years; and even though they are not paid, they have stayed out of loyalty to Mr. McCraggan's memory."

"Not paid!" Ian ejaculated, remembering the sum of money his mother had told him she sent to the Factor. "I must find out about that later. To return to your statement. . . . You tell me that you have moved in here because you have no home. Surely that is somewhat unprecedented behaviour."

"I expected you to think so," Moida replied, and there was a bitter intonation in the accent she put on the pronoun.

"Perhaps it would be easier if you explained the whole thing to me simply," Ian suggested. "Shall we sit down?"

The almost conciliatory tone in his voice, although Moida did not recognise it as a diplomatic move, took her unawares.

For a moment she seemed to hesitate and her defiance appeared to slacken a little; then she answered quickly:

"I would rather stand."

"As you please," Ian replied. "Now, supposing you start at the beginning."

Moida's hesitation was very evident now. After a moment she said:

"My brother-in-law and my sister were killed in a motor accident about a month after your great-uncle died. They had a small house here in the village where they lived with their two children. I came to look after Hamish and Cathy, and a week after I arrived your Factor sold the house over our heads and told us that we had to get out."

"That was Mr. Scott, I suppose?" Ian said.

"Yes, Mr. Scott," Moida replied. "He informed us that he was acting on your instructions."

"Indeed! And why did you obey him?"

"We had no choice in the matter. The people who bought the house arrived. They had paid for it and they expected to find it empty."

Moida's soft, full lips tightened for a moment and Ian guessed there must have been an unpleasant scene.

"So you came here," he said.

"It was only justice," Moida snapped at him.

She was no longer hesitating and embarrassed. Her gold-flecked eyes were flashing. She was, Ian thought with a faint smile, the personification of a champion fighting injustice.

"And the staff allowed you in?" he asked.

"There was no staff to prevent it," Moida replied. "The nurses who had attended Mr. McCraggan in his last illness had gone back to Inverness; the housemaids were only local girls; the cook and the butler had been engaged by the week, and when they did not receive their wages they also left."

"So you and your nephew and niece took up your abode in the castle without any opposition from anyone?" Ian said.

"Exactly. You had turned us out and we felt it was up to you to find us somewhere else to go."

"And supposing I say that it is none of my business?"

Moida shrugged her shoulders.

"I anticipated that that would be your attitude. We shall stay here unless you turn us out forcibly."

There was something in her attitude which got under Ian's skin and made him feel suddenly irritated.

"Now look here," he said; "I quite realise there has been some sort of muddle, since my great-uncle's death, and that you are doubtless justified in having a grievance. That must be gone into, but in the meantime I must ask you to leave here quietly and find yourself other accommodation. My mother and her guests are arriving to stay here. It is obviously quite impossible for you to be in the castle at the same time."

"That is what you think," Moida retorted. "I have told you that we have nowhere to go. You have taken away the children's home and it is up to you to provide them with another."

"Are there no houses empty in the village or on this estate?" Ian asked.

"Of course there aren't," Moida replied. "There is a housing shortage in Scotland as everywhere else."

"Then what exactly do you expect me to do?" Ian asked.

27

"Find us a roof over our heads," Moida replied, "and until you do, we stay here."

"That is impossible, and you know it," Ian answered. "And, incidentally, what right have you to exploit my property? I suppose it was your idea to open the castle to the public at sixpence a head?"

"We have to live," Moida informed him.

"And how did you live before you came here?" Ian asked.

There was a little smile of triumph on her lips as she answered him, as though she anticipated the question and knew the answer would disconcert him.

"My brother-in-law had an allowance made to him for many years. This ceased just before his death, but he augmented it by selling produce from his own garden. He and my sister worked very hard at growing vegetables, which had a ready sale here, where, as you may not know, vegetables are hard to obtain.

"They also had a greenhouse which they built with their own hands. There was no compensation for this when we were turned out of the house."

"I see that the whole problem is peculiarly difficult," Ian said; "but of course I cannot decide what happened until I find Mr. Scott and ask what were his reasons for selling the house."

Moida laughed.

"You will have a long way to go if you are going to find him," she said. "He has gone to Australia."

"To Australia!" Ian repeated in surprise. "But why?"

"There are various theories about that in the village," Moida replied; "but the most popular reason seems to be that he had enough money in his possession to make the journey well worth while. And, incidentally, the daughter of the schoolmaster went with him. Her husband is in the army in Malaya and no one has plucked up enough courage to write and tell him about it yet."

"You mean that Scott has absconded with some money?" Ian asked.

"That is what most people think," Moida answered.

"Of course, he may have left you the sums he obtained for our house and from various other transactions. You can go to his office and look. It has been empty ever since he went."

"Good Heavens, what a mess!" Ian exclaimed.

Already the pieces of the jigsaw were falling into place. He could hear his mother saying,

"I sent the man a thousand pounds and told him to be responsible for everything."

It was so like her, he thought—impulsive and overgenerous, not taking the trouble to wonder if it was wise before sending a man whom she did not know a very large cheque.

She had always been the same and he remembered how, as a child, it had embarrassed him when she always bought things in dozens while other people were deciding if they could afford to buy one.

"The Almighty Dollar!" He had squirmed when the boys at school had teased him because his mother had such lavish ideas.

His food parcels had always been four times the size of anyone else's and he had never confessed to Beatrice that he used to hide the presents she sent him —the gold-nibbed pens, the platinum wrist watch, the cufflinks encircled with small diamonds.

He had kept them locked in the very bottom of his tuck-box and bought himself their cheap counterparts so that he would be like the other boys.

Yes, this over-generosity on Beatrice's part had doubtless been responsible for making Scott into a crook; and yet this, or innumerable other occasions, would never convince her that money could be a curse as well as a blessing.

Yet whose-ever fault it was, it was obviously going to be impossible for his mother and Lynette to arrive and find Moida and two children already in possession of the castle. Something must be done about them, he could see that; but the difficulty was to know what.

"Who is in charge of the estate?" he asked.

"No one."

"But there must be someone," he said. "Are the keepers still here?"

"They are living in their crofts," she replied, "but I don't know whether, as they have received no wages for six months, they consider themselves employed by you."

"As you know so much about the whole estate and the people on it," Ian said with a hint of sarcasm in his voice, "perhaps you will suggest someone I could go and talk to about all this?"

"There is really no one in any position of responsibility, if that's what you mean," Moida answered. "Munro is in the Head Keeper's cottage, but he is an old man now and you will find it hard to make him talk about anything but the past. I doubt if he realises what is happening here today."

"The whole thing seems to be a pretty kettle of fish," Ian answered. "I suppose it is quite unnecessary to ask who is fishing the river?"

Moida did not answer, but he saw the faint smile on her lips and he added angrily.

"I suppose that was one of my salmon you were selling for five shillings a pound?"

"It was from the Skaig," Moida replied.

"And my lettuces and my fruit, too?"

"We planted the lettuces," Moida answered. "There has not been a gardener here for four months. Alex Tavish got another position in the Duke's gardens."

"Arkrae! That is whom I must go to see," Ian exclaimed. "In the meantime, perhaps you would be kind enough to remove your board from the gate and your stall from the ruins. There will be no more tourists in Skaig."

"I am afraid in that case you will have to feed us," Moida said.

"I shall make arrangements about you and the children," Ian said.

"Thank you," Moida replied, "but you do understand, don't you, Brigadier, that we expect accommodation that is not only adequate, but equal to that which we have lost?"

There was a steely note in her voice which told Ian that he was dealing with someone with a determination which it would be hard to circumvent. And yet she was only such a little person. Her head barely reached his shoulder and it seemed ridiculous that she should set herself in combat against him.

Ian stared at her for a moment.

She was a woman and she was pretty, and usually he could handle women, pretty or otherwise. But there was also a strength and courage about Moida MacDonald which was unexpected to say the least of it.

It was unusual for him to feel at a loss in any situation but he felt it now.

He wondered, with a sudden quirk of humour, what would happen if he kissed her and told her not to make such a fool of herself. He had solved problems in such a way before and the idea of kissing Moida was by no means unpleasant.

Her lips were sweetly curved—her looks grew on one, Ian thought. She was nearly as lovely in her own natural, unmade-up way as Lynette was in hers.

He felt almost guilty at the idea—how could he compare this intrusive stranger with Lynette?

"I am going over to see the Duke of Arkrae," he said. "In the morning we must make arrangements for your removal. In the meantime, may I ask what part of the castle you are occupying?"

"We are on the second floor," Moida answered. "I will tell Mrs. Mackay to prepare a bedroom for you."

"Thank you," Ian said, "but I prefer to give my own orders in my own house."

It was a snub he felt she deserved.

He saw the colour rise again in her small oval face, and then, as he wondered whether he had been too brutal, she moved across the hall and started to climb

31

the wide oak stairs before he could think of anything else to say to her.

He watched her go and then went in search of Mrs. Mackay. He found her in the big, high-ceilinged kitchen where he remembered going as a boy in search of white floured baps hot from the oven and golden brown pancakes lifted warm from the griddle.

Mrs. Mackay was nearly eighty. Her face was as wrinkled as a russet apple and she peered at Ian through her glasses as he introduced himself.

It took her a few minutes to remember who he was and why he was here, and then when she realised his identity she cackled with delight.

"Why, Master Ian! I've been a-wondering when ye would be turning up. 'Tis the Laird ye are the noo, but we'd almost given up hoping to see ye. Mackay was certain sure ye would come to your uncle's funeral, but we was told ye were away in those far-off foreign places and couldna get home."

"I was in Malaya," Ian said, "and did not hear of my uncle's death until three weeks after he died."

" 'Tis sad ye couldna see him," Mrs. Mackay said. "He made a lovely corpse. But there, it's mony a long year since ye've been here. Ye were but a wee laddie when last we saw ye."

"And it is too long," Ian agreed, "but now I have come home, Mrs. Mackay, and I want your help. My mother will be arriving in two or three days' time. She is bringing several of her staff up from London, but we shall want some daily women to clean the place and I am wondering if you could look after me in the meantime?"

"I'll be glad to do it, Master Ian, though I shouldna be calling ye that the noo. Ye've a military title, I've heard tell."

"Forget it while I'm here," Ian smiled.

"My, but ye've grown into a grand mon," Mrs. Mackay exclaimed.

"Thank you, Mrs. Mackay, and now there's a lot to

32

be done. Can you get some girls in from the village to help?"

"Aye, I can do that for sure," Mrs. Mackay replied. "I'll ask Miss Moida to run down and speak to ma cousin for me. She'll ken who would be likely to come."

"Miss MacDonald will be leaving," Ian said a little stiffly.

"Will she then? And where will ye be putting her an' the twa wee bairns?"

"I will find somewhere for them," Ian said with a confidence he was far from feeling.

He saw the curiosity in Mrs. Mackay's face and was determined not to indulge it.

"If you could manage a meal of some sort for me this evening, I shall be very grateful," he said. "I understand there is some salmon to be had at any rate."

He saw the expression on Mrs. Mackay's face and guessed who had caught the salmon for Moida to sell. Old Willie Mackay had always been a poacher.

Ian remembered one time when he had been staying with his great-uncle—the year before Beatrice had taken umbrage and left the castle for ever—Willie Mackay had been caught by one of the river watchers, fishing late at night with a silver minnow on his line.

Ian had been with his Great-Uncle Duncan when it was reported to him. The river watcher, spluttering with indignation at Willie's crime, had added:

"He saw me a-coming, Sir, and throwing his rod down on the bank, he snatched up the salmon he had already caught and slipped it down his trews. He hurried awa', but I caught up with him and made him tell me why he was walking so stiff."

Great-Uncle Duncan had roared with laughter.

"You will punish him, Sir?" the river watcher enquired.

"The punishment has fitted the crime," Duncan Mc-Craggan replied. "It is enough punishment for any man to have a wet salmon down his trousers."

The memory of what had happened sixteen years ago still made Ian want to laugh.

"Tell Willie I've always known him to be a good judge of a fish," he said to Mrs. Mackay as he left the kitchen.

He found himself chuckling as he walked back down the long, dark passage which led to the front hall.

The house was badly in need of decorating, he could see that. The wallpaper was peeling from the walls, the paint was cracked and blistered. He found himself wondering what Lynette would think of the castle.

When he had last stayed here, there had only been one bathroom, with a very old-fashioned bath framed in heavy mahogany and two steps to climb up into it.

His great-uncle had firmly refused to have a telephone in the place and the castle was lit by lamps or candles.

But Lynette would not have to endure such discomforts for long. Beatrice was longing to re-decorate. She would do it well, Ian was bound to admit that, for she had excellent taste and her ideas of comfort certainly made life easy.

At the same time, he felt a sudden regret that anything must be changed. For at least a century and a half the castle had remained unaltered, only the stags' heads in the hall had increased in number and the glass cases of stuffed eagles, ptarmigan and black game had been added to in the library.

Otherwise the furnishings were as they had been chosen by the McCraggan who had added the new part of the castle at the end of the eighteenth century.

"My great-great-great-grandfather," Ian thought to himself.

He felt a sudden kinship with all his ancestors who had lived at Skaig and looked across the blue waters of the loch to the heather-clad hills on the other side of it.

34

He walked out of the front door of the castle and along the drive where he had parked his car. The cars belonging to the tourists had gone now.

He saw the two children, Hamish and Cathy, coming up the driveway, carrying between them the board which had been fixed to the castle gates.

They stared at him for a moment with wide, inquisitive eyes, then Cathy smiled. Ian found himself thinking what a sweet face she had.

"Aunt Moida says you are the Laird," she remarked.

"I am."

"But we thought you would be old."

"I am sorry if I disappoint you." Ian smiled.

Cathy regarded him for a moment with her head twisted on one side. She had a bird-like grace about her and, unlike her brother, her skin, white against the vivid red of her hair, was not freckled.

"Aunt Moida said you would be angry with us when you came," she said. "Are you angry?"

Ian found the question disconcerting, and while he sought for a reply Hamish announced solemnly.

"He's our enemy, Cathy. We should not be talking to him."

"Did Aunt Moida say I was your enemy?" Ian enquired.

Hamish nodded.

"We're going to defy you," he said. "You will try to turn us out, but we shan't go. We belong here."

"So do I," Ian said, "and it happens to be my home, and I don't particularly want anyone to share it with me. You wouldn't like to share your home with me, would you?"

There was a long pause.

"I don't think we'd mind if you wanted to stay with us very much," Cathy lisped at length.

There was a look of the eternal coquette in her eyes and Ian suddenly threw back his head and laughed.

"Thank you, Cathy," he said. "I shan't forget your kindness. Hamish, as far as you are concerned, it is war to the knife."

He walked away and got into his car. As he started it up, Cathy waved to him, and as he drove away down the drive he felt almost angry that they were more at home in the castle than he was.

"An enemy" indeed! How dared that ridiculous girl put such ideas into the children's heads! He felt he was dealing with the whole situation in a most incompetent manner.

He might be good at settling international difficulties, but this situation was almost beyond him.

It was obvious that Scott had blundered badly, but the complications could be smoothed out, he was sure of that. His cousin, Arkrae, would have some suggestion to make. After all, he lived up here and he would know the right thing to do without creating too much local ill feeling.

All the same, Ian felt resentful that he had to ask help or advice from anyone at this particular moment.

He had been driving all day and had intended to spend the evening looking round the castle, inspecting the grounds, and enjoying every aspect of his new inheritance.

Instead of which, he was back on the road again, hurrying towards a relative whom he had always felt in his heart of hearts to be a fool.

Arkrae Castle was about twenty miles further along the coast, standing high on a cliff. Like Skaig it dated back to mediaeval times, but had been rebuilt time after time during the centuries, until little or nothing of its original walls remained.

The pseudo-Gothic style it had achieved in its last building was impressive, if not likely to be admired by the purists; but Ian, turning down the long drive, was concerned not with architecture, but with his own personal problems.

36

A stout red-faced butler, who smelt strongly of spirits, led him through a marble-paved hall to a shabby, untidy library facing the sea.

"Brigadier McCraggan, Your Grace," he announced, and the Duke, wearing a faded kilt and a bone-buttoned tweed jacket, rose from the writing-table and hurried across the room with outstretched hand.

He was a small man with water blue eyes and pale, mousy hair thinning rapidly at the top of his head. He had a fair, drooping moustache and a staccato manner of speaking which was at variance with the rest of his appearance.

One felt that his speech should have been as apologetic as his manner.

"Ian! A surprise! No idea you North, or in country that matter, Shoot at Skaig? They tell me grouse good."

"I came over to ask your advice, Archie," Ian replied.

"Glad give it, dear fellow. Have a drink?"

"Thanks, I will," Ian said, feeling that a strong whisky was exactly what he needed.

The Duke rang the bell and gave the necessary order to the butler, who had obviously been sampling the whisky himself in the nether regions of the castle and seemed reluctant to part with the decanter.

Then the Duke walked back across the room and sat down beside Ian in one of the shabby leather armchairs.

"Nice have you at Skaig," he said. "Miss old man."

"I thought you weren't on speaking terms," Ian remarked.

"No one on speaking terms with Duncan McCraggan more than few days at a time," the Duke remarked. "Miss him all same. One of us, you know. Aren't many left. Lodges and moors taken by upstarts these days—manufacturers and Americans."

The Duke remembered as he said it that Ian's mother was American and he gave an apologetic cough which made his eyes appear more watery than ever.

"Look here, Archie, things are in a hell of a mess at Skaig . . ." Ian began.

"Then they oughtn't to be," the Duke said positively. "Plenty birds there in spring. Saw them myself. Of course, keepers aren't what they used to be. Too many vermin about, but hatching was all right."

"I'm not talking about the grouse," Ian said patiently.

"What then?" the Duke enquired.

Briefly Ian explained what he had discovered so far. He told how the letter to Scott had been returned marked "Gone Away" and of how the man had turned Moida and the two children out of their house, obviously pocketing the money from the sale as well as Beatrice's cheque.

"Squatters at Skaig!" the Duke exclaimed as Ian finished. "By George, first I've heard of such a thing. Communism, that's what it is! Not even our castles our own these days. Bad enough people tramping over staterooms. Always thought that the limit. Spying on one! No private life, no privacy! By gum. If they're going move in on us, we shall have to do something."

"I don't think this is quite an ordinary case," Ian said. "This girl is a lady. I gather she considers it a bit of poetic justice more than anything else."

"Damn it, not the point," the Duke spluttered. "Real question is Skaig yours? If it is, what right lot of strangers come pushing in? Sleeping in best bedrooms, shouldn't wonder."

"They are on the second floor," Ian said.

"Enough to make your poor uncle turn in his grave!"

"The problem is, Archie, what am I to do about it? Is there any chance of finding a cottage for the girl? I could charge her a nominal rent, of course."

"Impossible!" the Duke answered. "Crofts disgracefully overcrowded. Said to Factor only last week, 'Insanitary, that's what it is!' Know what damn' fellow had cheek to say?"

"I have no idea," Ian answered.

"Said, 'What do you propose to do about it, Your

Grace?' Knew well as I did could no more afford build a cottage at moment than buy Koh-i-noor."

"Then if there are no cottages to be had," Ian said, "what do you suggest I do?"

"Turn 'em out, old boy."

"But how can I?" Ian asked. "Besides, they won't go, and it would be uncomfortable to go to the police."

"Police!" the Duke snorted. "Useless body. Never do damn' thing but drive fast cars up and down road. Poaching a disgrace! Tourists do exactly as they please! Why, one even had cheek to walk into greenhouse where I'm experimenting with blue heather. Left door open, nearly ruined new plants. Told police—said nothing they could do about it. Police! Might as well save your breath!"

"How are you getting on with the blue heather?" Ian enquired.

He knew this was the Duke's pet hobby. For years he had been trying to produce by pollination a heather that was vividly blue.

In answer to his question the Duke glanced over his shoulder, as if there might be someone standing behind him, and lowered his voice to a hissing whisper.

"Believe I've got it, old boy."

"A really blue heather?"

"Shush! Great secret! Been strange people snooping around lately. Don't trust them. There's firm in Glasgow trying out exactly same thing, and America's interested."

"You'll make a fortune, Archie—that's what will happen to you!"

The Duke shook his head.

"Don't mind about money—come in useful of course. Idea of being first in field. Not letting those Americans get ahead of me. Blue heather must belong to Scotland, nowhere else."

"What about the firm in Glasgow?" Ian asked.

"Haven't got it yet! Damn it, my idea in first place. If there hadn't been so much talk, no one known what

I was about until I'd got it perfect. Shall know for certain within next week or so if succeeded. Won't say a word, will you?"

"No, of course not, Archie. It's a great achievement."

"That's what I think," the Duke said with an almost beatific smile on his pale lips.

"And now to return to my problems," Ian said. "You haven't been very helpful so far."

"Don't know what to say," the Duke replied. "Heard this fellow Scott gone off with schoolmaster's daughter. Knew his father of course. Acted for me one time, until I took business to solicitors in Inverness. Old Scott all right—son never any good. Couldn't look you in the eye. Hate that type of chap! Warned Duncan trusting him too far. Wouldn't listen to me."

"I shall have to make some further enquiries," Ian said, "but the whole thing seems pretty conclusive. He has run away with every penny he could lay hands on."

"Bad luck!" the Duke murmured. "Better try my people, Anderson, Anderson and Anderson—not bad. Have difficulty remembering which is which. Always go to one with wart on nose."

"I'll remember that," Ian said gravely. "In the meantime I suppose, if there is nothing else I can do, I must send Miss MacDonald and the children to an hotel."

"Mustn't do that," the Duke said quickly. "Great mistake, old man. Make yourself responsible, acknowledge yourself under obligation, where will you find yourself?"

"I doubt if they would go anyway," Ian said. "They are expecting me to find them a cottage."

"Have build them one," the Duke said. "You can afford it."

There was a bitterness in his voice which made Ian feel embarrassed.

"It would take months," he said hastily. "Do you mean to say they are to live in the castle until then?"

"Big enough for them," the Duke remarked; "Communism, of course! Don't think I hold with it. But don't see what else you can do but keep them."

"Can you see my mother consenting to such a thing?" Ian asked. "Besides, she had everything planned for a huge party."

"Sorry can't help," the Duke replied. "Ask me come and shoot. Always enjoy day on Skaig."

"Yes, of course you must come," Ian said, "and I want you to meet Lynette Trent."

In speaking Lynette's name his voice softened and deepened. Even to speak of her made him see her all too vividly—her blue eyes raised to his, her gold hair framing the loveliness of her face.

"Lynette! Lynette!" his heart cried out for her— or was it his body lonely for the yielding softness of her?

The Duke was wrinkling his brow as if in an effort of recollecting something.

"Jove, yes. Forgotten," he said at length. "Had letter from Cedric three days ago. Seen your mother London told him you were engaged. Congratulations, old man."

"Thank you," Ian said. "She is very lovely."

"Hope she'll like Skaig. Want you stay there," the Duke said. "Landowners getting scarce."

"I don't think there's much chance of our settling there for long. I like it, but Lynette prefers London."

"Pity," the Duke remarked. "Still, never know, may alter with marriage. Sorry can't be help about squatters, old boy. If you can't push them out, better shut 'em up in dungeons. What our ancestors would have done. By Gad, those were the days!"

With a few more pleasantries Ian said good-by and left the castle. As he drove away, he reflected that the Duke had always been an ass.

He was fond of him, as one is fond of anyone one

41

has known from childhood; but it had been ridiculous to suppose that he would be any help in solving the problems at Skaig.

Arkrae only had two interests in life, grouse and his blue heather, and on any other subject he was ignorant and disinterested to the point of absurdity.

As Ian drove home, he decided that he would telephone to Inverness the following morning and ask the Duke's solicitors to send someone to cope with the problems of the estate; but even Anderson, Anderson and Anderson would find it difficult to know what to do about Moida MacDonald, Hamish and Cathy.

A cottage was what they wanted. And according to the Duke there was not likely to be one available.

It was with a feeling of depression that Ian hurried along the coast road and turned up the Skaig strath. The sun was sinking low, casting strange lights on the moors; the river was running gold with the reflections of the vivid sky. It was all very lovely and very peaceful.

Ahead the roofs and chimneys of the village came into view, and towering above them stood the castle, gaunt and grey, the empty windows for a moment seeming to be filled with light, as the red and gold of the sky shone through them.

Ian felt his spirits lift. There were difficulties ahead, but this was his home, these were the roots from which he had sprung.

He turned the car up the drive. There were a thousand problems ahead of him to be faced. He decided to see Moida MacDonald again and try to appeal to her better nature.

It was no use antagonising her, he decided. He must be subtle if he was to have her out of the house before his mother arrived.

It was then, as he swung round the corner of the ruins, that he saw a huge limousine standing outside the front door.

One glance at its silver-blue body, its shining chromium lamps and the pile of expensive luggage being disembowelled from the boot told Ian that his plans for diplomacy were too late.

He drew up his car with a sudden shriek of the brakes. Servants were hurrying up and down the steps. There was a sound of voices coming through the open door.

Yes, he was too late—his mother and Lynette had arrived, though why they should have hurried after him so quickly he had no idea.

With a sudden sense of urgency to find out what had happened, and perhaps to dispel a sudden sinking of his heart, Ian sprang out of his car and ran up the steps into the house.

The big hall seemed full of people. They were all in a circle round one small person—a woman swathed in sables, with diamonds glittering in her tiny ears.

She gave a sudden cry at the sight of Ian and held out her hands towards him with what in anyone else would have been a theatrical gesture but in Beatrice was just an expression of her impulsive nature.

"Ian, darling!" she exclaimed. "We could not get here quick enought to find you. Something terrible has happened!"

3

Lynette paid the bill and asked that the gloves she had bought should be sent to her at the hotel.

As she spelt out her name, the shop assistant gave her a quick glance and she knew by the expression on the girl's face that she had been recognised.

As always, it gave her a glow of pleasure, even though it was a fairly common occurrence. It was invariably the female sex who were aware of her identity.

As she passed into a theatre or stood at the brightly-lit portico of a fashionable hotel or moved through the crowded aisles of a department store, she would hear the whisper, "That's Lynette Trent," or see by the excitement in some woman's eyes that she had been spotted.

It was not only flattering, it was a tribute to the gossip and pictorial press who could make social stars as easily as the cinema and the television made their personalities famous to the general public.

Lynette's wide blue eyes and exquisite features had been plugged at the public week by week since her debut. There was hardly an issue of the glossy magazines which did not carry her photograph.

If she was not on the front page, she would be found attending a fashionable wedding, dancing energetically for charity, or among the groups captioned as ardent race-goers or enthusiastic ballet fans.

Wherever the social world was to be found, Lynette was there; and as she was very photogenic, the photographers never grew tired of taking her.

She was not exclusive to society gatherings; in *Vogue* and *Harper's Bazaar* she appeared month by month wearing Balmain or Dior's latest creation, jewellery by Cartier or Lacloche and posed against somebody or other's latest décor.

She was lovely, she had glamour, she had a figure which rivalled the measurements of any professional model, and she had a social background. What girl could ask for more? And yet Lynette was ambitious.

She had wanted to make a brilliant marriage since she emerged upon a startled, appreciative world at seventeen and a half. She wanted it far more urgently now at twenty-three.

Already she was beginning to be afraid of the younger and fresher rivals whom every season produced. Already she was giving her contemporaries christening presents and wondering if they talked about her behind her back as hanging fire.

It was not that she had not had the chance of marrying. She could count her proposals in dozens; but she wanted, as a great many young women had wanted before her, to marry a "catch".

It was her mother who had firmly instilled the idea in her head that above all things she must have a title.

Lynette's mother could speak with experience. She had been married four times. She had been Mrs. Trent, Lady Wilson-Jones, Mrs. Bangor and lastly— or rather for the moment—she was the Countess of Beckenham.

"It's hell being poor, darling," she told Lynette a hundred times, "but it is a bigger hell being poor and a commoner. A title counts more in a socialistic world than ever before, you can take my word for it."

Lynette took her word, not only because she thought

a title was glamorous, but because she had seen at firsthand the truth of her mother's assertions.

They had always been poor, ever since Lynette could remember—poor that was in comparison with their friends.

They were always trying to keep up with the other people without enough money to pay for the cars, the servants, the hunters, the houses and diamonds which, in the set in which they moved, were considered the absolute necessities of life.

Lynette had bought her clothes from her richer friends, or cadged them from those who were generous enough to give them to her, until sometimes she wondered if she had any opinions of her own, or whether, like her wardrobe, they were just a patch-work of other people's taste.

Even when she was dressed for a special occasion by a leading couturier who considered her an excellent advertisement, she was never allowed to pick out the things she wanted, but only to wear those which were chosen for her.

Sometimes she dreamed that she went out and bought thousands of pounds' worth of things, just because she wanted them, and paid for them out of an inexhaustible purse which never grew lighter.

It was only a dream; and when she came back to reality, it was to take part in one of the interminable conversations in her home when her mother and step-father of the moment argued as to how they could get to Deauville on the cheap or cadge a lift to Monte Carlo from someone who was either flying or motoring there.

Anyone even half as observant as Lynette would have been able to see that cadging favours of every sort and description was easier at the times when her mother was addressed respectfully as "M'lady"! A title by all means, Lynette said to herself; but money, too.

Yet somehow the success she achieved, both publicly in the newspapers and privately amongst the people who mattered, did not bring her the titled husband she required. Men with titles came her way, but there was always something terribly wrong with them.

One was an epileptic, another was a dissolute old man whose grandchildren were older than Lynette, the third was an undischarged bankrupt who thought Lynette herself had money until she disillusioned him.

There were other men, ordinary, charming, well-bred young men such as all nice girls meet at well-conducted dances; but there was always something to exclude them from filling the niche in Lynette's life which she had reserved exclusively for her husband.

A title and money! The two seemed incompatible.

She fell in love several times, but her head ruled her heart and she would not permit herself more than a few evenings of happiness before she was strong enough to cut them out completely from her life. She knew they must never mean more to her than they meant now.

"Does the fact that I love you mean nothing?" a poor young man had asked her once.

Then he pulled her into his arms and kissed her brutally with a desperation born of despair. She had felt herself quiver beneath his kisses and had been conscious of a strange fire mounting within her.

It was an ecstasy beyond anything she had ever experienced before and she wanted to surrender herself to it.

She felt herself weak in his arms, felt her breath come quickly between her lips, knew her hands were reaching out towards him . . . and then she remembered!

Remembered the cold, bare bedrooms of her childhood, the badly-cooked meals, the untrained and insolent servants. She could see her mother's ingratiating smile as she toadied to some wealthy friend, hear her

47

step-father's curses when the post brought only a sheaf of bills . . . .

With a desperate effort Lynette fought herself free.

"I can never see you again," she gasped and ran from the room lest her body should rebel against the dictatorship of her brain.

It was not true to say that where marriage was concerned Lynette was getting desperate. But she was beginning to find it hard to smile lightly and gaily when her mother's friends and inevitably her tiresome relations said, "And when shall we be coming to your wedding?" in arch tones which told Lynette all too clearly that they thought it was long overdue.

When she was asked to Beatrice McCraggan's dinner party she accepted because she had not received a better invitation for that particular night.

She had heard about Ian, but had never met him. She had spoken quite truly when she said he had become almost a legend; but she did not expect him to be quite so devastatingly attractive.

She felt a little tingle of pleasurable excitement in her throat when he suggested they should go to a night club.

She felt herself thrill as she had not done for a long time when he took her arm to help her into a taxi; and later, when she danced with him in the shrouded, musical darkness of *The Four Hundred,* she tried to pretend to herself that she had made up her mind to marry him before she remembered how rich he was.

As her mother had often said, "It's no use asking oneself if one would love a man if he hadn't got a title or if he had no money. Those things are part of him and one might just as well ask whether one would love someone without a nose or without ears."

Ian and money were indivisible in Lynette's mind and she loved him as she had never thought it possible for her to love anyone. There was something so experienced about him.

She liked his gravity, the way his hair grew back

from his square forehead, the faint tiredness of his eyes, the well-kept strength of his fingers.

"I would have married him without a penny," she told her dearest friends and knew it to be untrue. But she did love him.

She felt her heart beat more quickly when he came into the room. She found herself unable to eat for at least three days after he had asked her to marry him, which was good for her figure, besides being a sure indication that her emotions were actively interested.

"I love you; I love you," Ian whispered against her lips the first time he had kissed her.

"I love you," she replied.

It was so easy to say, so easy to mean.

"I love you! I love you!"

The words might have been the refrain of a song. They were lilting in the air, in Ian's smile, in his eyes, and on his lips.

"I'm in love!" Lynette told herself a thousand times a day, and knew an unspoken, irrepressible relief that for once she had not got to repress and refuse her own heart. Ian had everything except a title. Love and money, too! She was so lucky and so happy! Oh, how easy it was to love Ian!

It made everything perfect that Beatrice was delighted. She had wanted to announce their engagement immediately in *The Times,* but Lynette had to tell her mother first.

Lady Beckenham was in Kenya with her latest husband, trying to decide whether they could make more of a splash out there with the little money they had left than they would be able to do in England.

"You must write to her at once—by air mail of course," Beatrice said.

Lynette agreed only too willingly. If Beatrice was impatient, she, too, was impatient. If there had been a quicker method of transporting the tidings, they would have used it.

They had, indeed, wanted to telephone; but as the

only address Lynette had was a Bank, they felt it was too complicated.

"Mother has a great many friends in Kenya," Lynette said; "she might be staying with any of them."

"Ask her to wire her approval," Beatrice commanded, "and as soon as we hear from her, we can put it in *The Times*."

It was actually after Lynette had accepted Ian's proposal of marriage that she learned that he, too, might have a title. It seemed to her to set the seal of perfection on their engagement.

A Scottish title in itself had an air of romance about it and a Clan over which Ian could rule as Chieftain was the sort of information which any gossip column would call glamorous.

Lynette saw herself in a well-cut tartan skirt at the Braemar Games; she planned the white dress she would wear with the McCraggan sash at the Caledonian Ball. She could help Ian take his place as Chieftain, but an ancient title in abeyance would be front page news when it was proven.

She sighed to herself in a sudden ecstasy and remembered the look on Ian's face when he had asked her to marry him. They had known each other such a short time; but it was long enough for them both to know what they wanted.

They were dining together when Ian had looked at her across the table and said:

"Lynette! Are you happy?"

She raised her eyes to his, knowing that the softly-shaded light on the table was enhancing the clear purity of her skin and shining on the curling gold of her hair.

"Very, very happy," she replied, "and you?"

He put out his hand towards her and she laid her fingers with their Chinese red tips in his.

"I am happier than I ever believed it possible to be, and I think you know why."

"Do I?"

The question was artless. His hand closed over hers.

"I love you, Lynette. You know that already. Will you marry me?"

Just for a moment she had remained silent, savouring the joy and excitement of what was happening to her, feeling his fingers hard on the soft fragility of her skin, knowing, even though her eyes were downcast, that his were resting hungrily on her softly-parted lips.

"Lynette!"

His voice was now hoarse with anxiety.

"Darling, you know I will."

She spoke barely above a whisper, but he heard and knew it was the answer he wanted.

He lifted her fingers to his lips and they were engaged.

The sun was shining in Princes Street as Lynette came from the shop and walked slowly down the street—the most beautiful street in the world someone had called it—and Lynette, happy at being recognised by the shop assistant, felt it was a happy place for her today.

The castle, grim and gaunt as the centuries of Scottish history it represents, stood high above the gardens. The black cliff supporting it was lined with crevices and green with moss.

Below, the trim lawns, the toy bandstand and the flower beds seemed a strange contrast to the sullen battlements. On the other side of the street the shops were bright with tartans and tweeds.

Lynette felt that she was walking on air.

She had enjoyed driving north with Ian and Beatrice. She had liked the luxury of their big expensive car, the soft fur rugs which covered their knees, the attention which was waiting for them at every stop, the meals specially ordered ahead of them by Beatrice's efficient secretaries, the large, flower-filled suites of rooms into which they were shown on arrival at the hotels.

It was all so comfortable and never a sign of that nagging question whether the bill could be met.

How well Lynette could recall the hotels of her childhood, the bargaining which was part of every journey she took with her mother!

Arguments over extra items when the account was finally presented and the petty economies that must be thought of all the time—one cooked breakfast which had to do for two people, no coffee after any meal because it was extra, her mother's insistence that she was not to put the gas fire on in her room, however cold it was, because it was a waste of a shilling.

She found herself remembering those irritating, embarrassing journeys, as Beatrice ordered anything she fancied without a thought of whether they could possibly be classed as extras.

Now there was always a bathroom opening out of Lynette's bedroom, windows looking over the quietest and sunniest side of the hotel, a sitting-room filled with flowers and supplied with all the daily newspapers and the latest magazines, boxes of chocolates waiting to be eaten and several of the latest novels on a side-table in case they had time to read.

It was like being Royalty, Lynette thought, then chuckled because Beatrice was anything but royal with her trans-Atlantic energy and unflagging vitality that was exhausting for those who were perpetually with her.

She demanded the best and made certain at the same time of missing nothing, so that one had the impression that it was impossible for Beatrice McCraggan to relax lest the minutes that she might spend in such a manner might prove to have been wasted.

She was one hundred per cent efficient, one hundred per cent intelligent. In fact, taken all round, she was a very unusual person. And yet Lynette liked her future mother-in-law. It would have been impossible not to like anyone so generous.

She gave Lynette presents of clothes, jewels and any little *objet d'art* which took her fancy in the shops. Lynette found herself hesitating between three different coloured jumpers and was instantly the possessor of all three.

"Please! You are too kind to me," she expostulated, almost embarrassed by such generosity.

Beatrice had brushed her thanks on one side.

"If ever I want anything in life, I make up my mind to have it," she said. "It is a good motto for any woman. You try it."

Lynette bit back the reply that Beatrice had always been able to pay for anything she wanted. She only hoped that after they were married, Ian would be as openhanded as his mother.

Beatrice's arrangements for their journey were a well planned out campaign. Ian said it was "Operation Skaig".

When they reached Edinburgh, they all spent the night at the most comfortable and luxurious hotel that could be found for them, and then Beatrice informed Ian that he was to leave the next morning and go ahead of them to the castle.

"I guess it will take us about two or three days to get things fixed here with the Lord Lyon," she said, "and then we will join you. The servants are leaving London tomorrow evening. You must arrange for them to be met at Brora. I am bringing up Alphonse even though he loathes Scotland and old-fashioned kitchens; but if we are to entertain, we shall need him."

"Hadn't you better wait and see what the castle is like, before you ask too many guests?" Ian suggested cautiously.

"Darling, this is the right season for shooting," his mother replied, "and I know you want to be at Skaig, so Lynette and I will just have to make it as comfortable as possible. Next year I will do the place over so that you won't know it."

"That's what I'm afraid of," Ian said.

"Now, darling, Great-Uncle Duncan was the most antiquated, obstinate old stick-in-the-mud who ever existed. I remember, when I asked for some extra candles in my bedroom, he told me that his mother had always managed to dress with only two. Two candles! I ask you!"

"What did you do?" Lynette asked.

"I sent my maid down to the village and told her to buy a gross. She set them all round the room in saucers, and said it looked exactly like a garden illuminated for a dance; but the ceiling was still in darkness, however many candles I lit. I thought myself I was in some subterranean grotto."

"Mother, you are exaggerating!" Ian said. "The castle may not have many modern conveniences; but architecturally it is a fine example of Georgian building, as well you know; and if I remember rightly, the beds were comfortable."

"I'm taking no chances," Beatrice replied. "I'm bringing my own mattress and my own pillows, as I always do. If you and Lynette have to sleep hard, don't blame me."

Lynette felt rather apprehensive of what the future might hold, until, after Ian had gone out that morning, Beatrice told her with a smile that she had everything in hand.

"It is good for Ian to think that he is making arrangements for us. Actually my housekeeper is sending up quite a lot of things from London. There is bed linen, blankets and feather overlays for the mattresses. I have ordered a great deal of food from Fortnum and Mason; and Alphonse, my chef, is a genius when it comes to cooking game. I think we can make ourselves comfortable for a few weeks at any rate, though, from what I remember of Skaig, the washing arrangements are primitive in the extreme."

Beatrice had left the hotel to keep her appointment with the Lord Lyon at ten o'clock and Lynette had gone off shopping. She had very little money of her own. Her mother sent her a cheque occasionally, but just before she had got engaged to Ian she had made a little money by modelling the advance autumn fashions.

She meant to keep this prudently by her and spend as little as possible while she was staying with Beatrice and Ian; but the shops in Princes Street tempted her and she frittered away quite a considerable sum before she could check herself.

She told herself that she must not be extravagant until she was married.

There would be her trousseau to buy, and although she had already planned to obtain everything on credit and pay off her bills after she was married, there were always incidental expenses which had to be met day by day.

Her mother would not be able to help her for, black-listed at a great many shops in London, she was always engaged in paying off a small percentage of the bills she had incurred over years of extravagance.

Lynette's step-father, Lord Beckenham, was not much better when it came to ready cash. He was a gambler and could not help betting on anything and everything which took his fancy.

On one occasion, when he wagered a thousand pounds that his taxi could beat another in a race twice round Hyde Park, his wife had to pawn every jewel and fur she possessed, including her wedding ring, to pay the winner.

It was a sordid and precarious existence, being perpetually in debt and always on the point of being dunned for sums one could not raise. Lynette made up her mind that, when she was married to Ian, she would never owe another bill.

She wondered if her friends realised how rich he was. Of course she would not be able to tell them exactly how much he had, but it would be pleasant to hint that he was definitely a millionaire. Ian McCraggan—it was a nice name.

At the same time, she hoped Beatrice would find that it would not take long to unearth the ancient barony.

"Lady McCraggan!" Lynette repeated the words to herself as she walked up the steps of the hotel where she and Beatrice were staying.

A lift took her to the third floor. As Lynette opened the door of their sitting-room, the fragrance of great bowls of hot-house carnations and long-stemmed roses was almost overpowering. The room was empty.

There was a pile of parcels on the table; some were for her, Lynette noticed; but the majority were addressed to Beatrice. Her future mother-in-law must have been shopping again—the money she had already spent in Edinburgh ran into hundreds.

Lynette saw that the new *Tatler* had come, and she turned over the pages in an aimless manner.

As she had expected, there were two pictures of herself; one at Goodwood, surrounded by a group of distinguished racegoers, the other at a fashionable christening. She had been Godmother to a friend's first baby.

She made a little grimace as she remembered that the proud mother of the egg-shaped child was a year and a half younger than she was.

This was the last time they should write "Miss Lynette Trent" under such a group she thought to herself. Next time it would be "the beautiful Lady McCraggan".

She smiled at the reflection of herself in the glass over the mantelpiece. She was looking very lovely, there was no doubt about that. She might be twenty-three, but there was no one among the younger set who could hold a candle to her when it came to looks.

She saw herself walking down the aisle of St. Margaret's on Ian's arm. She imagined the envious glances of her friends, the admiration and exclamations from the crowd waiting outside. And Ian? He would be looking at her with that expression in his eyes which always left her breathless.

There was something so possessive about it, something which made her weak and helpless, so that she was thankful a thousand times a day that there was nothing to stop her loving him.

Supposing he had been poor and unimportant? Lynette trembled at the idea. But he was everything that was socially desirable and she did love him, she did, she did!

"Lady McCraggan!" She whispered the words, and at that moment the door was flung open.

Beatrice came hurrying into the room and one glance at her face told Lynette that there was something wrong.

"It's disgraceful," she said, "absolutely disgraceful that I have not been told of this before. I said to him, 'Surely my son or I should have been notified?' and he replied that it was not usual. My dear, I was so angry I really didn't know what to say."

"What has happened?" Lynette asked.

"I am telling you," Beatrice replied. "When I got there, I sensed there was something wrong from the way he greeted me."

"Who? The Lord Lyon?" Lynette asked.

Beatrice nodded.

"And then he told me there has been another claimant who made application two months ago—two months and nothing has been done in the meantime!"

"Another claimant—to what?" Lynette asked, knowing the answer even while she asked the question.

"The title, of course," Beatrice replied.

"Not to the barony?"

"Apparently they did not know about that, but to the chieftainship, and naturally the barony goes with it."

"I don't understand," Lynette gasped. "Isn't Ian the heir?"

"Of course he is," Beatrice answered fiercely. "The whole thing is ridiculous—a piece of impertinence from the very beginning. I shall get the best lawyers in Scotland to investigate the whole matter at once. There is no time to be lost. Ian must offer his claim and then these other imposters can be dismissed."

Beatrice rang the bell imperiously as she spoke.

"What are you going to do?" Lynette asked.

"Do? What do you expect I'm going to do?" Beatrice asked quite snappishly. "We are leaving here at once to join Ian at Skaig and find out what all this is about."

Lynette did not enjoy the journey from Edinburgh to Skaig. The chauffeur, commanded by Beatrice to go as quickly as possible, took her at her word and had seemed to Lynette to travel dangerously fast.

Besides feeling frightened, she found Beatrice's indignation and volubly expressed complaints tiring in the extreme.

It was the first time she had seen her future mother-in-law in this very different guise. The generous, entertaining hostess, which had been her role until now, disappeared; instead, here was a woman frustrated and denied something that she wanted and finding it almost impossible to believe that she could not get her way immediately merely because she wished it.

Beatrice crossed was a very different person from Beatrice placated; her prettiness, her air of fragility, even her femininity seemed to vanish.

One saw instead the square chin, determined lips and the expression of obstinacy which made her father, Sigmund B. Stevenson, a successful railroad king in the days when one outwitted one's enemies by gunfire if no other method was effective.

"Another claimant indeed!" she said not once but a hundred times as they travelled north. "There are no other relations except a lot of women cousins. There were only two brothers in the previous generation, Great-Uncle Duncan who has just died, and Ian's grandfather who died in 1916. He had only one son, Euan, whom I married, so how can there possibly be another claimant?"

58

"Great-Uncle Duncan never married?" Lynette asked tentatively.

"No, of course not. He was a born bachelor if ever there was one. No woman would have taken on such a disagreeable old curmudgeon."

"I suppose anyone can put in a claim and it has to be considered," Lynette said soothingly.

"I suppose so; and Heaven knows, there must be Mc-Craggans all over the world if it comes to that, and any one of them might pretend he is the Chieftain."

"Does the castle go to whoever is the Chief of the Clan?" Lynette asked.

"I don't know. That is a thing which has to be cleared up," Beatrice said. "The Lord Lyon spoke of the queer wording of Great-Uncle Duncan's Will. He was not very explicit and I was too angry to ask him much. I saw the Will when it came, but I did not read it very carefully. Ian has it on him. He had it among his papers when he left for Skaig."

"We shall know when we get there," Lynette said.

This was no comfort to Beatrice and she talked the whole way until with a sigh of relief Lynette realised they had nearly reached their destination.

The signpost turned them from the coast road and then they were speeding up the long narrow strath.

Lynette had a sudden yearning to see Ian. She felt that he not only would soothe his mother, but would find a way out of this unexpected difficulty.

He gave one a sense of security, she thought; he seemed always so sure of himself, so composed and dignified, so unruffled by minor irritations whatever they might be.

With a sigh of content, Lynette thought Ian would deal with this and they would very likely find the whole thing was a mare's nest.

She would be very sweet to him so that he would see how understanding she could be in a crisis.

She would let him kiss her as much as he wished! Lynette drew in a deep breath. But she must be careful not to be carried away by her emotions. How often her mother had warned her against surrendering herself too easily.

"Men don't run after a bus they've already caught," she had said once, with a cynical twist of her lips, to Lynette.

Her step-father had capped it with, "What your mother means is "don't be off before the flag drops'."

Marriage was the most important moment in a girl's life and anyone who didn't realise that was a fool. "Don't marry for money, but love where money is!" How often had she laughed at that old chestnut. But it was true and she was not going to lose Ian by losing her head.

"Keep him guessing"—that was what she must do until the wedding ring was actually on her finger.

When Lynette first saw the castle at the top of the strath, she had no eyes for the beauty of it against the darkening sky. She was conscious only of feeling desperately tired. It was a long way from Edinburgh.

The car swept round to the front of the castle. Lynette got out of the car with a swimming head and stiff legs, but eager to see Ian. It was with a feeling of being cheated that she entered the hall and found he was not there.

The chauffeur and Beatrice's lady's maid were carrying boxes into the hall for the door stood open when they arrived and they had walked straight in. Though the bell had been rung, no one came to answer it.

"Just as I remembered it," Beatrice said. "How I hate those stags' heads lowering down at one."

Lynette had not answered her. She was hoping that Ian would appear down the long flight of stairs or come from one of the many doors opening into the hall. She turned quickly at the sound of footsteps.

To her disappointment it was only a very wrinkled old woman who stood there and beside her two sturdy young women wearing aprons.

"Where's Brigadier McCraggan?" Beatrice asked in her clear, commanding voice.

The old woman opened her mouth to reply. At that moment there was the sound of another car drawing up outside, and the chauffeur, who was carrying in a suitcase, exclaimed, "Here he is, ma'am."

Ian came running up the steps and Lynette watched Beatrice hurry towards him, heard her start to tell him in her usual, impulsive manner that things were wrong and found herself suddenly weak with relief because he was there.

She had seen him that very morning and yet it seemed aeons of time ago. She, too, wanted to run towards him, to take hold of his arm, to lay her head against his shoulder and tell him how glad she was to see him.

Instead, she did nothing of the sort, but waited until he turned towards her with a smile of welcome; and then she smiled at him in return, slowly, provocatively and invitingly, in a manner she had perfected with constant practice.

She knew instinctively that he would not want her to join in the hubbub of conversation his mother was making, that he would want her to be composed and calm, and she played her part with an ease any experienced actress might have envied.

"I didn't expect you so soon and I am afraid there is nothing ready; but never mind, you are here. Explanations can wait for a moment until we are settled," Ian said.

He turned to the old woman standing in the doorway to the kitchen quarters.

"Mrs. Mackay, this is my mother. I was not expecting her for a few days as you know, but I am sure we can make her as comfortable as possible, and I see you've found someone to help you," he said, smiling at the girls.

"Joan and Bessie Ross are in service in Aberdeen," Mrs. Mackay explained, "but they're hame for a bit of a holiday and were willing to come in and gie me a hand."

"It is very kind of you," Ian told the Ross sisters. "Will you get a bedroom ready for my mother and one for Miss Trent?"

"We shall need more than that," Beatrice interrupted. "Miss Watson and Miss Murray are behind in another car; rooms will have to be got ready for them, and of course my other staff will be here tomorrow afternoon."

"My mother's two secretaries are arriving also, tonight," Ian explained to Mrs. Mackay.

"There isn't more than four rooms that can be used on the first floor," the old lady said. "Mr. McCraggan had the bedrooms at the back cleared of furniture. He said too many folk asked themselves to stay wi' him. 'If the rooms hae nae beds, Mrs. Mackay,' he says to me, 'naebody will want to sleep in them.' "

The expression on Beatrice's face told what she thought of Great-Uncle Duncan's eccentricity as clearly as if she had put it into words.

"If there are four rooms on the first floor in the front, there must be four rooms on the second floor," she calculated. "Are they furnished?"

Mrs. Mackay looked at Ian and he took the plunge.

"There's a little difficulty about them, Mother. You see, when I arrived here this afternoon, I discovered that some people had moved into the castle while it was empty."

"Moved into the castle!" Beatrice repeated the words almost mechanically.

"Yes, they call themselves squatters," Ian said.

"But I have never heard of such a thing! Tell them they must move out again, and at once. We need the rooms—we must have them. What does this squatting mean?"

"It's a long story," Ian said, "and for the moment, at any rate, they will have to stay here."

"But I forbid it. It is the most absurd thing I have

ever heard," Beatrice said. "We need the rooms, and yet you tell me there are strangers occupying them without permission. Why, it . . . it must be illegal!"

"We hae no moved anything from the servants' rooms on the top floor," Mrs. Mackay volunteered. "There's space for an army up there an' mair. Mony of the beds have no been slept in for a long while, but we can get twa off the mattresses doon and in front of a fire before the ladies arrive."

"Why should my secretaries sleep in the servants' rooms while the second floor is occupied by these squatters?" Beatrice enquired. "Who are they, what are their names?"

She spoke directly to Mrs. Mackay.

"It's Miss Moida MacDonald, ma'am, and twa wee bairns, her nephie and niece, Hamish and Cathy Holm."

To everyone's astonishment Beatrice gave a shrill scream.

"Moida MacDonald! Holm!" she exclaimed. "Those are the names, those are the names of the claimants! They have no right here, turn them out, turn them out at once!"

"Mother, what are you talking about?" Ian asked.

"They are the claimants. They have lodged their claim. That is the name—Hamish Holm and it is Moida MacDonald who has written on his behalf!"

4

Ian knocked at a door on the second floor. For a moment there was no reply. Then a small voice said, "Come in."

Ian entered to find Cathy alone in the room, seated at a table by the window, with a large bowl of bread and milk in front of her.

Ian remembered the room well. It was the one which, to his indignation, he had been allotted when he last stayed at the castle. He had been fifteen at the time and was insulted at being put in what had been known for generations as the nursery.

His hurt feelings had not been soothed by the fact that it was one of the most pleasant rooms in the whole castle. Three big windows looked south over the loch and beyond one could see the mountains, on the peaks of which there were always patches of snow, even in the hottest summer.

The nursery had remained unchanged, and though its occupants grew old and grey, there were always their children or their children's children to take their place.

There was a screen covered with scraps and Christmas cards which had protected many Nannies and babies from draught as they sat in the nursing-chair in front of the heavily guarded fire.

There was an ancient rocking-horse which had lost its tail and one eye, but it was still a shiny, dappled grey with fierce red nostrils. There was an ancient Noah's ark standing in one corner, although most of the animals had no paint left on them and the majority were lacking a limb or two.

The carpet was threadbare, the chairs were shabby and the pattern of the wallpaper had long faded into an indistinct blur.

But the atmosphere of peace and happiness remained the same and for a moment Ian thought how right and proper it was that there should be a child sitting at the sturdy, square table, using, in all probability, the same cup and saucer and the same spoon from which he had sucked his bread and milk in his infancy.

"Aunt Moida's bathing Hamish," Cathy told him informatively. "I've had my bath."

Ian saw that she was ready for bed, wearing a nightgown of some pretty, flowered material and a dressing gown of blue flannel which she had long outgrown.

"Will they be long do you think?" Ian asked, setting himself opposite her at the table.

"Hamish's knees were very dirty tonight," Cathy replied, "and it takes a long time to get them clean."

"How did he get them so dirty?" Ian asked, anxious to keep the conversation going.

"He went up to the tower to see if he could find a bow and arrow," Cathy explained. "Aunt Moida won't let him have a gun, so he thought he might find a bow and arrow there."

"I should think it more than likely," Ian said.

He remembered the junk which lay forgotten on the high towers and on the top floors of the castle and which was added to year by year.

Duncan McCraggan had been a hoarder. He would never allow anything to be destroyed or thrown away. Furniture that was beyond repair, china that was chipped and cracked, mats that were worn out, photographs that had faded until nothing was left but the frame, were all relegated to the junk rooms.

Ian remembered the excitement and sense of discovery that he himself had experienced when playing there.

"Aunt Moida was very angry with Hamish," Cathy said, and added with an air of self-righteousness, "I wouldn't go with him."

"Why not?" Ian asked.

"Because he might have hurted you."

Ian looked surprised for a minute, then understood.

"Hamish wanted to use the bow and arrow against me?"

"That's right. Aunt Moida wouldn't let him have a gun."

"I should think not, indeed," Ian said drily. "Hamish's blood-thirsty impulses must be curbed, I can see that."

"I'll try to stop him hurting you," Cathy said with a glance from under her long lashes which made Ian smile.

At that moment the door of the room opened and Hamish and Moida came in. Hamish, clean and somewhat subdued, was looking aggrieved, doubtless at the treatment he had received in the bathroom.

At the sight of Ian his expression turned to one of most ferocious enmity. Moida, carrying a lighted oil lamp in her hands, also looked at Ian with a hostile eye.

The sleeves of her green sweater were pulled up above her elbows, her cheeks were flushed, and there were soft, dark curls against her forehead, damp from the steam of the bath. Round her waist, to protect her skirt, she wore a towel pinned behind her to form an apron.

Ian rose to his feet, but nobody spoke.

"I wanted to have a talk with you," he said at length to Moida.

"I must put the children to bed first," she replied.

Her voice was cold, and without looking at him she walked across the room to set down the lamp and to

66

pick up another cup of bread and milk, which she put down on the table in front of Hamish.

Taking a clean napkin from the drawer she tied it round his neck.

"Try not to make a mess," she admonished.

"Did she get your knees clean?" Cathy asked her brother.

"She didn't really hurt," Hamish said stoutly in a voice which proclaimed all too clearly that the scrubbing had been unpleasant.

Moida turned towards Ian.

"It will be at least ten minutes before they are in bed," she said.

Ian's eyes met hers.

"I'll wait," he said pleasantly.

There was a battle of wills. He knew only too well that Moida wished him to go away and return when she had composed herself, when she was ready to do battle with him. But he was determined not to give ground.

After a second or so, her eyes fell before his and she turned away with a tiny flounce of her head.

"You are very comfortable up here," he said.

He glanced, as he spoke, towards the fire burning in the grate and a vase of flowers on a side table. There was a dish of apples on the dresser and suddenly he wondered whether to laugh at the sheer effrontery of it.

With an air of defiance which somehow failed to hide her embarrassment Moida was busying herself picking up the children's clothes which they had scattered on the floor and over a chair by the fire.

They had evidently undressed in here, playing while they did so, and a set of bagpipes in the vivid tartan of the McCraggans lay on the old bearskin rug which covered the hearth.

Moida picked them up and held them for a moment against her breast as if they gave her courage. Ian leaned on a high-backed chair and looked down at her.

"Those were mine," he said quietly.

The colour came and went in her face as she met his eyes. For a moment they were both very still, then Cathy's high, clear voice broke the tension between them:

"I told the Laird that you were going to shoot him with a bow and arrow if you found one," Cathy said to her brother in what was meant to be a whisper.

"I didn't find one," Hamish answered sullenly, and added, "I shall stick him with my skian dugh."

He put the sheath knife, which all Scots wear in their hose, on the table as he spoke. Moida rose to her feet, and, crossing the room picked up the knife.

"That's enough, Hamish," she said quickly. "Finish up your supper. It is long past your bedtime."

"Don't worry about me," Ian said. "Cathy has promised to protect me, haven't you, Cathy?"

He knew that he was deliberately inciting the little girl to take his side and realised that Moida was well aware of his intention when she said:

"Children, you are talking a great deal of nonsense. Come along, Cathy, you've finished, so say your Grace."

With her eyes tightly closed and her hands together, Cathy mumbled a few words, then opened her eyes.

"I'm going to say my prayers to the Laird."

"You will do nothing of the sort," Moida said. "I will hear them as usual."

"I should love to hear Cathy's prayers," Ian answered. "Come along, Cathy, do you say them here or in your bedroom?"

"In my bedroom," Cathy answered.

She slipped down from the table and put her hand in Ian's.

"Show me where you sleep," Ian smiled. "I expect I have often slept in the same bed myself."

"You are not to bother Brigadier McCraggan," Moida managed to say in a voice that sounded strangled.

68

Neither Cathy nor Ian paid any attention to her and hand in hand they disappeared through the door at the far end of the room into what had originally been the night nursery.

"I sleep here, all by myself," Cathy announced proudly.

The room was large and the furniture was white; an old-fashioned brass bedstead stood against the further wall on which were hung numerous photographs of people and children who had once used this nursery.

Ian recognised his grandfather and there were at least half a dozen photographs of his father as a boy, looking solemn and self-conscious and unnaturally tidy in his best clothes.

There was a picture of himself which seemed strangely out of place among the other photographs, for it had been taken by a most expensive Mayfair photographer.

It was not so much a photograph as a work of art and it looked very different from the pictures which had been obtained with much careful posing on the part of the local photographer from Inverness.

While Ian was looking around him, Cathy had pulled off her dressing gown. It was removed with some difficulty as the sleeves were too tight.

She laid it carefully on the end of the bed and looked up at Ian expectantly.

"Where do you say your prayers?" he asked.

"Sometimes I kneel on the floor," Cathy answered, "but it's nicer if I kneel on the bed. Aunt Moida stands; but as you are so tall, it would be easier if you sat."

Not quite understanding what she wanted, Ian did as she suggested. In a moment Cathy had sprung on to the bed, knelt beside him and slipped her arms round his neck.

It gave him a strange feeling he had never experienced before to have a child's soft arms holding him tight, the softness of her hair against his cheek, her face hidden against his shoulder.

Very softly she began her prayers, and as the long-familiar words, "Gentle Jesus . . ." were spoken in her soft, sometimes lisping voice, Ian felt the years roll back and he himself was saying the same prayer.

When he was young, they had always come to the castle for Christmas; and now he felt the same sense of excitement steal over him as had been his on Christmas Eve when he said his prayers, knowing in the morning that a fat, well-filled stocking would be lying at the end of this very bed.

"Please God, bless Mummy and Daddy. . . ."

There was a tremor in Cathy's voice now and her arms suddenly tightened about Ian's neck. Ian remembered his own feelings when his father had died.

He had been older than Cathy, of course, and better able to disguise his feelings; but that feeling of loss had been as sharp and painful as the physical wound he had received in the last war.

Nothing and nobody, he thought suddenly, could take the place of a father or a mother in a child's life.

He held Cathy a little closer to him. Her body was soft and warm beneath the thin cotton of her nightgown. Ian felt that he was holding something very precious, something as fragile and as easily broken as a piece of Dresden china.

He must do something for this child, he thought. She must not suffer more than he could help, and if it was in his power he would give her a home.

"Amen!" Cathy's voice was breathless as she raised her head. "That's all. I 'membered every word, didn't I?"

"Every word," Ian repeated.

She kissed his cheek lightly.

"Will you tuck me in?" she asked.

She climbed beneath the sheets and, awkwardly, for this was a task he had never been set before, Ian tucked her in the sheets and soft blankets and then stood looking down at her. Her hair was vividly red against the white pillows.

"Good-night," he said, and bent to kiss her.

Cathy's arms came up quickly.

"I like you very much," she whispered, "and if we do have a home of our own one day, you must come and live in it."

"Thank you, Cathy," Ian said.

Then as he straightened his back, he saw that Moida was watching through the doorway.

As he looked at her, she walked across the room and drew the blind down sharply and made the curtains on their old-fashioned brass rods rattle and clang as she closed them.

"Good-night, Aunt Moida," Cathy said.

"Good-night, my darling," Moida's voice was tender.

She might be angry, Ian thought, but she would not vent her rage on the child. He went back into the day nursery. It was empty. Hamish had obviously been put to bed. Ian waited, and after a few moments Moida came from Cathy's room, closing the door behind her.

She had removed the towel from her waist and pulled down the sleeves of her green jumper. Her hair still curled riotously around her forehead, but there was a wary look in her eyes such as a duellist might have as he faced his opponent rapier in hand.

"You wanted to speak to me?" Moida asked.

"You will not be surprised at that," Ian replied. "My mother has brought me some very strange news from Edinburgh."

Moida said nothing, and after a moment he added:

"It is obviously a very long story. May I sit down?"

"As you please," she indicated a hard chair beside the table, but deliberately he crossed the room and settled himself comfortably in an armchair by the fire.

Moida hesitated and then, because there was nothing else she could do, seated herself opposite him in the nursing-chair.

The screen of scraps, which had delighted so many

71

children since it was first made, made a background for her dark head and troubled eyes.

"It is indeed a long story," she said at length, and clasped her hands together in her lap.

She had lovely hands, Ian noticed, long, thin sensitive fingers and small, oval-shaped nails. They were not varnished, but were a natural pale pink with white half-moons.

Ian wondered how long it was since he had noticed a woman's fingers that were not tipped with crimson.

"When my sister and brother-in-law were killed in a motor accident, I came to Skaig to look after the children," Moida began. "I had been here many times before, as I use to spend my holidays with them. My sister was a few years older than I, but we were always close friends and companions. I had realised before they died that something was wrong.

"For the first time since I had known Rory there was talk of his having to get a job. I could not understand this for he always had money of his own and they had augmented it by selling the produce from their market garden.

"My sister had written to me that they were worried; and when I spoke to her on the telephone about a week before she was killed, she told me that the money which had always come to Rory in the form of an allowance had ceased.

"I did not connect this in any way, of course, with your Great-Uncle Duncan McCraggan. Not until I came to Skaig to look after the children had I any idea where Rory's money came from, or why it was paid to him. When I began to tidy up the house, I discovered in the drawer of his desk a big envelope marked 'Secret'.

"There seemed to me no reason why I should not look into the envelope, and what I found was certainly astounding."

Moida paused for a moment, and Ian said:

"Forgive my asking this question, but hadn't your brother-in-law any relations?"

"None that I knew of then," Moida answered. "His father, whom I knew well, was badly wounded in the first world war. He was semi-paralysed and was never expected to live more than a few years. Actually he did not die until three years ago."

"I see," Ian answered. "So you opened the secret documents?"

"Yes, I opened them," Moida said, "and I found first of all that my brother-in-law had received, in quarterly instalments, the sum of one thousand pounds a year, which was paid to him by your Great-Uncle Duncan."

"By cheque?" Ian asked.

Moida shook her head.

"No, in notes; but every time he received them he made an entry, 'received from Duncan McCraggan'."

"I see," Ian remarked. "Go on."

"This puzzled me, of course, until I found a bundle of old faded letters which were also in the envelope. They were letters written in 1894 by your grandfather, Angus McCraggan to Ula Holm, daughter of a shopkeeper in Brora. How they met it does not say in the letters, but that your grandfather fell very much in love with her is very evident.

"The first letters speak only of his deep affection, and make plans for their meeting where they will not be observed. The letters then get more ardent. Angus McCraggan is obviously terrified of losing Ula and he begs her to prove her affection for him by going away with him to Glasgow or Edinburgh.

"He tells her that he is frightened to tell his father of their love, but suggests that they could be married secretly and that once they are man and wife the Mc-Craggan family will have to accept her.

"There are many letters in the same vein and then Ula Holm must have agreed to your grandfather's sug-

73

gestion, for the next letter speaks of his delight and rapture at her consent, and promises that he will be at their usual place of assignation at nine o'clock that night.

"The next letters are addressed to Glasgow. It is obvious that while Ula is living there, Angus McCraggan is at home and that the secret of their marriage has not been told to his parents.

"Six months later he writes again. She is going to have a baby. He begs her to take care of herself and promises to be with her on the following Monday. After that there is only one more letter. It is a scribbled note, written in pencil, which says:

Our friend has just brought me the wonderful news, my Beloved. We have a son. I can hardly believe it. We will call him Malcolm. I shall be with you the day after tomorrow and till then, remember that I worship you."

Moida's voice throbbed into silence. The words of the letter she had learned by heart were strangely moving when said in her low voice, the firelight flickering on her face, giving it a strange beauty.

Ian felt that his own voice was a little strange as he asked:

"What happened then?"

"There are no more letters," Moida said. "The rest of the story I can piece together only from what Malcolm Holm himself told me from time to time. I remember his saying that his mother died three days after he was born.

"He often spoke, too, of his lonely childhood. He was brought up by two people whom he called Uncle and Aunt, but who were, in fact, no relation. He married in 1917, the year before he was wounded at Passchendaele.

"Rory's mother ran away and left her husband when their son was ten years old. Malcolm Holm came to Skaig soon after that with his son Rory and your

74

Great-Uncle Duncan gave him a house at a nominal rent of five pounds a year."

"That, at least, was kind," Ian suggested.

Moida answered quickly.

"It was part of the hush money which had obviously been paid all these years to keep the son of Ula Holm from inheriting his rightful place in the McCraggan family."

"Hush money?" Ian asked.

"That's what it was, of course," Moida said positively. "I have taken the trouble to look up in your family tree the date of your grandfather's marriage. We know from the letters that it was in 1895 that he was married to Ula Holm. Malcolm was born the same year.

"In 1897 your grandfather married Elizabeth, daughter of the Duke of Arkrae. Your father was born a year later and you are his only son. You believe that you are the heir to Skaig, but I am going to prove my contention that Hamish, great-grandson of your grandfather is Chieftain of the Clan and the owner of Skaig."

"Skaig, at any rate, was left to me," Ian said.

"Have you read the will carefully?" Moida asked.

"I have it among my papers," Ian replied.

"I have seen a copy in Mr. Scott's office," Moida said. "Your great-uncle left the castle and estate to 'my great-nephew and rightful heir—the Chief of the Clan McCraggan'. It was as if he expected that some day justice would be done and his other great-nephew, Rory, the descendant of your grandfather's first marriage, would come into his own."

Ian was silent for a moment.

"Are you not rather presuming there was a marriage?" he said at length. "You have no marriage certificate."

"No, but you forget that in Scotland at that date if a man and woman lived together as man and wife and

75

spoke of themselves as married in front of witnesses, they did in fact become so legally and irrefutably."

"I doubt if such a supposition would be upheld now, after such a long time," Ian said.

"That remains to be seen," Moida answered. "I have written to the Lord Lyon, giving my reasons for making the claim and sending him copies of the letters."

"May I see these letters?" Ian asked.

"Of course," Moida answered. "I have nothing to hide. I am merely fighting for justice and for my nephew's inheritance."

"I don't want to sound depressing," Ian said, "but I feel very doubtful that my grandfather actually did marry this girl who, you say, was the daughter of a shopkeeper.

"I never knew my grandfather, but I imagine he was rather like my great-uncle, fiercely proud, arrogant to the last degree, reverencing above all things, his family and the Clan.

"I cannot believe that such a marriage would have been contemplated by my grandfather, brought up as he was. He may have been in love with this girl, but she doesn't even sound Scottish."

"She was, I gather, of Scandinavian descent," Moida said. "She must have been very beautiful, for your grandfather's letters to her are the letters of a man who finds that nothing matters in life save his love."

Ian gave a little sigh.

"I shall, of course, fight the case. I wish to own Skaig. I have always thought of it as my real home, as my father did."

"I shall fight, too," Moida said fiercely.

"Do you have the money?"

"I will find the money," she answered, "if it takes me the whole of my life to do so."

"In the meantime?" Ian asked.

"In the meantime Hamish is living in his own home, the castle which will one day prove to be his."

Moida rose to her feet as she spoke. The lamp at

the far end of the room seemed to cast a little light on the two people by the fire.

The flames had died down for a moment and they seemed to speak to each other through the darkness.

"It all seems very obvious to me," Moida said, "a despicable plot to keep hidden the marriage of which a proud and stiff-necked family would not approve. Your grandfather paid for his son to be brought up by strangers while he made a marriage which could be applauded by the world in which he lived. When he died, he entrusted his secret to his elder brother."

"You are supposing a great many things which have to be proved," Ian said. "A lot of this is, as you know in your heart of hearts, sheer supposition. My great-uncle may have had many reasons for paying Malcolm Holm and later, his son, a thousand pounds a year.

"To jump to the conclusion that it was hush money or even the result of blackmail is to assume far more than is warranted by a collection of old love-letters. If there was anything secretive which must be hidden, do you really believe that my great-uncle would have allowed Malcolm Holm to come here and live in the village?"

"Perhaps he could not prevent it," Moida said softly.

"Exactly, blackmail!" Ian said.

"You can say what you like, you can sneer and protest and fight us with the strongest weapon you have, which is money," Moida said, "but in the end Hamish shall have what is rightfully his, and shall bear the name to which he is entitled."

"We shall see," Ian said.

He turned away as he spoke. Then, as he reached the door, he hesitated and turned back.

"I will ask a lawyer to come over here from Inverness tomorrow," he said. "We will put the case before him and see if there is some more obvious solution than you appear to have found."

"Thank you, but I will choose my own lawyer," Moida told him sharply.

There seemed to be nothing more to say, so Ian shut the door and went down the wide oak stairs in search of his mother. Already Beatrice had contrived to get both light and warmth into the house.

The big library, where Ian remembered his great-uncle had always sat, was cheerful and bright with the light of half a dozen lamps, a huge log fire was blazing in the hearth and a tray of drinks, a shining silver cocktail shaker amongst them, had been placed on the table in the corner.

There was no sign of Beatrice, but Lynette was sitting in a chair by the fireplace.

She rose as Ian entered and walked towards him, holding out her hands invitingly. She had changed for dinner, he noted, and thought how in every possible circumstance she always managed to look right and wear the right thing.

Her short dinner frock of green wool was embroidered with gold sequins and she had a necklace of gold around her neck and innumerable little hanging bracelets around her wrist.

She looked lovely; but Ian, annoyed and irritated with everything to do with the new developments, felt that her first question jarred.

"Is it all right? Have you shown them up as imposters?"

"It isn't exactly a question of that," Ian said a little stiffly.

With her usual adaptability Lynette realised that she had said the wrong thing. She put up her hand and touched his cheek.

"Darling, you look tired," she said. "Mix yourself a cocktail, and I would like one, too."

"Has Mother gone to change?" Ian asked.

Lynette nodded.

"I think so," she said. "She had no idea what time we should have dinner, but she promised that, when we did have it, it would be good. We brought lots of stuff with us you know."

"Mother always thinks of everything."

Ian hoped that his mother had not offended Mrs. Mackay who had been willing to look after him when he asked her. It was no use worrying, he thought; this sort of thing was always happening where Beatrice was concerned.

A crisis was what she really enjoyed. Like most Americans, she was a good cook and if the worst came to the worst she would cook excellent meals herself on a chafing-dish.

He sipped the cocktail he had made and though it was warm because there was no ice, he found it delicious. He gave one to Lynette. He finished his own glass quickly. It had been a long day and he was tired.

"That girl, who your mother tells me is the aunt of the two children, does she really intend to stay here unless we throw her out bodily?"

"We can't do that," Ian said. "It would cause a scandal, and that is the last thing we want."

"It is a ridiculous story, isn't it?" Lynnete said. "But these people will make up anything to draw attention to themselves. I imagine she is the sort of girl who would stick at nothing."

Quite suddenly Ian was annoyed. Moida was sincere, he was sure of that, though he believed her entirely wrong in her suppositions.

"Let's talk about something else," he said to Lynette. "Tell me about yourself. Have you missed me?"

"A great deal," Lynette answered. "And, it is lovely to see you again so soon. I didn't expect to be here until the end of the week."

"You are very sweet, Lynette," Ian said softly.

She put out a hand towards him and he raised it to his lips.

"You're the loveliest person I have ever seen," he said.

He bent towards her and would have found her lips, but at that moment the door opened and Beatrice came in. She was wearing a blue velvet dinner gown with a stole of white mink round her shoulders.

She looked as if she had just stepped out of a band-box and Ian felt a sudden impulse of admiration.

His mother was tremendous. There was no doubt about that. She had driven from Edinburgh, reorganised the household, and they would doubtless, in a few moments, be given a perfectly cooked and perfectly served dinner; and yet she managed to look as if she had just stepped out of Elizabeth Arden's.

"A cocktail is just what I want," Beatrice said. "We must remember to see about some ice tomorrow."

As she spoke, there was the sound of a car being driven up outside at tremendous speed.

"Who can that be?" Beatrice asked, her hand arrested as she raised the cocktail glass to her lips.

"I've no idea," Ian replied. "Are you expecting anybody?"

There was a sound of a voice in the hall; and then, as they all three waited, the door was flung open and one of the Ross girls, looking flustered, announced in a breathless voice: "The Duke of Arkrae, Madam."

Before she had finished speaking, the Duke had pushed past her. What hair he had appeared to be standing on end, and his eyes were not only watery, but protruding.

He had eyes for no one save Ian and strode across the room towards him in what appeared to be an agitated and yet somehow nervous manner.

"Ian, old chap," he stuttered, his words almost falling over each other. "Came see you at once. Need your help! It's gone . . . ! Went look at it found it had gone."

"What's gone?" Ian asked, and then remembered. "Not the blue heather?"

"That's right. Vanished. Place where it stood absolutely empty! I'll get it back—if have to shoot somebody."

80

5

Beatrice, changing her dress before dinner, listened to her lady's maid moaning about the discomforts of the castle.

"I've never seen a more uncomfortable place, Madam. It's hardly what I call civilised. The staff they have had here in the past have been prepared to put up with anything."

Beatrice paid no attention. She was used to Mathieson's disagreeableness whenever she was faced with a change of any sort; but she was an excellent maid, neat, methodical and skilful with her needle, besides having been with Beatrice for ten years, so she was entitled to a certain amount of licence.

"What's more, I don't believe Madam's bath will work here with this inadequate plumbing."

This was meant to be a blow beneath the belt, for Mathieson knew quite well that Beatrice's bath was one of the most important things in her life.

She had long ago despaired of finding any sort of comfort in English bathrooms—most of which she considered both insanitary and dirty—and she had, therefore, evolved a contraption of her own which created consternation wherever she went.

It was a rubber bath of deep azure blue, made soft and collapsible so as to be carried in a suitcase. To it were attached literally miles of rubber pipes which could extend along passages and be adjusted to fit any hotwater tap.

The other occupants of the house or hotel where Beatrice was staying fell over the pipes in the corridors, became entangled with them on the stairs and found it impossible to get a bath themselves, as the taps were engaged in supplying Beatrice. But the latter washed in comfort in the privacy of her own room and in her own elegant and unique tub.

She was well aware, as Mathieson spoke, that her maid intended to be difficult and if possible to goad her into leaving the castle as soon as possible.

She had not expected the servants to like it and she was already anticipating that there would be a scene when her chef, Alphonse, saw the kitchen.

But this made her, if anything, more determined to stay where she was.

There was a streak of obstinacy in her which she had inherited from her father. He had made his railroad against great opposition and against every possible natural difficulty.

Where a meeker man would have crumpled up, Sigmund Stevenson had set his jaw and gone ahead. As he got older, he had really thrived on opposition and had been suspicious of things which he attained too easily.

Beatrice was becoming like him. All her life, everything she wanted had fallen into her lap like an overripe peach. She found everything too easy. She could pay for what she wanted and there was very little that could not be bought with money.

The mere fact that there was some difficulty over proving that Ian was the Chieftain of the Clan and that the castle was his, made it, for the moment, seem infinitely more desirable than any other place in the whole world.

She had hated Skaig and all it stood for ever since her row with Great-Uncle Duncan, when she had shaken the dust of the family residence from her feet and taken her son with her, threatening never to return.

She managed, through sheer feminine subtlety to prevent Ian from going back. There had always been some wonderful excuse to sidetrack the demand that he should spend a part of his holidays there.

She had even taken grouse moors for him in Yorkshire and a forest on the West Coast so that he should not miss Skaig, and she had no idea that in his heart he still thought of it as home.

Now Beatrice was prepared to forget the way she had raged against Skaig and decried it during those years when she kept Ian in exile.

"A mouldy heap of ruins" she had called it not once but many times, yet now that its ownership was in doubt she was as devoted to it as if she had been a McCraggan herself.

"I can't think where I'm going to put your things, Madam," Mathieson said with a sniff. "The paper in the chests of drawers has not been changed for years to judge by the colour, and there's sure to be moth in these old-fashioned wardrobes."

"You should have brought your DDT spray with you," Beatrice said unsympathetically. "I'll wear the blue velvet tonight, Mathieson, and my ermine wrap."

"You'll need it, Madam," Mathieson remarked gloomily. "This place is like an ice-house."

"I have given orders for fires to be lit in every room," Beatrice replied. "The staff will be arriving tomorrow and I am sure there is plenty of local help to be had."

"If there is, they are usually more trouble than they are worth, Madam," Mathieson retorted, rustling among the tissue paper in the suit cases so aggressively that Beatrice could hardly hear what she said.

"I'm afraid you don't like Scotland, Mathieson."

"There's Scotland and Scotland, Madam," Mathieson answered reprovingly. "When I was with the Duchess of Torrish, we stayed in a great many castles, but they were always most comfortable and well heated."

"This will be the same by the time I have finished with it," Beatrice remarked.

The Duchess of Torrish was Mathieson's standard of perfection to judge by the times her Grace was quoted. Nevertheless, Mathieson had left the Duchess to come to Beatrice for reasons best known to herself.

"There's some places as can't stand renovation," Mathieson sighed.

"Judging by the look of them, the walls here are strong enough to stand anything," Beatrice answered. "When we have electric light and central heating, you will hardly know the place."

"That is if I'm here to see it," Mathieson said gloomily. "The room I am in, Madam, wouldn't be suitable for a dog. Damp is literally pouring down the walls, and as for the bed—one might just as well sleep in a bog!"

"I'm sorry about that, Mathieson," Beatrice told her, "I will go up after dinner and see what we can do to improve the room."

It was the last thing Mathieson wanted, as Beatrice well knew.

She was perfectly capable of choosing for herself the most comfortable room available, and whoever else went without, Mathieson would be warm and waited on. She liked to grumble, and a legitimate grievance was exactly what suited her best.

"I will wear my sapphires," Beatrice said, as Mathieson finished doing up her dress.

Her jewel case was produced and she chose from it a necklace, brooch and bracelet of sapphires skilfully set with diamonds. Like everything else she bought, Beatrice's jewels were large and expensive.

She looked at herself in the looking-glass and was well pleased with the reflection. She had to admit that candles were far more becoming than electric light.

Already she was playing with the idea of having only candles in the chandelier and cut-glass sconces in the big drawingroom in Grosvenor Square. Soft lights took literally years off a woman, she thought.

It was as if Mathieson guessed her thoughts, for she said sourly:

"And I hope, Madam, with so many candles about, you will give instructions for everyone to be particularly careful, otherwise we shall all be burnt to death in our beds for a certainty."

"What with the damp and the thickness of the walls, I don't think the castle will burn easily," Beatrice smiled.

As she walked downstairs, she considered how fortunate it was that Mrs. Mackay had so many candles put by in the store cupboard. Great-Uncle Duncan had so far conceded to modernity as to use oil lamps, but there were only about half a dozen of these to light the whole castle.

Beatrice could well remember how gloomy and frightening the place had been when he was alive.

One had groped one's way along the passage, felt rather than seen the stairs, and peered across the gloom of the great dining-room with only two paltry lamps to illuminate it.

Ridiculous old man, bigotted and set in his ways! How she had disliked him, and yet she had a respect for him, too. He said what he thought and was not afraid of God or man.

Beatrice admired that attitude towards life. It was what she had always wanted to feel herself; yet despite her every effort at superiority some people over-awed her.

Great-Uncle Duncan had been one; and now, though she hesitated to admit it herself, Ian was another. It was the self-sufficiency of her son that frightened her and made her often feel at a loss in his presence.

Even as a little boy he had always been the same; and even when he had been sweet and loving towards her, she had always sensed a reserve that she could not dispel.

Being a strong character, Beatrice liked those around her to be weak. She would have wished her son to cling to her, to let her do the fighting, to let her order and direct his life.

But Ian had done none of these things. From the moment he had gone to Eton when he was thirteen years old, it seemed to Beatrice that he had become a man.

He had still been gratifyingly affectionate; he had still wanted her to do things with him and told her flatteringly she was a jolly sight prettier than any of the other fellows' mothers.

But he had stood on his own feet; and then, as he grew older, he had developed, most irritatingly as far as Beatrice was concerned, a strong character of his own.

Strangely enough, Beatrice could see little of herself or her father in Ian. It was the McCraggans he took after, and most of all, though she hated to admit it, he was like his Great-Uncle.

There was the same directness about him, the same quickness of decision, the same determination which made them both so often get their own way before people realised they were doing it. There was, too, that same twinkling sense of humour.

Yes, Great-Uncle Duncan had had that, although Beatrice always felt uncomfortably that he regarded her as a joke.

She was well aware that Euan's marriage to an American had been received not only with astonishment but with a certain amount of disapproval by the McCraggan family.

There were plenty of nice, well-behaved Scottish young women whom Euan could have chosen as a bride, girls who in tweeds woven in every shade of porridge strode over the moors, their unwaved hair blowing untidily against their shiny, unpowdered faces.

Beside them Beatrice had looked like a tiny, exquisite doll. Her beautiful clothes, her small, elegant feet and thin ankles, her perfectly-coiffured hair and skilfully made-up face made her seem like a creature from another world—which indeed she was.

She was polished, assured, sophisticated and extremely well educated at eighteen. She had nothing in common with Euan's friends, who appeared gauche and out of place anywhere except on the moors.

But Euan himself had looked romantic enough in a kilt to satisfy Beatrice's yearning for romanticism, and handsome enough to keep her proud of him until his dying day.

"Darling, I just love to look at you," she would say sometimes.

To which Euan, squirming uncomfortably, would reply: "Silly girl, it's you who are worth looking at!"

But he was pleased all the same and he was passionate enough by nature to justify his appearance.

"You are mine—mine, do you hear me?" he would demand fiercely of Beatrice when he was jealous.

Once, driven beyond endurance, he dragged her away from a party by sheer force and beat her most effectively when he got her home. A lot of champagne had given him Dutch courage on this occasion and when his anger died away he was appalled by what he had done.

But Beatrice would not listen to his apologies; she loved him at that moment more passionately, more completely than she had ever loved him before.

It was a pity that Euan never again forgot he was a gentleman and repeated the performance.

Beatrice had found him, when the first rapture of their honeymoon was over, slow brained, obstinate and an unmitigated bore when it came to talking about sport; but she had only to see him in his kilt to fall in love with him all over again, and their marriage was on the whole an extraordinarily happy one.

It was of Euan that Beatrice was thinking as she came down the wide staircase.

How often he had bored her by talking about the

castle, telling her long stories about his childhood which had been spent there when his father had been abroad in the Army.

"One day it will belong to Ian," Euan had said, not once but a thousand times in their married life.

Once Beatrice, driven almost beyond endurance by her husband's praises of Skaig, had replied:

"Why should Ian want that dilapidated castle? Let us buy him a decent estate in Inverness-shire or on the West Coast!"

Euan had stared at her in amazement.

"Buy a place! What on earth for?"

"To live there, of course," Beatrice answered defiantly feeling that in some way she did not understand she had made some monstrous gaffe.

"Buy an estate? Make somebody else's land ours when we have Skaig?"

There was scorn and contempt in Euan's voice which told Beatrice far more clearly than his words how terribly she had affronted him. She forced a laugh to her lips and tucked her arm into her husband's.

"Don't look so shocked. I was only teasing you."

The shadow in his eyes cleared.

"Thought you meant it," he muttered. "I can't always tell when you're making fun of me."

Yes, it had been Skaig! Skaig! Skaig! until Beatrice felt she would scream at the mention of the word; and when Euan had died, Ian had been no better.

"Why can't we go to Skaig?" he asked every holiday.

"Your Great-Uncle is getting old and does not really want young people about him," Beatrice had lied. "I have rented you a grouse moor of which I have heard the most glowing reports and I have invited a most amusing party. You will like it."

"Thank you, Mother, but it won't be the same as going to Skaig." Ian had said.

Sometimes she could hardly bear the disappointment in his eyes, and yet she would not toady to the Highland monster who had been so rude to her.

She knew Great-Uncle Duncan was sitting there like some rapacious spider, waiting for her to go back so that he could get his clutches into Ian again.

So she had managed to hold out all these years. She would not have succeeded much longer.

At eighteen Ian had said in strong, unmistakable terms that he intended to go back to Skaig in the autumn; but the war had saved her and Ian's visit had been postponed indefinitely.

Now for the first time Beatrice wondered if she had made a mistake in keeping him away from Skaig. Perhaps, if Ian had seen his uncle, this trouble might have been avoided.

What was there in the Will which made there seem some doubt about Ian's being the rightful heir? She felt herself shiver at the thought that Great-Uncle Duncan had played a trick on her after all.

Was this his revenge because she had defied him fifteen years ago?

The shadows in the great hall seemed suddenly deep and menacing, despite the fact that there were several lamps and dozens of candles arranged on the heavy furniture.

Beatrice hurried towards the library. She could hear voices in there and guessed that Ian and Lynette would be waiting for her. What they all wanted was a good meal.

After dinner everything would seem more cheerful and perhaps Ian would have news for her about that tiresome girl and the children on the second floor.

The whole thing was ridiculous of course, Beatrice told herself soothingly. The idea of anyone being a claimand to the Chieftainship was merely ludicrous.

It was just another piece of impertinence like their daring to move in here as squatters or whatever they called themselves.

Beatrice threw open the library door, and the sight of Ian bending towards Lynette made her feel suddenly gay and cheerful. Everything would be all right—of course it would be. Why, he seemed to fit into the place as if it had always been his.

Even the ponderous, heavy furniture, which Beatrice had secretly resolved to remove as soon as possible, seemed to be the right background for Ian with his height, great breadth of shoulder and clear-cut features.

Beatrice felt a great rush of pride. This was her son and she would fight for him if it took every ounce of energy in her body, every dollar she had in the bank.

Lynette would be the right wife for him. Beatrice congratulated herself that she had been very clever in bringing the two together.

She had made up her mind a long time ago, that, when the moment came, she would choose Ian's wife and find him someone who would fill the position with grace, dignity and intelligence.

Most of the young women Beatrice met in London she had dismissed as being far too dull and unpolished to be the right type of wife for Ian. To Beatrice, elegance and the ability to wear clothes well were as important as knowing the right knife and fork to use at the dinner table.

The casual, unpolished appearance of the average English debutante shocked Beatrice, who had spent two or three years of her girlhood in Paris and whose smartness dated from those days.

She had liked Lynette and admired her from the first time she saw her; and then, after the girl had accepted several invitations to her flat in Grosvenor Square, Beatrice began to plan for Lynette to meet Ian.

When he came back so unexpectedly and telephoned her, her first impulse had been to cancel her party for that evening and have him all to herself.

She wanted to talk to him, she wanted to hear what he had been doing; and then she remembered that Lynette was to be one of the guests.

It had been the work of a few seconds to place them side by side, and exactly what she hoped for had come to pass. Ian had been attracted by Lynette; and Beatrice, seeing them disappearing together, had been elated beyond words.

She had been wise not to question Ian too closely, but merely to mention Lynette among a host of friends.

"She's such a sweet girl—I don't suppose you noticed her last night. I must get you to meet her some time. She is quite lovely and every man in London is mad about her."

It was only a fortnight after that that Ian had said with elaborate casualness:

"You might ask Lynette to dinner, Mother, and alone. We want to talk to you."

Everything was exactly as she had planned it, Beatrice thought; and now, seeing them together in the library at Skaig, she thought how suited they were to each other.

But there was another girl in the house, Beatrice remembered with a sense of irritation. This trouble-making MacDonald whom Ian had been to see.

She must ask him what had transpired; but even as Beatrice opened her lips to speak, the door was flung open and the Duke of Arkrae came in.

The Duke's aunt had been Ian's grandmother, which made them cousins. Beatrice had known Archie ever since she had married Euan, but she thought he did not alter with the years. He still had the same schoolboy mentality as when she first knew him.

He was agitated and fussed now in a manner which appealed immediately to Beatrice's sense of organisation. She would have to organise Archie, she could see that; and before he knew quite what was happening to him, he had been given two strong cocktails and taken in to dinner.

"Nothing seems quite so bad after a good meal" was one of Beatrice's mottoes, and the Duke certainly felt better after several excellent courses and a glass of champagne.

"I brought this wine with me," Beatrice said, raising the glass to her lips. "Tomorrow Ian had better see what is left in the cellar."

"Not much," the Duke told her. "Duncan, condemned to water last few years of his life! Grudged everyone else able to drink."

"He must have hated giving up his whisky," Ian exclaimed.

"Doctors told him he'd die if he didn't," the Duke remarked. "Better dead than teetotal when one's eighty."

A decanter of port was put down in front of Ian at the head of the table and the servants departed.

"Now we can talk," Beatrice said. "I didn't want you to say anything in front of Hull. He's my chauffeur, but he always helps wait if there is an emergency. He's a nice man, but a terrible talker. Whatever you said about your blue heather would have been repeated to everyone in the house and doubtless in the village, too."

"No secret. It's gone," the Duke said in a voice of gloom.

"Start at the beginning," Ian suggested. "When did you discover the loss?"

"Two hours ago," the Duke replied. "Usually look in greenhouses before dressing for dinner. Tonight agent came see me and you'd called, so a bit late. Changed first, then remembered I hadn't been down to gardens. Still a quarter of an hour before dinner—dine sharp at eight o'clock when alone. Toddled off to gardens. Walked into greenhouse—gone!"

"Was it in a pot?" Beatrice asked.

"Thirty of 'em. Most had bloomed, but this one just beginning bud. Blue—no doubt of it. Just waiting for first flower come out."

"Why wasn't the door of the greenhouse locked?" Lynette asked.

The Duke looked sheepish.

"Key lost for years. Always meant fit new lock. There's one on grape house and peach house. Isn't as if heather kept in one place—too cold, too hot—you know what gardeners are. Hadn't been in this house more than week."

"Seems a bit careless," Ian remarked.

"Knew people were interested, trying it themselves. But expect honesty and all that. Can't lock up whole estate."

"Are you absolutely certain it's gone?" Beatrice asked.

"Searched whole place. Called gardeners, made hell of hullabaloo. All knew which it was of course. Not a sign nor sight of it—definitely pinched."

"What are you going to do?" Ian asked.

"Don't know what the devil to do. Came over ask your advice—you asked mine. After all, you're clever sort of chap. Used dealing communists and that sort of person."

"You think this might be the work of a communist?" Lynette asked.

The Duke pursed his lips.

"Those chaps everywhere. Would be just like 'em. Blow against Scotland. Blue heather's going mean lot to country properly handled. Bring in tourists. Good as Loch Ness monster any day."

"You were telling me this afternoon that there were two groups of people especially interested in the heather," Ian said. "I remember that one was a firm in Glasgow; who was the other?"

"Americans! Had letter from some busybody in America week ago," the Duke replied.

He stopped suddenly and brought his clenched fist down on the table with a crash.

"Got it!" he exclaimed. "Bet it's that damned American who's taken Benuire this year. Talked to him about it only last week. Curious, kept asking questions."

"What's his name?" Ian asked.

"Struther," the Duke replied. "Talks through his nose. Always did loathe that sort of fellow." He stopped and looked at Beatrice apologetically. "Know you're American, Beatrice, but damn it, you don't talk like one."

"I imagine this Mr. Struther is a Yankee," Beatrice said stiffly.

She was intensely proud of the fact that she was a Southerner—a Virginian, and it was certainly true that she spoke without a trace of accent of any sort. Ian, who was well aware of the strong feelings between the North and the South, of her great country, smiled across the table at her as he said,

"Yankees will do anything, even to stealing blue heather, eh, Mother?"

"It might as easily be Mr. Struther as anyone else," Beatrice replied.

Ian, with a smile, turned to his cousin.

"This Struther is a possibility," he said. "What did he say about the heather when you saw him?"

"Heard I was experimenting. Father horticulturist. Knew nothing himself. Drew me out tell him what I'd done."

"And did you show him the heather?" Lynette asked.

The Duke looked uncomfortable.

"Matter of fact, yes. Chap seemed interested and . . . know what it is when you're keen on thing."

"Oh, Archie, a clear case of boasting!" Ian teased.

The Duke twisted the ends of his fair moustache.

"Sounds like it now. By Jingo! If I'd know what he was after, have had him out of place quick enough."

"You've got to prove it, you know," Ian said. "You can't just jump to conclusions like that. You say this fellow is at Benuire?"

"Yes. Rented for season. Gave old Fraser couple of thousand. Pleased as Punch. Never got more than thousand before and grouse aren't as good there as they are with us."

"What are you going to do?" Beatrice enquired.

"Asking you that," the Duke replied.

"We must plan this very carefully," Ian said. "You can't just barge in on a strange man and accuse him of pinching your plant. Have you thought of telling the police?"

The Duke hit the table again furiously.

"Not telling those damn' fellows," he said. "No good anyone, driving about in checked hat bands. Always make me think of draughts I played with my old father up to day of his death. Great man for draughts. Always had to win. Cut me out of his Will if I beat him."

"Well, we won't tell the police then," Ian said. "We shall just have to try to get it back on our own. It's too late to do anything tonight."

The Duke pulled at his moustache with a gesture of anguish.

"Will flower tomorrow. Five years' hard work, and show next week!"

"What show?" Beatrice asked with interest.

"Flower show Inverness," the Duke replied. "Made regular thing of it this year. Exhibits from all over Highlands. Slap-up effort. Intended show my blue heather. Thought that would surprise 'em. Make it clear once and for all I'd got there first."

"I see," Ian said; "then we've got to get the blue heather by next week, whatever happens."

"Would have suspected Colonel Lofts but car's out of action, crippled with arthritis. His idea prize for most original exhibit. Pestering me for weeks find out if succeeded with blue heather. Showing multi-coloured fuchsia himself. If I'm out of running, he'll win. Never seen such a cock-eyed-looking plant in life."

"Are you sure it can't be him?" Ian asked.

"No. Lofts can't move. Not sort of chap ask anyone else do his dirty work for him. That Struther fellow. Isn't going in for flower show. Out bigger game— blue heather for America!"

"I do wish I could have seen it," Lynette said wistfully.

She was looking very lovely in the candlelight; but the Duke's eyes, watery and miserable, seemed hardly to see her.

"Five years' work!" he murmured brokenly.

"Well, the best thing you can do," Beatrice said crisply, "is to go home, Archie; make absolutely sure there's been no mistake and that the blue heather has not been left in another greenhouse or dropped down behind a stand. Then come back here first thing in the morning. Ian will go with you to see this Struther man. You can't go alone."

"Why? Think he might shoot me?" the Duke asked nervously.

"No, but you can't just walk in and accuse him of stealing your heather. You can say Ian's just arrived at Skaig and you've brought him over to introduce him."

"Good idea," the Duke said. "Better come, too, Beatrice—you able talk to him better than we—both Americans."

"I'm a Southerner and we should have very little in common," Beatrice said coldly. "Nevertheless, if you think I can be of any assistance, I shall be only too delighted to come with you."

"The more the better," Ian said. "We needn't all sit in the drawing-room making polite conversation. One of us might take a turn round the gardens and see what we can find."

"And if we can find it, steal it back!" Lynette said. "Oh, what a wonderful idea."

"If heather been put in greenhouse at Benuire it will die," the Duke said mournfully. "Not a pane of glass left. Old Fraser drunk on New Year's Eve six years ago. Went round estate shooting everything he could see. Only things hit were greenhouses and clock in stable yard—never gone since."

"Well, don't let's look on the gloomy side," Ian said cheerfully. "If this Struther chap wants the blue heather enough to steal it, he will obviously keep it carefully, especially if he is going to send it to his father in America."

"Wouldn't trust chap like that look after common daisy," the Duke sighed.

"We shall have to be careful how we approach him," Ian went on. "Are any of Fraser's servants still there?"

"Took over lock, stock and barrel."

"Then we'll have to talk to them. Find out if he was out earlier this evening in a car. Does he drive himself or have a chauffeur?"

"Drives himself," the Duke answered. "Peculiar looking machine—backside before."

"Well, we'll ask where he's been this evening," Ian said; "but you will have to be careful of what you say, Archie, or you'll be had up for slander."

"If he's a thief, lock him up," the Duke replied.

"You've got to prove it first," Ian cautioned.

"Well, anyway, that's settled," Beatrice said, rising to her feet. "Come, Lynette, we'll leave the men to their port." As Ian opened the door for her, she said, "I haven't had time to ask you—did you get any satisfaction out of Miss MacDonald or whatever her name is?"

"She undoubtedly has a claim," Ian replied quietly.

The sapphires glittered in Beatrice's ears as she moved her head sharply.

"Nonsense!" she said. "There's no possibility of her having anything she could possibly substantiate. I suppose you are trying to tell me that your Great-Uncle Duncan was married in his youth?"

"Not Great-Uncle Duncan," Ian replied: "my grandfather."

"It's a lie," Beatrice said positively.

She swept from the room, her small head held high. Lynette followed her, after looking up into Ian's eyes as she passed him in a manner which made him want to kiss her. He would have done no more than wish, if Lynette had not turned back in the corridor and waited expectantly.

Ian closed the dining-room door behind him and held out his arms. Lynette hesitated, looked over her shoulder and then ran forward eagerly.

"Darling, you haven't thought about me all evening," she pouted as Ian caught hold of her possessively.

"Do I ever think of anything or anyone else?" he asked.

"Yes, you do," she accused. "I'm feeling unwanted."

"My poor, sweet, ridiculous darling!" His lips were seeking hers but her mouth evaded him.

"Say you're sorry!"

"I'm sorry—no, I'm not—I won't be bullied. Kiss me!" It was a command.

"And if I don't?" Lynette only breathed the words.

"I'll make you."

Ian put his hand under her chin as he spoke and turned her face up to his. For one moment he looked down at her glowing pink and white and gold loveliness before he kissed her as if he would never stop.

"I must go!" Flushed and adorable Lynette slipped away from him and sped to the library. As she entered the room a little guiltily, Beatrice, with an air of determination, was ringing the bell.

"Do you want something?" Lynette asked. Her breath was coming quickly from between her lips.

"I am going to send for this Miss MacDonald," Beatrice said, too intent on her own concerns to notice Lynette; "and get her to tell me her story. I should have gone with Ian in the first place. Men are so credulous. They believe anything a woman tells them."

"She's obviously a very tiresome sort of person," Lynette said. "Can you imagine wanting to move into someone else's house when they were not there?"

"My dear, there are some women who will do anything to attract attention to themselves," Beatrice answered.

The bell was answered by one of the girls from Skaig.

"Ask Miss MacDonald, who is on the second floor, to come down and speak to me," Beatrice commanded.

98

"Yes ma'am."

The girl closed the door and Beatrice, lighting one of the small Turkish cigarettes which were made specially for her, settled herself in a comfortable chair by the fire.

"You look very pretty tonight, Lynette," she remarked.

Lynette tried to blush deprecatingly, but it was too big an effort and she merely looked coy.

"If you and Ian think so," she said, "then I am more than happy."

"Don't fail Ian," Beatrice said unexpectedly.

"Fail him?" Lynette echoed in surprise.

Beatrice threw away her cigarette.

"He expects so much—too much," she explained. "But you will be able to manage him—I'm sure of it . . . yes, quite sure."

"I don't understand," Lynette faltered.

Beatrice looked at her for a long moment, and if Lynette could have read her thoughts she would have been insulted, for her future mother-in-law was thinking that it was a pity she was such a fool.

"Forget it," Beatrice said briskly, as the door opened and Bessie returned.

"If you please, Ma'am," she said breathlessly, "Miss MacDonald says it's half past ten and she's in bed. She's afraid she can't see you now, but will be ready to do so any time in the morning."

"Thank you, Bessie," Beatrice said with composure.

Then, as the girl shut the door behind her, she looked at Lynette and they both exclaimed together,

"What impertinence!"

"To think," Beatrice continued, "that she's pushed her way in here, annexed some of the best bedrooms, and then, when I send for her, refuses to come. Really, what next? I ask you, what next?"

6

Ian opened the front door quietly and let himself out.

The sun was already shining in the loch although it was not yet six o'clock. In the distance the sea was vividly emerald against the pale morning sky, and dew hung heavily on the heather as he walked towards the river.

Before he left the terrace, he paused for a moment and looked back at the castle. The curtains were tightly drawn over the bedroom windows on the first floor.

He resisted an impulse to wake up Lynette and ask her to come with him. He would have liked to show her the beauties of Skaig when no one was about, when the peaks of the mountains were pearl-grey and the strath had a radiance which belonged only to the break of day.

But he had already learned that Lynette must not be disturbed until the world was well aired.

He had found in London that if he telephoned to her too early, he was met by a blank, "Miss Lynette has not yet been called, Sir," or an annoying conversation with Lynette's aunt with whom she lived, an ingratiating woman whose arch coyness made Ian avoid her as far as possible.

No, Lynette would not wish to come out with him at six o'clock in the morning; and yet she was with him in thought, as with his rod on his shoulder he tramped through the heather.

Last night he had managed to get her to himself for a few moments before they went to bed.

He made the excuse that he wanted to show her a picture in the big, shrouded drawing-room, that by the look of it had not been open for many years.

They walked hand in hand between the furniture covered with dust sheets and the musty airless atmosphere added to the sense of mystery created by the light of the candle which Ian held shoulder high.

He found the picture he sought and set down the candle on a table so that they could examine it; but when he turned to look at Lynette, he forgot the picture and everything else.

She was so lovely, with her fair hair shining against the darkness, her eyes raised to his and her red lips parted a little, that he swept her masterfully into his arms.

For a long time they stood there, clinging to each other, their lips pressed together.

"My sweet darling," Ian murmured at length.

He looked down at her face close against his shoulder, her eyes half shut, her face flushed and her breath coming quickly.

He knew then, with a sense of triumph, that his own rising passion had awakened a response in her so that she trembled and her voice was low and sweet as she whispered: "Kiss me again."

Time stood still. How long they remained together in the drawing-room Ian had no idea. He only knew that Lynette was utterly desirable and that his tiredness had vanished.

He was ecstatically, vibrantly alive, thrilling with an excitement such as he had not known for a very long time.

It was Lynette who came back to earth first and remembered they must return to the library.

She withdrew herself from Ian's arms and taking the candle from the table in front of the picture, carried it to the mantelpiece so that she could see to powder her nose and redden her lips in the carved and gilt mirror which hung above it.

"Have I made you untidy?" Ian asked.

She turned her head to flash him a glance, provocative and inviting.

"I'll forgive you," she smiled.

He put out his hand then to cup her chin with his fingers.

"You're wasting time," he said, looking at the lipstick she still held in her hand, but she turned her lips away from him when he would have kissed her again.

"We must go back to your mother," she said.

Ian did not know that Lynette found it hard to keep her head and to control the rising emotion within herself. He was only a little hurt that she could switch so quickly from the magic of their embrace back to the commonplace.

He did not attempt to kiss her again and was only slightly mollified when, as they reached the bright lights and the warmth of the big hall, Lynette laid her hand on his arm for a moment and said softly:

"I am so very happy."

For a moment he contemplated picking her up in his arms and carrying her back to the drawing-room. But he knew she did not wish it and his own urgency ebbed away, leaving him with only a feeling of quite unwarranted frustration.

"I've been conventional all my life," Ian told himself later that evening; "but now, because I'm in love, I want to be unconventional."

He was dead tired and yet he did not want to go to bed. He wanted to take Lynette out beneath the star-strewn sky, he wanted her to row with him across the loch, he wanted her to climb the battlements and look out towards the sea as his ancestors had done in the past; and yet he knew all these desires were ridiculous.

He was tired, Lynette was tired; Ian realised that

he was being absurd and wishing for the moon, yet he wanted to do wild, mad things with Lynette instead of being alone with the blood racing in his veins.

He lay awake for a long time before finally he fell into a troubled sleep to dream that he was a stag and Hamish was stalking him.

As dawn broke, Ian had awakened with a feeling of well-being and known himself to be as excited as a schoolboy. How often had he experienced that same thrill in the past on the first day of the holidays when as he opened his eyes he had remembered that he was not at school, but at Skaig and that his rod was waiting for him downstairs.

It was a recaptured joy to be nearing the river now; and yet, perversely, he felt lonely. He would have liked Lynette to be with him; but because he knew that such a desire was unreasonable, he felt annoyed by his desire for her company.

But even Lynette was forgotten when he saw that the river, owing to a recent spate, was at exactly the right level and then as he reached the bank, a big silver salmon leapt out of the water a few feet away from him.

Five minutes later Ian had put up his rod, tied on a fly and was casting downstream. As he drew the line through his fingers, he hummed a little tune beneath his breath.

And soon with the warmth of the sun on his head he began to feel that calm detachment which every fisherman knows so well.

He ceased to become a person and became one with the river, the sunshine and the soft gurgle of the water. He moved slowly along the bank, remembering, as he fished, every pool, every twist and turn of the river.

Here it had altered a little, there a bank had fallen in; but it was Skaig, the river of which he had dreamed in many far-away places.

It was then, as he made a long cast under the bank on the other side, that he felt the line tighten, and with a sudden leap of his heart he struck.

The line ran out with a shriek; the salmon darted upstream.

It was not a heavy fish, but a high-spirited one, leaping, jumping and making quick dashes up and down the river until Ian was quite breathless with following it over the rough stones and under the high banks.

It was when the fish was beginning to tire that he remembered to feel for the gaff and with a sense of dismay realised that he must have left it on the bank when he tied on his fly.

That was a good quarter of a mile upstream, and knowing the predicament he was in, Ian looked hopefully around in case there should be a shepherd in sight.

As he did so, a quiet voice beside him said:

"Are you looking for your gaff?"

Ian started, for he had not heard Moida approach.

"I've left it on the bank," he replied.

"I saw it there at the same time as I saw you had a fish on," Moida told him, "so I brought it along,"

"Thank you!"

Ian's words were brief, but his tone was heartfelt. The salmon made a last despairing run at that moment and he was forced to hurry after it. But the fish was tired and as Ian reeled in he could see it coming unprotestingly towards him.

"I'll gaff it for you, if you like," Moida offered.

"Do you know how?" Ian was about to say and then checked the words on his lips.

There was a purposeful air about her which told him that she was by no means inexperienced. She crouched down at the waterline and slowly he walked backwards, drawing the salmon towards her.

She moved suddenly, the sharp steel of the gaff

lashed in the sunshine, then she was lifting the fish out of the water and carrying it on to the bank.

"Well done!" Ian exclaimed.

The fish was still alive. He put down his rod and hit it on the head with a stone so that it should suffer no longer.

"About nine pounds, I should think," he said proudly.

"It's fresh run," Moida remarked.

Ian gave a sigh of contentment and took out his cigarette case.

"Do you smoke?" he asked.

She shook her head.

"Quite right," he approved; "I dislike women who smoke."

She raised her eyebrows a little at that.

"Are you being old fashioned or merely economical?"

"Old fashioned," Ian answered.

He lit his cigarette and sat down on the river bank; then he looked up at Moida.

"Sit down for a moment and tell me how you happened to come to my rescue," he said.

"I was going down to the village to beg, borrow or steal some eggs for your breakfast," she replied.

Ian threw back his head and laughed.

"Beware of the enemy when he brings gifts," he remarked.

"Mrs. Mackay is in a panic that you won't have enough to eat," Moida went on; "and apparently every egg already in the house was finished up for dinner last night."

"So you are being charitably munificent," Ian stated.

Moida nodded.

"Mrs. Mackay knows I am always up early, so she asked me to fetch them as a favour."

"And the children?"

"They are still asleep, I hope."

Moida looked across the loch to the mountains.

"This is the one time in the day when I can be on my own," she said. "I love my sister's children, but at the same time I sometimes like to be alone."

She spoke almost as she were talking to herself and not to Ian; then he saw by the sudden change in her expression that she remembered who he was and regretted that she should have confided in him anything that was personal.

It was then, for the first time he noted not only that she was pretty, but that her face was one of unusual intelligence.

Her mouth was beautifully shaped and there was a strength and determination in the moulding of her lips; her eyelashes were long and dark, but they did not hide the depth of thought which seemed to lie behind her eyes.

Her forehead was broad and her eyebrows lay against it dark and winged. There was nothing ordinary about her, Ian thought suddenly, and he asked out loud:

"What do you do when you are not here?"

She looked at him for a moment and he saw the hostility slowly return to her face.

"Why should it matter?" she asked.

"I just wondered," Ian replied. "You are no relation, I suppose, of the MacDonald who is always writing rude things about my exploits in the East?"

He was speaking more to be conversational than anything else, without previous consideration, with no reason for his question other than the fact that it suddenly occurred to him the name was the same.

To his astonishment he saw a wave of crimson appear suddenly in Moida's cheeks, a blush as vivid and startling as the one which had stained the whiteness of her skin when he first told her his name.

"Then it is some relation?" he said as she did not speak. "Who is it . . . your father?"

"My father is dead," Moida replied. "He was Murdoe MacDonald."

"The economist?" Ian ejaculated.

Moida nodded.

"Good God! I would never have imagined such a thing!"

Murdoe MacDonald had been a powerful force in politics. He had been hated or respected according to whether one agreed or disagreed with him. No one could ignore him.

He had caused a sensation in America by his revolutionary ideas on finance. In England one had only to mention his name to start a bitter controversy in which feelings ran high and tempers became overheated.

He had been killed tragically during a civil uprising in Mexico. A stray bullet from some trigger-happy rioter had pierced his lung as he watched the crowd from a balcony, and he had died within a few seconds of being shot.

No one had denied Murdoe MacDonald's brilliance though a great many people opposed his conclusions; and yet, already, so many things he had prophesied were coming true and governments were being forced to adopt his suggestions because there was no alternative.

Ian had intuitively distrusted his ideas, but had come to the reluctant decision that many of them were necessary owing to world conditions.

Yet somehow, he had never managed to think of Murdoe MacDonald as anything but a revolutionary figure, a man without a home or country.

To find his daughter here on the river bank at Skaig left Ian breathless; looking up at Moida with his mouth open and his hand suspended with his cigarette halfway to his lips, he ejaculated:

"Murdoe MacDonald's daughter! Well, I'm damned!"

Then, as he watched the colour slowly receding from Moida's cheeks, he added, "and you are the 'M. MacDonald' of the articles."

"I am not ashamed to acknowledge it," Moida replied defiantly.

"Of course not," Ian answered quickly, and added, "but I can't believe it. It can't be possible. How can you write as you do and be here at Skaig?"

"It does seem rather like cheating," Moida agreed.

She sat down as she spoke and, staring across the river, went on:

"I am really studying to be an economist like my father, but I have to keep myself. I need money, you see, so I take in typing as homework and write for the newspapers when I have something to say. I have always been interested in what are commonly called 'world affairs'."

"Interested!" Ian said with a snort. "I should think you are. You pretty well flayed me alive in the *Telegraph* last month."

"There was nothing personal about it," Moida said. "I know that you were representing Government policy, but it is that with which I disagree."

"What do you know about such things?" Ian asked.

She turned to look at him then and he saw there was a faint smile at the corner of her lips.

"This is supposed to be a free country," she said. "I am only expressing my own opinions in any criticism I may make."

Ian thought back. He could remember several articles which had been signed "M. MacDonald." They had been brilliant, provocative and extremely critical.

He had often wondered to himself who this new MacDonald might be, remembering that Murdoe was dead. But it was a common name and he had not even suspected a relationship.

Of one thing he had been quite certain, that was the "M. MacDonald" who had written so scathingly of his last mission was a man.

In fact, several people with whom he had been discussing the matter had suggested that it might be the pseudonym of a well-known Member of Parliament who was known to have somewhat similar views.

To find it was this girl, someone whom he had thought on first acquaintance a simple Scottish lassie, put a different complexion on the whole thing.

That the squatter in the castle, aunt to the claimant to the Chieftainship, should be the daughter of Murdoe MacDonald, that tenacious, intrepid and infuriating man who set half the world by the ears and whom no Government had ever been able to ignore, was sensational and astounding to say the least of it.

"Well, since I now know who you are," Ian said abruptly, "why on earth do you take up the attitude you do over China?"

Moida turned round to face him.

"Now look at it this way . . ." she began; and in a few seconds they were oblivious to everything but their own argument.

Words flashed between them like winged arrows. Suddenly Ian said forcibly:

"You are wrong—quite, quite wrong!"

He gesticulated with his right hand as he spoke and brought it down with a slap on the salmon which was lying on the ground between them. It was the feeling of the cold fish beneath his hand which recalled him to where they were.

His action made Moida rise to her feet with a little cry.

"What on earth am I thinking about?" she exclaimed, "sitting here talking while the household will be waiting for their breakfast? The children will be waking up to find no one there. I must be mad! You are as bigotted and narrow-minded in what you say as you were wrong in your statement over Korea."

"I was nothing of the sort," Ian replied furiously; but even as he spoke, he saw that she was almost out of hearing.

She was running away from him towards the village and as he said the last words, he realised that the wind was blowing them away from his mouth and it was doubtful if she could hear them.

He watched her go, then threw his cigarette into the river. He drew his cigarette case from his pocket only to find that he had already smoked his last one.

While they had been arguing, he had been smoking all the time. He frowned for a moment, remembering how the shrewdness of her arguments had got under his skin.

Then suddenly he had began to laugh. It was all too ridiculous, too impossible to be believed that Murdoe MacDonald's daughter should have been sitting here, fighting with him, with a dead salmon between them.

It was just not possible, and yet now there was no doubt at all in his mind that she was the MacDonald who had written those extremely able and well-informed articles in the Press which had been irritating him for some time.

He picked up his rod and fish and started to walk back towards the castle.

It had been an incredible morning, and yet one he would remember all the days of his life. He repeated the name to himself and again found himself laughing.

The only sad thing was there was no one to share the joke with him. He doubted if Beatrice ever had time for the more serious utterances of the newspapers. He was quite certain that Lynette read nothing but the gossip columns and the fashion notes.

No, it was a joke he would have to keep to himself for the moment, although he could imagine the astonishment on the faces of some of his colleagues when he told them that "M. MacDonald" was a girl.

He felt suddenly intensely curious about Moida. Where had she lived, how had she been brought up?

It was almost impossible to imagine Murdoe Mac-Donald with his thin, cadaverous face, untidy dark hair and eyes that always seemed to be burning with a fierce indignation, being a loving father, or even an unloving one.

The man had never seemed human. He had just been a mouthpiece for his tempestuous, brilliant brain.

No one had ever denied his brilliance; and when he died, there had been expressions of sympathy from almost every nation in the world.

Had his wife been alive? Ian wished he could remember, and knew that there were many other questions he wanted to ask Moida.

He was stunned and surprised by the revelation of who she was and at the same time he was curious. She knew what she was talking about.

Of course, he disagreed with her; he was convinced that many of her assertions were absolutely wrong and without foundation; and yet he was forced into an admiration of her intimate knowledge of the nations and peoples of whom they had spoken.

There was no guess work behind her arguments—they were solid facts.

Often, when he had been dealing with peoples of whom he had only a superficial knowledge, Ian had felt appalled at his own ignorance of the history, customs and behaviour of such peoples; and yet men like himself were allowed to recommend far-reaching decisions with only a most superficial acquaintance of those directly concerned.

Because he was conscientious, Ian had tried to study not only the things with which he was directly concerned himself, but everything which affected both the past and the future of those with whom he came in contact.

He well knew the immense amount of work this entailed, and he thought now how hard Moida must have studied to know as much as she did, to have gained such a lot of information without the easy contacts which smoothed the path for him.

Murdoe MacDonald's daughter! And with undoubtedly much of his brilliance.

The clock was striking the hour as Ian entered the castle door. He counted the strokes and then thought he must be mistaken and went to look at the grandfather clock which stood in the corner of the hall. Nine o'clock! It was two hours they had sat arguing on the river bank, not one.

He rang the bell and gave his salmon to the maid, Bessie, who appeared after some minutes' wait.

"Tell Mrs. Mackay I am ready for breakfast," Ian said.

"It is already laid in the dining-room, Sir," Bessie answered. "I'll wet the tea and bring it up to you this minute."

"Thank you, Bessie," Ian smiled.

He ate his breakfast, noting there were no eggs, and he was just finishing the meal with an apple when Bessie came hurrying into the room.

"Mrs. Mackay says the eggs have just come, Sir, and would you like a couple?"

"Thank you, Bessie, but I have finished. Tell Mrs. Mackay that it is my fault the eggs were late."

"I will, Sir," Bessie answered.

Ian left the dining-room to go upstairs to his mother.

Beatrice always held court in her bedroom first thing in the morning. Propped up by lace and satin cushions, wearing a dressing-jacket of white velvet trimmed with bands of sable, she was dictating her letters, ordering the meals and giving instructions to the rest of the household, usually at one and the same time.

Only one thing was missing from the castle, Ian thought, and that was the telephone. It was usually at his mother's hand so that she could carry on a conversation while everyone else waited, expectant and silent, around her bed.

"Good morning, darling," she said to Ian, adding in almost the same breath, " 'I shall expect to hear from you by return of post . . . Yours truly'."

Ian, from long practice, realised that the last sentence was for Miss Watson's dictation and not for him. He crossed the room, kissed his mother, and saw that Hull, the chauffeur, was waiting for his orders.

"Good morning, Hull," Ian greeted him. "Did you have a good night?"

"Indeed I did not, Sir," Hull said positively.

"It shall all be seen to today," Beatrice interrupted. "Everyone was uncomfortable last night, but tonight will be different. Miss Watson is going to telephone to Inverness for a large number of things to be sent off immediately. You will take her down to the village in the car, Hull, and bring her back as quickly as possible.

"Miss Watson will be arranging for decorators and carpenters to come here from Inverness. You will meet them, Hull, and you'd better find somewhere for them to lodge in the village while you are down there."

"Yes, Madam."

The chauffeur, with an air of resignation, turned to the door. Miss Watson went after him, clutching a sheaf of letters in her hand and making last feverish entries in her shorthand notebook.

"Everything will soon be perfectly all right," Beatrice said to Ian. "I have not seen this tiresome MacDonald girl yet, but I shall make it quite clear that, if she intends to remain in the castle, she cannot sleep in the best bedrooms."

"I want to talk to you about Miss MacDonald," Ian said.

"Yes, I know you do, but not now, dear. I have to get up because Archie will be here at quarter to ten."

"Quarter to ten!" Ian ejaculated. "We can't go calling on this American fellow at that hour."

"Of course we can," Beatrice contradicted. "The sooner we get to the bottom of things the better. Archie is in a state of nerves and quite insupportable; and as he is our nearest neighbour and a relative, I prefer him in his usual state of inanity. Is my bath ready, Mathieson?"

113

"Yes, Madam," Mathieson replied, and added triumphantly, "but the water is only lukewarm."

"Miss Murray will arrange for the coke to be delivered today," Beatrice said. "Go and find Miss Watson, Ian, and tell her not to forget the primus stove and oil lamps."

But Ian had already disappeared through the door and shut it behind him. He knew, if he remained much longer, he would be given a list of things to do, for his mother could not bear to see anyone standing about without an immediate job.

Miss Murray and Miss Watson were conversing in the hall as he came downstairs. He knew by the worried expressions on their pale faces that upon their shoulders had been laid the burden of making the castle habitable.

Beatrice would have gone to bed with a list of things that she needed written on a pad beside her, and during the night she would have awakened innumerable times to pencil down another instruction.

It was obvious to Ian from the hurrying to and fro in the house that by nightfall the place would be a hive of activity. Beatrice had her own way of getting things done.

It was not only money, it was the inexhaustible supply of vitality and enthusiasm which made people work for her harder than they would ever work for anyone else.

If she made up her mind to have something done, it was achieved in half the time it would take other people; and though there were often tears, grumbles and occasional resignations among her staff, everybody on the whole liked working for Beatrice.

As one secretary had said, "There's never a dull moment, for the Lord only knows what's going to happen next."

Ian had only reached the bottom of the stairs when he heard a car draw up outside, and a moment later the Duke came hurrying into the hall.

114

"Morning, Ian. Ready?"

"You're early, Archie," Ian replied. "We weren't expecting you till a quarter to ten."

"Know that, haven't slept. Up at five this morning having another look round. Not a sign of anything. Thought perhaps thief might have had attack of conscience, brought it back."

"Not much chance of that if the thief is who you think it is," Ian said cheerfully.

"Yes, I know," the Duke replied, pulling miserably at his moustache.

"You are sure it is this American chap? You want to be careful how you tell him so."

"I know, I know. Been rehearsing all time I was coming here."

"Well, we'll leave the talking to you," Ian suggested. "Mother and I will just sit around and look pleasant."

They were standing in the hall, and now there was a sudden cry of excitement from behind them and Cathy came running downstairs.

"Good morning, Laird," she said, running up to Ian and putting her hand into his. "Aunt Moida says you caught a big fish this morning. It made her very late for breakfast. Hamish and I were up and dressed when she got back."

"Yes, I'm sorry about that," Ian smiled. He looked at the Duke to see a question in his expression. "Oh, Archie, this is Cathy," he said, "one of the squatters I told you about."

"Ha, indeed!" the Duke exclaimed, and stared down at Cathy who politely held out her hand to him.

"That's right, say 'how-do-you-do' ," Ian said. "This is the Duke of Arkrae and he lives near here."

"Are you really and truly a Duke?" Cathy asked.

"Hum. Suppose so," the Duke replied.

"You're not very tall," Cathy said critically.

"Should one be tall to be a Duke?" Ian asked.

Cathy had no time to answer before Moida's voice was heard calling her from the stairs.

"Cathy, where are you?"

"I'm here, Aunt Moida, talking to the Laird and . . . a Duke."

Moida came hurrying into the hall.

"You are not supposed to come down the front stairs," she said sternly. "You know I told you we are to use the others. I'm sorry," she apologised to Ian, "she escaped from the nursery."

The Duke gave a sudden cough and Ian realised that he was drawing attention to his presence.

"May I introduce my cousin, the Duke of Arkrae?"

Moida held out her hand.

"How do you do?" she said. "I am sorry if Cathy has been a nuisance."

"Not at all," the Duke replied. "Thought I was a bit small for my position. Dare say people have thought so before, been too polite to say so."

"I am sorry!" Moida exclaimed. "Cathy must learn not to make personal remarks about people."

"Do you think you are qualified to teach her that?" Ian asked, with an accent on the pronoun, and Moida flushed.

"As I said before," she replied, "I was not being personal, I was only attacking your policy."

"It seemed very personal to me," Ian retorted.

"Oh! there you are, Archie," came Beatrice's voice from the top of the staircase.

She walked quickly down into the hall, exquisitely dressed in a beautifully-cut tweed coat and skirt with a felt hat to match and a narrow fur round her shoulders. She gave her hand to Archie with a friendly gesture, and at the same time turned to Moida with an air of rebuke.

"I was expecting to see you this morning, Miss MacDonald; but now I am afraid I can't spare the time. Kindly be ready to see me when we return, which I anticipate will be about twelve o'clock. I shall not expect to receive an excuse this time."

Beatrice's tone as she spoke to Moida was the same

116

as she might have used to a servant who had been found stealing the silver spoons.

There was the lash of a whip in her tones, and then she turned to Ian with a smile of honeyed sweetness on her lips.

"Come, darling, we mustn't keep Archie waiting. We have to find his blue heather."

Beatrice moved towards the front door. Ian tried to smile apologetically at Moida; he wanted to make some excuse for his mother's rudeness, but was not certain how he could say it.

While he hesitated, she had gone.

Holding Cathy tightly by the hand, she hurried quickly up the staircase, her back, Ian thought uncomfortably, eloquent of disapproval.

7

Moida took the children into the kitchen garden and told them to weed the lettuce bed.

She found her own thoughts strangely chaotic this morning. In planning her offensive against the Mc-Craggans and deciding to take up residence at the castle after she and the children had been turned out of their house in the village, she had been fired by a burning sense of injustice which made everything she did and planned to do seem comparatively easy.

It had been easy in theory to feel indignant that both Malcolm and Rory had been forced to live in obscurity all these years because of the autocratic, overbearing pride of the McCraggan family.

She felt that she was being a crusader in championing the cause of Hamish and fighting that he should take his rightful place as Chief of the Clan and Laird of Skaig Castle.

Indeed, she had looked forward to meeting Ian and confronting him with the truth. She had imagined that he would be angry, that he would defy her and that it would require all her intelligence to outwit him.

He had even become, in her mind, a kind of stage villain, grinding down the face of the poor and being quite oblivious to the suffering of those he persecuted.

But somehow, in reality, the fight between them was neither as easy nor as violent as she had anticipated.

Ian had indeed told her that he intended to fight for

Skaig because it was his home and because he believed that he had a right to the inheritance.

But he had smiled at her this morning when she had gaffed his fish; and although they had argued fiercely about world affairs, he had treated her as an intellectual equal, which had been curiously disarming.

She had expected much more active opposition, and although she knew that she still had Ian's mother to cope with, the sense of self-righteousness which she expected to feel in these encounters had vanished, leaving her curiously deflated and somehow reluctant to continue to be aggressive.

She told herself she was being idiotic and she had only to look at Hamish to realise that he was worth fighting for and that in no circumstance could she leave him penniless and without the comfort of the name to which he was entitled.

At the same time, it was one thing to plan what one would say and do, and then to find that one's opponents were behaving very differently from what one had expected.

What was more, Beatrice, although she had been rude and autocratic as she swept away into the car, followed by the Duke and Ian, had contrived to make Moida feel comparatively unimportant.

She wanted to fight, she wanted to stand up to the attacks of the enemy, but it was disconcerting when the enemy seemed to be preoccupied with other matters and one was relegated to what appeared to be a place of unimportance in their thoughts.

The children enjoyed working in the garden and Hamish and Cathy were soon competing with each other to see who could collect the bigger pile of weeds, but Moida found herself resting on her hoe.

She wondered suddenly why she was taking the trouble to weed the lettuces.

There was no stall now on which to sell the results of her labours. It had amused her these past weeks to discover how many things there were at Skaig that could be sold.

There had been a satisfaction in selling salmon, grapes, apples, and in planting the lettuces, feeling that they were being made to replace the things that were no longer theirs and which had been unjustly wrenched away from them.

Now she had a sudden impulse to pack her box, to take the children away; and yet, even as she thought of it, she chided herself for weakness.

She had made up her mind to do this because it was the right and just thing to do. It was ridiculous at the first onslaught to feel weak and curiously depressed.

A delighted shriek of laughter from Cathy brought a faint smile to her lips and a sudden tenderness to her eyes.

At least the children were happy—happier than they would be in some cramped and cheap lodging, which would be all she would be able to afford for them if she took them to Edinburgh.

What sort of life would she be able to give them if she tried to keep them on her own? She could, of course, give up her studies and take a regular job.

But even if she were to obtain a position in an office or as secretary to some private person, her salary would not be large enough to clothe and feed the children, educate them and in the meantime find someone to look after them while she was at work.

It was a big problem and she had considered it many times; but it grew no easier, however often she considered it. What was more, she was well aware that she would require money, and quite a considerable amount of it, to fight Hamish's claim to Skaig.

She had pondered over this until her head ached, but so far she was no nearer a solution.

She had a little money of her own; and the furniture and personal belongings of her sister and Rory had

120

been sold for a few hundred pounds. Moida had deposited this money in the Bank.

She was determined not to touch it if it could be avoided. This was the only fund Hamish and Cathy would have to pay for their education and anything else they might require in the future.

In the meantime, she felt it was up to her to keep them; but however hard she worked, however successful her articles in the newspaper, she could not really see how she could accumulate enough to pay the large fees which would be required by the Court of the Lord Lyon. And yet, as her mother had said often enough:

"It's no use fussing about tomorrow. When tomorrow comes, you may be dead!"

That had been Dolly MacDonald's whole philosophy ever since Moida could remember. It was likely to continue to be hers until she died. It was not the sort of outlook which encouraged one to save.

However much she earned, Dolly seldom had a penny to her name, and though Moida had considered writing to her for help, she knew it would be a waste of a twopence-halfpenny stamp.

Surely no one, Moida often thought, had a more extraordinary upbringing than she and her sister Janet. Her father had married, when he was a young man, a north-country concert singer called Dorothy Durham.

She had never been very successful and it had been no hardship for her, when she first married, to settle down to domestic life and become the mother of two girls, Janet and Moida.

It was when they were very hard up and Murdoe was getting a great deal of publicity and very little money that Dorothy decided she must go back to the stage, so that she could pay the baker's bills.

Murdoe's father was the curator at the Palace of Holyroodhouse, a brilliant scholar who lived in a world of his own and knew very little of what went on outside the walls of the Palace.

He was a dreamer and a visionary and it was, perhaps, to be expected that his son should demand action in the present where he had been content to meander in the past.

It was to her father-in-law at Holyrood that Dorothy MacDonald sent her two little girls, begging him to keep them for a short time while she tried to get back some of her previous engagements.

Then began a life of extraordinary contrasts. For a few months the two children would live with their grandfather.

They would listen to his quiet, gentle voice telling them the history of the people who had once walked in the Long Gallery or had wept and died in the State Apartments. Sometimes they imagined they saw the ghost of Mary, Queen of Scots, in the Audience Chamber.

Their grandfather had described to them that it was in this room the Queen, in a gown of purple velvet and ablaze with jewels, had received John Knox. One of the most memorable interviews in history, it had been a bitter, tearful scene between two strong and angry people.

The two little girls would tremble, too, in the Queen's bedroom; and when they gazed into a delicately engraved, but sadly tarnished mirror which hung in a recess, they expected to see in its dull surface not their own pale faces and startled eyes, but the vivid, glowing beauty of the red-haired Queen.

Sometimes they would creep into each other's bed as they imagined the screams of Rizzio still echoing from the Queen's supper-room in which he had been brutally murdered by Darnley and Ruthven and a band of their followers.

Was it really his terrified voice they heard, or merely the wind whistling down the narrow staircases and twisting passages? The people who were dead often seemed as real to Moida as those who were living.

She loved to think of Prince Charles Edward in Royal Stuart coat, scarlet breeches and blue velvet bonnet, riding with his Highlanders across Queen's park and dancing in the Long Gallery.

She loathed the Duke of Cumberland who, after the tragic horror of the battle of Culloden, where the handsome young Chevalier had been defeated, had lorded it in the Palace of the Stuart kings.

"Stop dreaming, Moida!" her teacher would say at school; but Moida was never certain when she lived at Holyrood where reality began and dreams ended.

Then unexpectedly, without any warning, their mother would arrive and whisk Moida and Janet away with her to spend a week in Manchester, Glasgow, Leeds or Halifax, wherever she might be performing at the moment, and where sometimes, and sometimes not, their father would join them.

It was three years after she went back to the concert platform that Dorothy MacDonald discovered she had a talent for burlesque.

She had been asked to sing in a provincial town and arrived to find that the hall in which she was to appear had been burnt down the night before.

She was sitting disconsolate in the station hotel, wondering what to do when she got into conversation with the manager of the local theatre. He, too, had a hardluck story.

One of his turns was down with influenza and though he had telegraphed to several agents, they had no one to offer him.

Dorothy had offered to stand in, at least for a night or two, until he got someone else. She hoped that she sounded as if she was being generous, but she knew in her heart that she was desperately in need of the money.

She went on the stage that night to find a noisy, good-humoured audience who wanted to be amused. There had been a market in the town that day, a large number of farmers from all over the country had crowded there.

They came to the theatre that night because there

123

was nothing else to do and because for many of them it was the one outing of the year and they wanted a bit of fun.

Dorothy was preceded by some clowns who had the audience roaring with laughter. She felt their faces fall as the curtain rose and revealed her, looking very ladylike in her elegant evening dress.

She was artist enough to feel the drop in the atmosphere, the boredom with which the audience turned to their programmes and found the slip of paper which announced that she was deputising for an old favourite.

She began to sing and then suddenly knew that she could not go on with it.

She started to burlesque her own song; she found herself making faces and gestures which never, in her wildest dreams, had occurred to her as being those which might amuse an audience.

She was a riot—there was no other word to describe it.

As she came off the stage after nearly a dozen curtain calls, the manager hurried up to her, pale with excitement.

"God Almighty, woman! Why didn't you tell me you were as good as that?" he said. "I thought you did a straight act."

"I thought so, too," Dorothy replied and started to laugh.

Her future altered from that moment, and funnily enough, her character altered too.

She had been brought up by staid, respectable parents who took life seriously. She had married Murdoe, who was excessively serious, and never until now had she learned to laugh.

Making other people laugh, she laughed herself and was ridiculously and irresponsibly happy. She found it impossible to take anything seriously, not even her husband and her children.

She made money and spent it or gave it away just

as quickly as she made it. She behaved in a manner which her parents would have called "reprehensible" and which her husband called "damned silly."

But she enjoyed life; she enjoyed every moment of it.

It did not worry Dorothy, who automatically became "Dolly" to her friends, her public and everyone who met her, whether things were comfortable or uncomfortable, whether she had money or not, so long as there was an audience and she could make them laugh and could laugh with them.

She loved her two solemn little girls and she had them with her as much as possible; but Moida had the feeling that, as soon as they were gone, their mother forgot all about them and that at times she found their presence somewhat of a strain.

Nevertheless, they adored going to stay with her. Dingy, often dirty lodgings were always an adventure, just as it was an adventure to come down to the theatre and to sit in the small, stuffy dressing-room with its messy grease-paint, an untidy tangle of clothes, flowers and half-finished bottles of beer.

The chaos and darkness behind the stage remained always as thrilling as the first time they saw it.

They would stand behind the curtains and watch their mother go on, hear a burst of applause, followed almost immediately by a shriek of laughter as she tripped over her train or started off on the wrong note.

"She's a born comic, your ma; that's what she is," one of the other actors said to Moida.

No one ever spoke a truer word. Dolly was a "natural". She had always used her maiden name and now the billing was changed from "Dorothy Durham" to "Wee Dolly Durham"—the "Wee" of course referred to her size.

It was certainly true of Dolly that she "laughed and grew fat". She ate enormously, too, and grew fatter and fatter, till even the sight of her would start the audience laughing.

As her size and reputation increased, so the gulf

between her and her husband grew wider and wider. Murdoe had become the fiery prophet of gloom and disaster, the man whom many men feared and few men loved. He had no time for laughter.

As Moida grew older, she realised that he found her mother an embarrassment. Dorothy had become someone he did not understand, with whom he had nothing in common.

He did not find her amusing on the stage and thought she made herself ridiculous. He was ashamed that people should know that this large, fat gesticulating woman was married to Murdoe MacDonald.

They became strangers to each other; when they met, they had nothing to say and Dolly began to be as glad as Murdoe when the intervals between their meetings grew longer and longer.

Moida guessed rather than knew that there were other men in her mother's life. She would hear Dolly talk about 'Sam' or "Tom", letting the names slip out by mistake when she was telling them where she had been or what she had been doing.

"Sam and I saw that play in Manchester," or, "We went to Blackpool last week-end. I felt I needed a rest."

The "we" was dropped unintentionally, and yet it had been said. There was no talk of a divorce or even of a legal separation. Dolly and Murdoe just lived apart, and even their children preferred it that way.

It was far easier, they found, to be alone with Mummy or alone with Daddy. If they were both there, there was an atmosphere which was almost insupportable and made them feel miserable and upset long after both parents had gone away again.

It was inevitable, Moida supposed, that as she and Janet grew older they, too, found they had little in common with their mother. The times they spent with her were fewer.

When Janet was eighteen, she got a job as a typist in a solicitor's office and stayed there until she married;

and then she swore that never again would she raise a finger to earn her own living.

"I hate work," she said to Moida. "I want a house of my own. I like cooking, I adore babies. I am just boringly domesticated."

She was extremely happy with her husband. Rory was one of the best-tempered, most easy-going people Moida had ever met. She could quite understand why Janet was in love with him. It was very easy to see that he was very much in love with her.

Dolly gave them a silver tea service for a wedding present—it was the last thing they wanted—and came to the wedding, wept happy tears which she thought were expected of her as the bride's mother, and hurried away long before the reception was over because she was playing in Glasgow that night.

"You wouldn't want me to be late, would you ducks?"

She had grown into the way of talking as she did on the stage.

She had a north country accent now and her conversation was bespattered with endearments. Moida had seen a look of distaste on her father's face as Dolly drove away from Janet's wedding, blowing indiscriminate kisses on her fat fingers.

Murdoe was looking ill, she thought. His eyes seemed sunk in his thin white face, his hair was more untidy than ever and she noticed that he was eating ravenously at the buffet after Dolly had gone. Going up to him she put her hand on his arm.

"When did you last have a good meal?" she asked.

He looked at her in surprise before he helped himself to another sandwich.

"Haven't time to eat these days," he said. "I must leave in five minutes. I've a meeting in London tomorrow morning."

"I'm coming with you," Moida said. "It's time you had someone to look after you."

He expostulated, but she got her own way. She threw up her work in Edinburgh and went south with him, making the rooms in which he lived as comfortable as possible, cooking his meals whatever time of night he came in, forcing him to eat a sensible breakfast before he set out in the morning.

She never regretted those years they spent together. He taught her more than she would ever have learned at any University or from any course.

She typed his notes for him, listened to his speeches, went with him to his meetings whenever she could do so. She met a lot of interesting people; she found herself in violent disagreement with many of them.

Inevitably she became enthused with much of the fire which burned within her father like an inexhaustible flame. He suffered and bled for his convictions.

He never spared himself any more than he spared anyone else. He spoke the truth as he saw it and his sincerity was like a very large cane which left weals on those against whom he used it.

He was magnificent, awe-inspiring and rather pathetic, all at the same time.

When her father was killed in Mexico, Moida realised that she was, to all intents and purposes, alone in the world. Her grandfather was dead, Janet was happily married, her mother lived a life of her own into which she could never intrude or be a participant.

She had not loved her father—he had not been human enough for that; but she admired him and she knew, too, that he was essentially a pioneer. What he fought for would come to pass, but he would not get the credit. Those who came after would get that.

She saw her future quite clearly. Much of what her father had said and done had died with him, but the rest could be preserved.

She began to write, and then, gradually, as she tried to present her father's idealism in simpler form to be understood by the general public, her own ideas crystallised and formed, so that it was hard to know where Murdoe MacDonald's thoughts ended and his daughter's began.

Moida went back to Edinburgh because she had always been happy there. The Palace of Holyroodhouse had been the one stable, sane place she could, remembering her childhood, call home.

Through a friend of her father's she obtained typing work at the University, and in her spare time she attended lectures and classes.

She studied all the subjects in which she knew she must excel if she were to carry on her father's work and her father's mission. She worked hard; she had no time for amusement; but she was happy in a vague, unemotional sort of way.

Sometimes she felt she had driven her brain too far and she must relax or go mad. When this happened, she would go up to Skaig to stay with Janet and Rory, and to find that she was still young and that the world was not peopled only with serious and often pedantic students.

Occasionally she would get a postcard from her mother, saying that she was coming to Glasgow or some other nearby town and that she hoped to see her.

However tired or busy she might be, Moida would force herself to go and see her mother. Dolly would greet her with cries of delight. She would seem to envelop her with love and affection, with endearments and kisses.

Moida would hate herself because she would feel cold and anxious to withdraw from Dolly's fat and overwhelming sentimentality.

It was wrong not to love Dolly. She was such a generous, warm-hearted person, and yet Moida could not help her reserve. She had nothing in common with her mother.

"We have never been a family," Janet said once with a note of sadness in her voice.

Moida, sitting with her in front of the fire at Skaig,

129

had understood what she meant. The room was small but it was homely. The chintz curtains were fresh and clean, flowers on the table in front of the window were beautifully arranged.

There was a big, comfy sofa on one side of the fireplace, and lying on it, with his feet up, Rory was reading to Hamish from a book of nursery rhymes.

There was a dog on the hearth-rug and a cat curled up in another armchair. Janet was seated with Cathy in her arms, giving her a bottle. Looking back, Moida could never remember a moment like this when she had been a child.

There was only the smell of grease-paint and the stale vegetables flowing up the stairs of a boarding house to remind her of her mother; cold draughty halls and the scrape of hard chairs to make her think of her father.

She added, to herself, the ghosts of Holyrood Palace and the impersonal grandeur of State Apartments, the books which their grandfather treasured and treated as if they were children, and the long, dark evenings when, home from school, there would be no one to look after them, no one to play with, and they would sit alone, two frightened, forgotten little girls without a family.

"It shan't happen to Hamish and Cathy," Moida thought suddenly as she stood in the garden, resting on a hoe.

She looked at the castle, its turrets gleaming in the morning sun, and wondered if she could ever make a home there for Hamish if he owned it. She and Cathy would stay there while Hamish went away to school, and would be ready to welcome him when he returned.

She thought of herself sitting alone at Skaig in the evening when the children had gone to bed, and then felt herself shiver at the thought of it. She had been lonely all her life, and yet the thought of living at Skaig made her feel lonelier still.

It was not children who made a family—it was a husband she said to herself, and then tried to laugh at the idea. She would never marry.

How could she, with Hamish and Cathy to look after, with no money and no prospect of every having any?

The children had grown bored with working and, not being kept at their task, they were chasing each other round the cabbage bed.

Moida was about to call them back when she saw someone come from the door of the castle and start to walk along the path which led to the gate opening into the kitchen garden.

She knew it was Lynette Trent, and she watched the girl approach with a feeling of curiosity. Lynette was hatless, and her hair was the pale gold of the April sun as she walked up the garden in the sunshine.

Her eyes were very blue, matching the exquisitely-cut tweed suit she wore with a silk blouse to match. She wore loose-fitting gloves of pale hogskin, and as she advanced towards Moida, the latter was suddenly conscious of her own appearance.

Her tartan skirt and green jumper seemed very rough beside Lynette's beautifully-cut suit; her hands were sunburnt and there were tiny freckles on the back of them. She felt that her hair wanted combing and her nose powdering.

"Good morning," Lynette's tone was pleasant, her red lips smiling, but her eyes were cold.

"Good morning," Moida replied.

"You are Miss MacDonald, are you not?" Lynette asked. "I saw you from the windows and I thought I would come out and make your acquaintance."

"That is kind of you," Moida replied in her deep voice.

"Not really," Lynette replied. "I was anxious to know what you looked like. I felt you must be very tough to force your way into a castle like this and stay here despite everyone's desire to be rid of you."

131

Moida felt herself stiffen. Lynette was speaking pleasantly, with an almost studied sweetness in her voice, yet this was certainly an attack from the enemy.

"Poor Ian, it is so worrying for him," Lynette continued with a little laugh, "as we hope to have a lot of friends to stay. It is going to be troublesome to have you occupying so much of the second floor if we want to fill the castle with guests, you can see that for yourself."

"It is far more troublesome to have no home and nowhere to go," Moida answered.

"I can quite understand that," Lynette replied, "but if everyone who was homeless moved into other people's houses, the country would soon be reduced to a state of chaos, wouldn't it?"

"Have you ever been without a roof over your head?" Moida asked.

"No, I haven't," Lynette answered. "And I think I would have the sense to find somewhere to go if I were in that position."

"I wonder!" Moida replied. She looked Lynette straight in the eyes; then she added, "I am not staying here because of my personal troubles. It is my sister's two children who are homeless. And, as I expect you already know, I consider that Hamish, my nephew has a right to be here."

"That's ridiculous!" Lynette exclaimed. "Brigadier McCraggan is undoubtedly the Chieftain and owner of the castle. If you try to prove the contrary, you will only make yourself ridiculous and waste a great deal of money—that is, if you have it to waste!"

Moida's lips tightened. For a moment she resented, bitterly and with her whole heart, that this girl, beautifully dressed, engaged to a very rich man, should be in a position to make her feel a beggar. As she did not speak, Lynette went on:

"I know how uncomfortable it is to be without money. I have often been in the same position myself; but Mrs. McCraggan is so rich and so generous. I feel

132

sure she would not like you to suffer. She will do something for your nephew and your little niece, if you make it clear to her that that is what you want."

Lynette spoke so pleasantly and so sweetly that for a moment Moida did not take in the full import of her words; but when she did, she felt the colour come into her face, and a sudden fury within her heart.

"If you think I am here to try to get money out of the McCraggans, you are mistaken," she said angrily. "They managed to buy off Hamish's father and his grandfather; but as long as I am in charge of the child, his silence is not purchasable. If you are speaking on behalf of Mrs. McCraggan, you can tell her that."

Lynette shrugged her shoulders.

"I was only making a suggestion," she said. "I thought it might be helpful; but if you are determined to fight the case, there is nothing that can be done about it; but it seems a pity."

She looked Moida up and down, then strolled off down the garden path, the beautiful lines of her figure very evident as she moved away.

Moida watched her go and thought that she disliked Miss Lynette Trent more than anyone she had ever met before. That Lynette had come up the garden with the deliberate intention of being disagreeable was very obvious.

Lynette turned at the end of the path and, going down a flight of steps, pushed open a wrought-iron gate which led on to the terrace. She did not look back, but walked across the gravel, turned the corner of the castle, and disappeared.

"Who is that pretty lady?" a voice asked.

Moida turned to look and found Cathy standing beside her.

"That is Miss Lynette Trent," she said, and the bitterness of her voice was very apparent.

"Where's the Laird?" Hamish called, a little way

133

down the garden. "I've got a big stone to shoot at him with my catapult."

"You are not to, you are not to!" Cathy screamed in a sudden panic.

"Don't scream like that," Moida said automatically, "and, Hamish, you are not to keep threatening to hurt Brigadier McCraggan—you know it upsets Cathy."

"I want to hurt him," Hamish retorted stoutly.

"He's not to, is he, Aunt Moida? He's a horrid, unkind boy," Cathy stormed.

"That's quite enough, Hamish," Moida said. "You had better come in now, it must be nearly lunchtime; and put that stone down, or I will confiscate your catapult."

Hamish did as he was told with a bad grace. Cathy took hold of Moida's hand.

"I like the Laird," she said in a soft voice. "Where has he gone to, Aunt Moida?"

"He said he was going to look for some blue heather," Moida said. "Isn't that a funny thing to say? I have never heard of blue heather, have you?"

"I thought all heather was purple or white," Cathy answered.

"So did I," Moida said, "but perhaps heather can be blue like forget-me-nots or delphiniums."

She was talking to try to interest the children and keep them quiet as they walked down towards the castle. She was ashamed of her feelings where Lynette was concerned, and ashamed, too, that she had wasted the whole morning thinking about herself and not entertaining the children or playing with them.

"I tell you what we will do," she said. "We will go out this afternoon on to the moors and see if we can pick some white heather."

"Are we going to sell it?" Hamish asked.

"No," Moida answered. "We have nowhere to sell it now; but we will keep it ourselves and see if it brings us luck."

"I should like to do that," Cathy said, giving a little skip as she held on to Moida's hand.

"We could put it in a pot," Hamish said, "and then it would grow, wouldn't it?"

"Hamish, what a good idea! What made you think of it?"

"There was a girl who came to the stall the other day." Hamish answered. "She had a pot of heather. She wanted to buy one of our bunches, but her mother wouldn't let her—said she had enough. The girl was cross, she kept saying, 'I want some white heather'."

"Was it blue heather in her pot?" Cathy asked.

"It might have been," Hamish answered. "It wasn't cut."

"I think blue heather's silly," Cathy said. "Purple and white are much prettier."

The children went on chattering together and Moida led them into the castle. She heard the car draw up at the front and guessed that Ian, the Duke and Mrs. McCraggan had returned.

"Hush, don't make a noise," she said, thinking it was best they should not draw attention to themselves.

But before she could stop her, Cathy had already run from the garden entrance across the hall towards Ian.

"Hello, Laird. I'm so glad you're back. Aunt Moida said you had gone to find some blue heather. Do show it to me."

"I'm afraid we haven't got it," Ian answered.

"Empty-handed," the Duke muttered gloomily.

"What was it like?" Cathy asked.

"Nobody knows yet except the Duke," Ian replied. "You must ask him."

Cathy waited for information, but before the Duke could speak, Beatrice, who had been taking off her fur and putting her bag and gloves on the chair, said sharply:

135

"That child should be in the nursery!"

Embarrassed and at the same time conscious that she was at fault, Moida came forward from the doorway.

"Come along, Cathy," she said sharply.

"But I want to hear about the blue heather," Cathy wailed. "Hamish said that the little girl who came to the stall might have had blue heather in her pot, but he isn't certain."

"What's that?"

The Duke stared at Cathy and then at Ian.

"Do you hear that?" he asked. "Child's seen thief who stole heather."

"Nonsense," Ian answered, "she doesn't know what she is talking about . . . or does she? Tell us again, Cathy. What is that about a little girl at the stall?"

Moida took Cathy by the hand and would have dragged her away, but Ian stopped her.

"Wait a minute," he said. "What is this about a child coming to the stall?"

"It was Hamish who told me," Cathy said.

"I don't think it is of consequence," Moida said. "Hamish said that a child who came to the stall had some heather in a pot. That was all. Cathy asked him what colour it was and he said it wasn't out, but it might have been blue."

"My blue heather!" the Duke cried. "What was the thief like, quick?"

"It was Hamish who saw her, not Cathy," Ian explained patiently. "Where is Hamish?"

Moida did not answer but walked across the hall to the door through which Cathy had entered.

Sitting at the foot of the back stairs with his catapult in his hand, was Hamish with a weary look of resignation on his face which almost made Moida laugh.

"Come along, Hamish. You've heard they want to ask about the child with the pot of heather."

"I am not speaking to that man," Hamish answered.

136

"Don't be tiresome," Moida replied.

"I'm not. Daddy said one of the first rules of war is 'give no information to the enemy'."

"But you are not having war about the heather!"

"What is all this about?" Beatrice asked.

She had followed Moida and now stood looking through the doorway into the stone passage. Hamish looked up at the sound of her voice and then stared at her with large unblinking eyes.

Beatrice moved past Moida in a manner which expressed her contempt far more effectively than if she had said anything in words, then she held out her hand to Hamish.

"You are a big boy," she said, "and you appear to know something that everyone wants to hear. Come into the hall and tell us. It might be very helpful."

There was a beguilement in her voice which Hamish apparently found irresistible.

As usual, Beatrice had her way. His hand went out and clasped hers and she pulled him to his feet.

"Is that a catapult?" she remarked conversationally. "I remember my son used to be a very good shot with one when he was a boy."

"I can shoot miles and miles with it," Hamish boasted.

"I'm sure of it," Beatrice remarked.

She led him back to the hall, Moida following them somewhat uncomfortably.

"I am a great believer in coincidences," Beatrice remarked as she reached the Duke and Ian. "I have a premonition in my bones that this child is going to tell us something we all want to hear, but there is no reason why we should hear it standing in a draught. Let us go into the library and sit down."

"Don't want waste time," the Duke murmured.

"It doesn't take any longer to listen to someone speaking when you are sitting than when you are standing," Beatrice replied. "Come along, Archie."

She led the way, still holding Hamish by the hand, and the Duke followed her, while Ian turned towards Moida.

"Does he really know anything?" he asked.

"I haven't the slightest idea," Moida answered tartly, her voice bristling with indignation.

Ian smiled at her disarmingly.

"Don't be annoyed. If you knew the ghastly morning we've had, you wouldn't be cross. The Duke's blue heather has got to be found soon, or we shall all be raving lunatics!"

8

As Beatrice walked towards the library holding Hamish by the hand, she thought to herself that she had had enough of Archie and his troubles.

And yet, being a bossy woman, she could not resist the appeal of someone limp and inefficient; and as had often happened before, she found herself giving more energy and thought to the Duke's problems than there was any necessity for her to do.

She wanted to concentrate on redecorating the castle; she wanted to get down to the task of turning out Moida MacDonald and the children; but instead she found herself involved in the Duke's ridiculous search for his pot of blue heather.

"Never again! I'm a fool!" she had told herself as she sat in the stiff, ugly drawing-room at Benuire and listened to the Duke pumping Douglas Struther about what he had done the day before.

The young American had looked rather surprised at their coming to call so early in the morning. He was indeed only finishing his breakfast when the car containing Beatrice, the Duke and Ian swept up to the front door.

Mr. Struther was not, however, abashed at their finding him in the dining-room at such a late hour, but explained cheerfully that he had been playing poker until the early hours of the morning.

He had obviously been drinking, too, to judge by

his voice and the lines under his eyes; and Beatrice, who was strictly abstemious in the matter of alcohol, spoke to her countryman with a sharp note in her voice, which Ian knew only too well proclaimed her disapproval.

Ian, however, could not resist a smile when he caught the expression on the Duke's face as he saw how the American was clothed.

Struther had been told that it was correct to wear a kilt in Scotland, and he sported one in a large check tweed which stuck out over his heavy hips like a ballet dancer's skirt and was at least three inches too long, so that it hid his knees and gave him the appearance of being disguised as a woman.

He wore a wind-jammer instead of a coat, and his feet were encased in wool-lined flying boots.

The Duke's pale blue eyes seemed almost to start from his head as the American shook hands and then with an effort he averted his gaze and spoke to him thereafter looking anywhere except at him.

"Dropped in introduce cousin—Brigadier McCraggan," he said. "Just arrived Skaig with his mother—Mrs. McCraggan."

"I'm sure pleased to meet you," Douglas Struther said genially. "Will you join me at breakfast or is it too late?"

"Too late, thank you," Ian said briefly.

"What about a cup of cauffee?" the American enquired, but again his guests refused.

There was an uncomfortable silence and Ian cleared his throat. The Duke glanced at him and realised that this was a signal for action.

"Wondering where you were yesterday," the Duke began.

"Yesterday?" the American repeated. "Now, let me see. I had breakfast early—I remember remarking as I came downstairs that it was vurry surprising for me to be down so early. I ate alone, for my house guests have theirs in their rooms."

"Yes, yes," the Duke said testily; "afternoon more important."

"The afternoon?" Douglas Struther repeated slowly. "We went out shooting in the morning, but came back for lunch. We mean to make it a short day, but we were late and it was nearly two o'clock before we sat down to . . ."

"No, no," the Duke interrupted. "Tea-time."

"Waal," the American drawled, "that's quite a question, Dook, because I don't take tea."

"Four, five . . . six o'clock," the Duke insisted.

"What's all this?" the American asked. "Am I wanted by the cops or something?"

Beatrice felt that it was time for her to intervene.

"The Duke is just interested to know if you were anywhere near his castle at that time," she said.

"Why?"

The question was direct. The American might not be very quick-brained, but he had gathered by this time that something was afoot and he was beginning to resent the Duke's manner.

"We have reason to believe there were some thieves about at that time," Ian explained, "and we thought you might have seen something of them."

"Thieves!" the American ejaculated. "What have they taken?"

"My . . ." the Duke began, only to be drowned by Beatrice and Ian speaking simultaneously.

"Nothing . . . nothing of importance. We just heard they were about and are trying to gather any information we can."

The Duke, realising that he had nearly put his foot in it, sat back suddenly in his chair, looking guilty and uncomfortable.

"This doesn't sound quite right to me," the American drawled.

He rose and walked across the room to pick up a packet of Chesterfields. His ridiculously-long kilt swung

141

as he moved, and his heavy flying boots gave him the appearance of taking part in a Russian burlesque.

"Let's get disentangled," he suggested, offering round the cigarettes. "You say nothing has been lifted?"

"Nothing of importance," Ian said firmly.

"Important to me, old man," the Duke protested.

"What is?" the American enquired.

"It's purely a private matter," Ian replied. "We don't want to say too much about it, but we thought you might know something and be able to help us."

"How can I help if you don't tell me what it is all about?" the American asked, bewildered.

"Where were you between four and six o'clock last night?" the Duke demanded fiercely.

"To hell with it—why should I answer," the American replied, "if you don't come clean?"

He stared at the Duke, and suddenly a suspicious look came into his eyes.

"Say, you're not suggesting that I'm the thief?" he asked.

"No! No, of course not!" Ian replied hastily before the Duke could reply. "Such a thought never crossed our minds. We only wanted your help. It is most unfortunate that we can't tell you exactly what has gone, but something is missing. You haven't seen any suspicious characters about?"

"A great many folk in Scotland look suspicious to me," the American replied; "but that doesn't say they are thieves or that they have this mysterious something the Dook has had stolen."

"Where were you between four and six o'clock?" the Duke repeated in a voice of thunder.

The American stared at him for a long moment and then replied slowly and distinctly:

"That's my business, Dook."

There was nothing else to do but go. Ian tried to pour oil on troubled waters, and Beatrice set herself out to be her most charming, inviting Douglas Struther to dinner—an invitation which he refused most firmly.

142

They walked out of Benuire feeling like schoolboys leaving the Headmaster's study after a good caning. They had gained nothing. Douglas Struther was obviously as suspicious of them as they were of him.

"Thief, no doubt about it," the Duke said as they got into the car. "Why are we leaving?"

"You'll gain nothing by saying he is a thief except to advertise the loss of your heather," Ian replied.

"You should have let me do the talking, Archie," Beatrice said. "You know as well as I do that Americans like to take their time in telling a story."

"Damn the fellow, meandering on as if all day listen to him," the Duke answered.

"Well, hurrying him hasn't been very helpful," Beatrice snapped.

They were driving down the pot-holed, ill-kept road which led to the lodge when the Duke suddenly shouted:

"Stop!"

Ian had no need to ask why. A very antiquated vehicle was approaching up the road, driven by a dour-faced man wearing a chauffeur's cap.

"Sutherland!" the Duke exclaimed excitedly. "Chauffeur to Frazer. May know something."

Ian brought the car to a standstill. The Duke got out and walked down the road to where the chauffeur had drawn up the ancient shooting-brake preparatory to letting them pass.

" 'Morning, Sutherland," he said.

"Guid morning, Your Grace," Sutherland replied gloomily.

"Want ask you something, Sutherland," the Duke said in the pregnant tones of one about to divulge a state secret.

"Aye, Your Grace."

The Duke glanced over his shoulder as if he were afraid he would be overheard.

"Mr. Struther take car out yesterday evening between four and six?"

143

Sutherland scratched his chin.

" 'Tween four an' six?" he repeated reflectively. "Ma mem'ry's getting awfu' bad the noo, Your Grace."

The Duke realised what he was being asked; and after fumbling fruitlessly in several pockets of his tweed jacket found a very creased ten shilling note in the breast pocket. He held it delicately between his fingers. There was a sudden gleam of intelligence in Sutherland's eyes.

"Nay, Your Grace. Mr. Struther weren't oot in th' car. He were wi' auld Donald havin' a shot or twa wi' the rifle at a target on th' hill. Th' worst mon wi' a gun, Donald says, tha' he ever did ken."

"Quite sure there 'till six o'clock or later?" the Duke insisted in a desperate voice.

"Aye, Your Grace. 'Twere nigh on seven when he came walkin' back to th' hoose. I seed him wi' ma ain eyes; I canna mistake tha' strange kilt he wears. For sure, it bears na resemblance ta th' real thing."

"Thank you, Sutherland. All I wanted to know," the Duke said.

He hesitated a moment and then put the ten shilling note back into his breast pocket.

"All I wanted to know," he repeated almost to himself, and turned away, completely oblivious of the disappointment and chagrin on Sutherland's face.

He got back into the car and there was no need for Beatrice or Ian to ask him what had transpired. The pathetic droop of his pale moustache was answer enough.

It was absurd to feel sorry for him, Beatrice told herself; and yet she could not help hoping that they would find his blue heather.

The Duke's enthusiasms—and he had had many in the years she had known him—were incredibly boring to other people and usually exhausting in some way or another.

Yet Beatrice knew that it was because he had had absolutely no affection in his life that he would take up

144

some extraordinary thing and devote all his energy to it while his interest lasted.

The Duke had been a comparatively young man when she first knew him; but it seemed to her that even then he had been pathetic, so that, though in some ways she despised him, she instinctively found herself mothering him and trying to protect him from the results of his own folly.

His father had been an autocrat of the days when Dukes had power and prestige and were looked up to with both awe and respect.

Nevertheless, he did his duty in a heavy-handed manner which made those who benefited from his benevolence resent everything they took from him.

His wife, Archie's mother, had been a beautiful fool. She adored being a Duchess and the only other thing she loved in her whole life was her own pretty face. She had flitted through life as prettily and with about as much sense of reality as the proverbial butterfly.

She had everything she wanted—flattery, adulation, social success and attentive young men. She spent a great deal of time in London, standing at the top of a long flight of marble stairs in Arkrae House, receiving hundreds of distinguished guests as they arrived and saying good-bye as they left.

She was never photographed except in full evening dress with tiara and dog collar of diamonds. She was painted by Sargent wearing the same jewels, and the papers described them in detail at every Opening of Parliament and whenever she went to Court.

She was not interested in children, and having produced an heir she refused to have any more. She even found it difficult at times to remember the very existence of her only son.

He, too, was painted by Sargent and the portrait was hung in the picture gallery alongside those of his ancestors. In his childhood he was left with his nurses; on his holidays from Eton he had a tutor to look after him and keep him from getting into mischief.

He gave the impression of being alone, even in the gayest and noisiest crowd. And he had a disconcerting habit, like many other lonely people, of turning up when least expected and vanishing again before one had even got used to his presence.

When he came to London, the Duke called on Beatrice.

"Why didn't you let me know you were coming, Archie?" she would say when he arrived at the flat in Grosvenor Square at the most inconvenient times, usually when she had a Committee meeting or a women's luncheon party.

"Don't want to be any trouble," the Duke would answer apologetically. "Dropped in to see if you were all right."

"I have to go out to dinner tonight," Beatrice would say, "but what about tomorrow? Will you dine with me, Archie? I've got a few people coming whom I think you would like."

"Not sure," the Duke would answer. "Let you know later."

Beatrice began to know that this was his formula for getting out of engagements, for invariably she would receive a message which began, "The Duke Arkrae regrets . . ."

What he did with himself in London and who were his friends Beatrice had no idea. She knew he went to his Club; she would occasionally meet people who had seen him in the most unexpected places, like Battersea Park or the British Museum.

Otherwise his doings were as mysterious as his arrival, and one morning she would telephone Arkrae House to find that he had gone back to Scotland.

"It's time you got married, Archie," she said to him once.

"Don't know any girls," he replied.

"That's easily remedied," Beatrice suggested.

The impulse towards matchmaking which lies latent in every woman springing enthusiastically into life.

But the Duke shook his head.

"Shouldn't know what to say to 'em," he said. "Too busy, anyway. Drainage at Arkrae."

Beatrice had suppressed the impulse to giggle.

"You would do much better with a Duchess to look after you, Archie, and you've got to have an heir, you know."

"No hurry . . . no hurry," the Duke said quickly. "Never cared for babies myself."

With persistence Beatrice had managed to introduce him to several charming young women when he came to London; but he had stared at them with his watery blue eyes and had, to Beatrice's astonishment, been extremely critical.

"No beauty," he said of one of Beatrice's introductions. "Too long in nose; too short in leg."

"But, Archie, she is most attractive and comes from such a nice family," Beatrice expostulated.

"Wouldn't look good in tiara," was the reply.

Beatrice, remembering pictures of the last Duchess, suddenly realised that Archie was comparing everyone he met with his mother. That beautiful, stupid face had set a standard in his mind of what his wife, when he had one, must look like.

With a sense of dismay Beatrice realised that there were few girls today who could even begin to rival the regal loveliness of Archie's mother.

She had been of the period when beautiful women were tall and golden-haired, with full, curved figures, large busts and tiny waists and hips such as Rubens liked to paint in the nude.

There was no girl living who would wear the tiara with the dignified grace with which Gwendoline, Duchess of Arkrae, had worn it; no girl appeared to have a neck long enough for the famous dog collar and certainly none of them had enough bust to support the row upon row of the famous Arkrae pearls.

Beatrice was wise enough to know she was beaten; she gave up trying to produce young women for the

Duke, and out of sheer pity let him bore her for hours on end about the extensive alterations he was doing to the drains.

And yet, as always when she saw him, he reminded her of a spaniel who had been left outside in the cold, and she found herself longing to comfort and minister to him as she had never longed to comfort and minister to her own son.

They had driven back from Benuire in silence.

Despite the Duke's high hopes of finding the blue heather in Douglas Struther's possession, Beatrice had thought it unlikely from the first that the American, however enthusiastic a horticulturist his father might be, would stoop to stealing the precious plant from Arkrae. And as soon as she saw him, she knew his type only too well.

Douglas Struther was an American who wished to cut a social dash. He had taken a grouse moor because it was the right thing to do. He was interested only in himself and in showing his friends what an international sportsman he could be. His aspirations certainly did not include stealing.

He was angry now because he thought the Duke was making a fool of him. But when he thought it over in cold blood, he would be only too willing to make friends and forget his indignation.

He liked being able to speak of "my friend, the Duke of Arkrae" to his friends who came up to Benuire for the first time.

No real harm had been done by temporarily offending him Beatrice decided; but they had certainly not found the Duke's blue heather and now had to consider where else to look.

Ian had given up thinking about it. He was going over his arguments with Moida that morning and remembering several points which he might have made with effect.

Funny how, when she argued, her eyes seemd to get bigger and bigger and the gold flecks in them more

148

prominent. He had enjoyed fighting with her over foreign affairs—but he couldn't say he had won the contest.

She was an opponent worthy of his steel. It was almost impossible to believe that her pretty dark head should hold so much real knowledge.

In Ian's experience pretty women were usually fools and clever women had faces like the back of a cab. Looking at Moida one admired her looks; talking with her one almost forgot them.

Ian wondered what she would be like when she fell in love. Was she soft and tender and clinging? Or was she commanding, inspiring and tantalising? He had a sudden desire to see her eyes dark and languorous with passion and her lips parted a little to receive a kiss.

He pulled himself up with a jerk. They were home at Skaig—and Heaven knows where his thoughts had been leading him.

As Beatrice came into the hall and began to take off her furs, she did not at first listen to Cathy's prattle, but was planning something scathing to say to Moida for permitting the children to run about the house as if they owned it.

The Duke's interests took a back place when she remembered that she had not had an opportunity to speak to the squatters.

Then, as she heard Cathy speak of what Hamish had seen and Moida vainly tried to coax Hamish into telling what he knew, Beatrice found herself, willy-nilly, taking part in what was going on.

She could never forbear to have her finger in the pie, no matter what it might be or to whom it might belong. She had to play a leading part in every drama however unimportant.

To her life was only a play in which she monopolised the centre of the stage to the exclusion of everyone else. Her strong will, her dominant personality and her intense, unflagging vitality rendered this very easy.

In most cases people were too tired or too limp to oppose Beatrice in any way. Those who found her insupportable merely drifted out of her life and ignored her, while she, for her part, had no idea they even existed.

In reality, for all her exquisitely feminine appearance, she should have been born a man. She would have made a shrewd and successful business man.

She wanted to command and control; and because she was hampered by being a woman, she made the very best and the very most of what power she had.

Leading Hamish by the hand into the library, she was at her most charming. She was the centre of interest. She had mesmerised away Hamish's hostility. She had everyone else following her like patient sheep.

She sat down on the sofa and kept Hamish's attention fixed on her while the others filed into the room.

"Listen to me, Hamish," she said. "What do you want more than anything else in the whole world?"

"A gun," Hamish replied promptly.

"I don't know whether I could get you a real gun," Beatrice replied, "but I know I can get a two-barrelled gun which will fire corks and pieces of wood. They can fire quite a long way, and look exactly like a man's gun. Would you like one of those?"

"She should not bribe him," Moida said fiercely to Ian.

She spoke in a low voice, but everyone in the room heard her.

She spoke with spirit, and Ian, turning to smile at her reassuringly, thought how lovely she looked with her eyes flashing and a pink flush in her cheeks.

Beatrice appeared to be oblivious of everyone save Hamish.

"Would anybody know it wasn't real?" Hamish asked.

"Nobody except you," Beatrice answered.

"Then I'll have one," Hamish said solemnly, adding after a little pause . . . "please."

"We'll telephone for it today. It should be here by the day after tomorrow. But, if I give you this gun, will you do something for me?"

Hamish paused before he replied. He was shrewd enough to realise a bargain was being struck.

"Y . . . yes," he said at length, a little reluctantly.

"Then tell me about the little girl who came to the stall for the white heather. Tell me everything you can remember. Let us begin at the beginning. It was yesterday afternoon, wasn't it?"

Hamish nodded.

"Who else was there?"

"Cathy. Aunt Moida was showing people round the castle."

"People? The people who had the little girl with the pot of heather?"

"Yes, but the little girl didn't go into the castle. She said she was tired and her mother told her she could play about till they came out."

"I remember now," Cathy ejaculated, "because she gave me sixpence for the little girl and then made me give it back again because she said the little girl wasn't going in."

"What happened then?" Beatrice asked.

"The little girl stood about," Hamish replied. "She kept looking at me and smiling. But I wouldn't smile at her."

"Why not?" Beatrice asked.

"She was a girl," Hamish said simply.

"Oh, I see!" Beatrice remarked solemnly. "Had she anything in her hand?"

"No," Hamish replied, "but after a bit she climbed into the car."

"She couldn't open the car door for a long time," Cathy said scornfully. "She was bigger than me, but she couldn't get it open for ages. I can open car doors, can't I, Aunt Moida?"

"Yes, darling," Moida answered.

"She got the door open," Beatrice said. "Then what did she do?"

"She came back to the stall with a pot of heather in her hands, and a lollipop," Hamish replied. "She sucked the lollipop to make me want it."

"Did you speak to her?" Beatrice asked.

Hamish shook his head.

"It was a red lollipop," Cathy said. "She might have given it to you if you had spoken to her."

Hamish said nothing. He was staring at a stag's head over the mantelpiece, and Beatrice could see that he was counting the points on its horns. His attention was wandering, so she said quickly:

"I will get you some red lollipops as well as your gun, but you haven't finished your story yet, Hamish. She was standing by your stall with her pot of heather and a lollipop."

"She stood there till her mother came out," Hamish said in a bored voice. "There was another lady with her, and a man, too. They bought some apples and the lady said. 'Do you want some white heather, Bertha? It would be nice to take home with you to . . .'" Hamish hesitated. "I can't remember where she said."

"Think," the Duke pleaded.

He was standing with his back to the fireplace, pulling at his moustache, his eyes fixed on Hamish's as Beatrice extracted the story.

"I don't remember," Hamish repeated stubbornly.

"I do," Cathy said. "It was Glasgow."

"It wasn't," Hamish replied fiercely, annoyed at his sister's interference.

"Yes, it was," Cathy retorted. "They said Glasgow, and when the man finished paying for the apples, he said to her, 'Come on now, it's nearly a hundred miles to Inverness. You'll be complaining before we get there.' I thought it was funny 'cos she said she was going to Glasgow."

"I didn't hear her say that," Hamish said firmly.

152

"Never mind," Beatrice interposed. "What was said about the heather?"

"The little girl started crying, 'I want some heather, Mummy. I want some white heather,' and her mother said, 'You don't want any more heather. You've got a pot of it there. That ought to be enough for you'; and the little girl said, 'It isn't white. I want some white heather 'cos it's lucky'; but her mother wouldn't let her have any, although the other lady bought a piece, and then they went away."

Hamish gave a big sigh as though the telling of the story had been exhausting.

"That's all," he said. "Can I have my gun?"

"Yes, of course," Beatrice answered.

"Did you look at the heather?" the Duke asked. "Did you see it? What colour was it?"

"It was just heather in a pot," Hamish answered stoutly.

"It wasn't white," Cathy said helpfully.

"Was it blue?" the Duke asked.

Everyone waited for Hamish's answer.

"It might have been," he said unconvincingly.

The Duke gave an audible groan.

"Got to find out," he said; "Inverness and Glasgow big places. Needle in haystack without knowing names."

"I know their names," Moida said quietly.

Beatrice turned towards her sharply and looked at her for the first time.

"Why on earth didn't you say so?"

"I haven't had the opportunity to say anything, as yet," Moida replied.

There was nothing rude in her reply. She was just stating a fact.

"Tell us," the Duke begged.

"I remember the people distinctly," Moida said. "They were about the second lot who came yesterday afternoon. We seemed to be rather slack at first, which was surprising because there are usually more sight-

153

seers then than at any other time. So I was glad to see these people and perhaps I took more trouble over them than usual.

"There was a woman of about thirty, who was the mother of the little girl, and her sister, a little older. I gather that it was the sister's husband who was driving the car. I got the impression, though how I don't know, that the mother and the little girl were staying with the man and woman—they were visitors, if you know what I mean."

"Yes, go on!" Ian said encouragingly.

"You know how difficult it is to remember everything that has been said when one was not paying particular attention at the time," Moida said; "but piecing together my impressions with what Hamish has told you, I think the mother and the little girl lived in Glasgow, and the woman and husband live in Inverness or somewhere near it."

"And their names?" Beatrice asked.

"The name of the man and woman was Stewart," Moida replied. "I know that because the wife said to me, 'We must come another day as Mr. Stewart wants to take some photos. We forgot the camera, which is a pity as there's so much sun.'

"Then Mr. Stewart said,

'We'll be back, sure enough, and I'll take a snap of you, Miss!'

"I thanked him, although I could see that his wife was rather annoyed when he said it and hurried him away after that. I think that shows they were the ones from Inverness."

"Yes, of course," Ian said, "they wouldn't be so ready to come again for a day if they lived in Glasgow. Mr. and Mrs. Stewart of Inverness! Well, that gives us something to go on."

"There must be thousands of them," Beatrice said.

"Hundreds," corrected Ian. "We shall have to get a telephone book."

"Yes, yes of course," Beatrice said, "and Miss Murray and Miss Watson can ring up from the village."

"You mean and ask the people who answer if they are the Mr. and Mrs. Stewart who visited Skaig Castle?"

"Of course. I'll tell them to go and do it at once. Ring the bell, Ian."

"Will they telephone for my gun?" Hamish asked.

"Yes, of course," Beatrice answered. "I hadn't forgotten. They shall do that first, then they shall try the Stewarts. It will take time as they will have to go down to the village. Really, Ian, I could break Great-Uncle Duncan's neck for not having a telephone here."

"He was horrified, as you well know, at the very idea of such modern contraptions."

"Useful things," the Duke remarked, "especially on occasions like this."

"Which, thank goodness, don't occur very often," Ian replied.

"Hope not, indeed. Get blue heather back and I'll put it under lock and key," the Duke muttered.

"Which you ought to have done in the first place," Ian said severely; "and don't forget, if you do find it, it will be entirely due to Miss MacDonald and to Hamish."

"Entirely to Hamish," Moida corrected. "I had no idea the little girl had a pot of heather in her hands. I'm afraid I am not as observant as I thought I was."

"Very few people are," Ian smiled at her.

"Why doesn't somebody answer the bell?" Beatrice asked, getting to her feet.

"It probably isn't working," Ian said.

"I'll go and find the secretaries myself," Beatrice said. "It must be nearly luncheon time."

As she spoke, she looked at Moida, who realised that she was being dismissed.

"Come, Hamish! Come, Cathy," she said.

"Don't go," the Duke said suddenly. "Might remember something else."

"I must go and see to the children's luncheon," Moida replied. "If we do remember anything else, we'll let you know at once."

"Most grateful," the Duke said.

They moved towards the open door just as Lynette came in. Moida stood on one side to let her pass. She seemed to brush by her as she hurried towards Ian.

"No one told me you were back," she said. "I do think it's unkind. I've been alone here all the morning."

"Mother said you were in bed when we left," Ian replied. "We were as quick as we could be."

"Good-bye, Laird."

It was Cathy waving from the door, and Ian waved in reply.

"Good-bye, Cathy."

"Are the squatters invading us here as well as keeping a floor to themselves?" Lynette enquired, a little edge in her voice.

"Miss MacDonald and the children have been most helpful about Archie's blue heather," Ian explained.

"Clever girl that," the Duke said. "Must waste no time finding those people. Heather should be in bloom today."

"You mean Miss MacDonald knows who stole the heather?" Lynette enquired.

"They were people who must have been making a tour of the neighbourhood," Ian said. "They visited Arkrae, went over the rooms that were open to the public and then went into the gardens and stole the heather from the greenhouse."

"Trespassing, of course," the Duke said. "Disgraceful! No privacy these days. Strangers prying into every corner. Won't be able to have a bath soon for them staring at one."

"Do you know who has done it, so that you can get the heather back and have them up for stealing?" Lynette said.

"We have to find them first," Ian explained.

"Yes, of course, but you know their name."

"Stewart, and they come from Inverness. But there must be quite a lot of Stewarts living there. It's a common name."

"Oh, I see. You haven't got the exact address?"

"No, unfortunately," Ian replied.

He fancied Lynette was being rather dense. But she looked so lovely, her skin very fair against the blue of her tweed, that he felt it didn't matter what she said as long as her eyes continued to shine and her lips moved enticingly as she spoke.

"Clever girl that," the Duke repeated.

Ian thought for a moment that he was referring to Lynette, then realised he was still speaking of Moida. He thought again of his argument with her on the river bank that morning and smiled reminiscently to himself.

Yes, she was clever—there was no doubt about it; but she was wrong, dead wrong about many of the things she had said.

He looked forward to convincing her that he was right.

9

"Excuse me, but are you Mrs. Stewart?"

"Aye, that I be."

The elderly woman in the doorway looked in surprise at the good-looking young man addressing her and at the big car standing outside her gate, through the windows of which several eager faces were looking out.

"I wonder if by any chance you and your husband were motoring north on Tuesday and called at Arkrae Castle?"

"Arkrae Castle?" The woman seemed astounded. "I dinna ken sich a place, an' ma mon has been deed these past fifteen year."

"Then I must apologise for bothering you, Madam. Good morning."

Ian took off his hat politely and turned and hurried down the small front garden, shut the gate behind him with a clang and got into the car that was waiting for him.

"Another blank," he said. "It's your turn next, Archie."

"Many more?" the Duke asked with a groan.

Moida in the back seat, the children on each side of her, turned to some sheets of typewritten names.

"Twenty-one," she announced.

"It isn't possible," Ian expostulated. "You've made

a mistake. We've done at least fifty houses already, and there were only fifty-three in all."

"We've done thirty-two," Moida contradicted.

"Well, I shall go on strike soon," Ian said. "I didn't believe there would be so many tiresome people called Stewart."

"Mustn't give up, old boy," the Duke said cheerily; "one of 'em has my blue heather."

"Don't you believe it," Ian retorted. "Moida thought the name was Stewart, but it was quite likely 'Tuart' or 'Stewed eel' or something vaguely resembling it."

Hamish and Cathy gave a shriek of laughter.

"That would be a funny name, wouldn't it?" Cathy giggled.

"I'm quite sure it was Stewart," Moida said.

She looked worried all the same. Supposing, when they had done all the twenty-one remaining houses, they were still without the blue heather?

"Where next?" Ian asked resignedly.

"148A Union Street," Moida said. "Perhaps that will be a lucky number."

Ian turned the car and drove back towards the town. They crossed the red sandstone bridge spanning the River Ness and came into the busy shopping centre.

As they passed Macpherson's, the famous gun and rod shop, Ian wondered if he should suggest stopping so that he could buy some salmon flies, and then decided against it. The sooner they got on with their business, the better.

Life was likely to be insupportable until Archie had his blue heather restored to him.

Beatrice's secretaries had spent the whole of the previous afternoon telephoning every Stewart listed in the telephone book; but they had drawn a blank.

Then from the list of electors and the publishers in charge of a street directory they managed to compile a list of all the other Stewarts living in Inverness.

There had been a conference then as to how it

159

would be best to approach them. Ian suggested sending them a pre-paid telegram, but this had been vetoed on the grounds that no one who had stolen the heather would be willing to admit it, and even if whoever had it was merely asked if he had visited Arkrae Castle, he might become suspicious and lie.

"There is only one thing to do," Ian said at length, "we shall have to visit every house."

"Good idea," the Duke approved. "What odds our picking right Stewart first time?"

"About a million to one against," Ian told him; but when he saw the list of fifty-three householders of the name Stewart, he groaned and lengthened the odds to another million or so.

The Duke arrived at Skaig long before anyone was ready or had even finished breakfast. It had been decided that Ian, Moida, Hamish and Cathy should go with him.

The children were certain that they would know the little girl if they saw her again, and Moida was equally sure she would recognise the grown-ups.

The Duke, who was determined not to be left alone to face his difficulties, had wanted Beatrice and Lynette to join the party; but Beatrice had been very positive in her refusal.

"I've got too much to do here, Archie," she said. "Besides, I can't see that I shall be of any help, and it would bore Lynette to tears as well as being extremely tiring for her."

Lynette had agreed with this, even though privately she resented Ian's absorption in the Duke's affairs. She wanted to have him to herself; and the way he was becoming involved with Moida and the children made her furious, although she was wise enough not to show it.

She disliked, more than she thought it possible to dislike anyone, Moida, whom she described to herself as "that pushing squatter".

Nobody in her hearing had mentioned Moida's good

160

looks, but Lynette had noticed them; and although, as she told herself, she was not in the least jealous of Ian, she thought the less he saw of any woman under the age of fifty, the better.

She managed to get Ian to herself after dinner, and taking him away from Beatrice and the Duke, led him into one of the other sitting-rooms on the ground floor.

"Let us be alone for a little while," she said invitingly. "I'm tired of talking about blue heather, and any other sort for that matter."

Ian knew what she wanted.

"We will talk about you, darling," he said soothingly, putting his arm around her.

"Us," Lynette corrected, "you and me together."

"The two are indivisible," he smiled, putting his cheek against hers.

Even as he said it, he thought how untrue it was. He and Lynette were joined together only by their love; in everything else they were poles apart. But he loved her! Loved her beautiful face, her tiny tip-tilted nose, her exquisitely moulded lips.

"Kiss me," he commanded her urgently; "kiss me as if you meant it."

Lynette turned her lips to his. For a moment Ian looked down at her and then his mouth possessed hers with a hard, fierce, possessiveness which left her breathless.

To himself he knew he was seeking something from her and, afraid she could not or would not give it to him, was determined to take it, if necessary, by force. Yet, he asked, what was it that he wanted? And how could he explain to Lynette the urgent, aching need within his heart?

An hour later, when they returned to the library, there was a becoming flush on Lynette's cheeks and her eyes were shining like the proverbial stars.

It was Ian, this time, who had suggested they must be polite and return to "civilisation".

Actually, however much Lynette might deprecate it, Ian was really interested in the Duke's search for his stolen plant.

It was the sort of thing which appealed to his sense of humour; and although he might complain after visiting thirty-two houses without, as he put it, any positive reaction, his sporting instincts were aroused and he was prepared to go anywhere or do anything rather than admit defeat.

Moida was inclined to think the same. As with Beatrice, the Duke appealed to her maternal instincts. It was the thought of his disappointment that made her worry and wonder if she had in fact made a mistake in the people's name.

She had been positive enough at first; but—as always happens when something is queried—one begins to question one's own memory.

"I'm sure it was Stewart," she murmured now, and Cathy, knowing she was worried, slipped her hand into hers.

To the children it was all a huge adventure.

Even Hamish had found it difficult to keep up his private war with Ian when they were whisked away in a magnificent car, fed with ice-cream and orangeade at frequent intervals, and had all the thrills and excitement of coming to Inverness—a treat which they enjoyed only about once a year.

"What about another ice-cream?" Ian asked as he passed the Station and saw that the clock over the entrance said three o'clock.

"We must visit at least two more houses before Hamish and Cathy can have another."

Hamish and Cathy gave a whoop of joy at the permission, even if it was delayed. Hamish was not the only person who was finding it difficult to stand on his dignity.

After visiting a dozen houses that morning Ian had started to call Moida by her Christian name and she found it impossible to rebuke him.

The way he made the children laugh and kept them amused during the long drive, the considerate manner in which he remembered to stop for food and to let them stretch their legs had endeared him to Moida despite her every resolution to the contrary.

She found herself laughing and talking with him as easily and as comfortably as if she had known him all her life; and once the barriers were down, it was impossible to erect them again.

"You are a martinet, Moida—that's what you are," Ian said now. "What do you say children? Instead of Aunt Moida, shall we call her Aunt Martinet?"

"No," Cathy answered, "you are not to be unkind to Aunt Moida, 'cos we love her very much."

"I'm not surprised," Ian said, and this time he didn't sound as if he were teasing.

The Duke was peering at the houses as they passed.

"138," he called. "Can't be far. Stop! There—on right."

"Your turn to enquire, Archie," Ian said, "and don't bully them; the last woman you spoke to nearly sent for the police."

"Thought she was lying," the Duke said gloomily.

He got out of the car and rapped on the door. There was no garden to this house as it opened off the street. There was a pause, and the Duke rapped again. There was the sound of footsteps and then the door was opened.

Moida, watching from the car, gave a sudden gasp.

"That's her! I'm sure it is," she said to Ian.

"Good," he answered. "Out you jump and make sure."

Moida scrambled out on to the pavement, followed by the two children. She was right, the woman talking to the Duke was the one who had referred to her husband as "Mr. Stewart".

"Yes, we did visit Arkrae Castle," she was saying, "and a lovely place it is, too."

163

The Duke was so surprised at her admitting that she had been there, after so many people had refused any knowledge of Arkrae, that for a moment he was rendered speechless. With his mouth open he pulled at his moustache and merely goggled at her.

The woman waited for a moment and then, as he did not speak, she looked round her at Moida and Hamish and Ian also approaching from the other side of the car.

"Why do you ask?" she said. "What's it all about?"

"Heather," said the Duke, in a strangled voice. "You took my heather."

This wasn't what they had rehearsed. A look of fright appeared on the woman's face and her jocularity vanished immediately.

"I'm sure I don't know what you're talking about," she said. "I think you must have come to the wrong house."

She started to shut the door, but Ian, moving quickly, managed to save the situation.

"One minute, Madam. We are so sorry to trouble you. We heard you had been at Arkrae on Tuesday and we thought perhaps you might be able to help us."

"I don't think that's at all likely," the woman said, her eyes wary, her lips pursed together.

"I'm sure you'll do your best," Ian said. "First of all, let me introduce you. This is the Duke of Arkrae, owner of the castle you visited."

The woman looked astonished and also disbelieving. It was true that the Duke, pulling at his moustache and in his agitation appearing more indecisive and insignificant than usual, looked very unlike what one might expect of a Scottish Duke, but Ian gave his listener little time to think.

"I am Brigadier McCraggan," he said, "and I own Skaig Castle, which I think you visited after you had been to Arkrae. This is Miss MacDonald, who took you round—you remember her of course."

"I suppose so," the woman admitted reluctantly.

164

"Now, this is the position," Ian said, "and I am sure you won't mind my being frank with you. You had a little girl with you—Miss MacDonald thought it was your niece; and when she came to Skaig, she was carrying a pot of heather in her hand. Now, we think she may have picked this up by accident from the greenhouse in Arkrae."

Mrs. Stewart seemed about to make a hot denial, but Ian prevented the words passing her lips.

"Wait one moment before you tell us about it. You see, ordinarily it would not matter in the slightest if your niece had taken half a dozen pots of heather from the greenhouse. As a general rule the Duke is only too delighted for anyone to take a souvenir after they have visited Arkrae—in fact, it is very flattering for him that they should want to."

As Ian spoke he saw the bewilderment on the Duke's face and the frown appearing between his eyes, but by edging a little in front of him, Ian managed to distract Mrs. Stewart's attention so that she did not notice.

"But on Tuesday, by sheer misfortune, your niece took not an ordinary pot of heather, which the Duke would have been only too pleased to give her if he had been there, but a rather special plant which is to be shown next week at the Flower Show—you've heard about that, of course, and I expect you will be going."

"I don't know anything about a pot . . ." the woman began, only to be interrupted once again by Ian.

"Now, I can see," he smiled, "that we can trust you with our secret. It isn't the sort of thing we should say to anyone, but quite frankly, Mrs. Stewart, the Duke believes he will win first prize for the most original exhibit if he had the pot of heather.

"So we must appeal to you to help us in every possible way—I know you would hate to deprive the Duke of the prize after he has worked so hard for it and set his heart on winning it. It means everything to you, doesn't it, Archie?"

Ian kicked the Duke sharply on the ankle as he spoke. The Duke groaned as he replied:

"Jolly well think so. Must have heather—can't win without it."

"There you are, you see, Mrs. Stewart. Now, please, tell us where it is. You will tell us, won't you?"

The pleading in his voice and the charm which Ian could exude when he wished was irresistible.

After a moment's pause, when she was quite obviously debating whether to follow her instinct and deny all knowledge of the heather or to succumb to Ian's blandishments, Mrs. Stewart capitulated.

"Well, I don't hold with people taking things," she said, "and I didn't notice what the child had got hold of until we'd left the castle well behind; and then when I saw it was only a bit of heather in a pot I thought there was no harm in it, otherwise I'd have made Mr. Stewart turn round and we'd have gone straight back, I can tell you that."

"I'm sure you would," Ian said. "As I have explained, ordinarily the heather would have been quite unimportant."

"It's not exactly what you might call stealing, though some might think so," Mrs. Stewart continued. "I don't hold with it myself, mind you. Souvenirs is souvenirs, but as I said to Mr. Stewart afterwards, the pot's worth a few pence, whatever's planted in it. . . ."

"Let me tell you, woman . . ." the Duke began, only to receive a kick on the ankle from his cousin which nearly lamed him.

"Mrs. Stewart, you are a very kind person and I don't want you to worry in the slightest about the moral aspect of the situation. All we want is that particular pot of heather and your little niece shall have something she would much rather have to replace it—a doll or a picture book."

"I hope as you'll give her nothing of the sort," Mrs.

Stewart said sharply, "for she had no right to take the Duke's pot in the first place, and well she knows it; but there, it was done before we could say anything about it, and it did seem a waste of petrol to go back three or four miles for a bit of heather when you can pick armfuls of it on every side of the road."

"Of course, of course," Ian said soothingly, "no one would expect you to waste time or petrol for such a stupid reason, but we do want this particular pot of heather for the Flower Show. Have you got it here?"

"No, indeed, I haven't, or you should have it this very minute. No, my sister's gone back to Glasgow and taken the little girl with her. As it happens she wanted her to leave the pot behind, but the child was that pleased with it. It was coming into flower and she insisted on taking it with her."

"Into flower!" the Duke ejaculated the words in a manner which made them half a groan of agony and half a cry of triumph. "Colour? Quickly, what colour?"

"Well, there you have me," Mrs. Stewart replied. "I didn't take much notice of it, to tell the truth. Now I come to think of it, my sister did say to Mr. Stewart—he's more interested in gardening than I am—she says to him, she says, 'Funny sort of heather that, it don't seem to me to be the right colour'."

"Blue!" the Duke ejaculated. "Was it blue?"

"Well, now, as I was saying, I didn't have a look at it myself. I'll ask Mr. Stewart when he comes home. But he won't be in before seven tonight."

"In the meantime, perhaps you could tell us where your niece has taken the heather?" Ian said.

"Why, back to Glasgow with her, of course. I was telling you, they went yesterday on the morning train."

"And their address?" Ian asked, seeing that Moida already had a pencil ready.

"292 West Campbell Street," Mrs. Stewart replied.

"What is your sister's name?" Moida enquired, speaking for the first time.

"Oh, of course, you'll want to know that, won't

167

you?" Mrs. Stewart said; "though I suppose I'm right in giving it. She'll be ever so upset at you wanting that pot of heather. Many a time I've said to her that she spoils the child, but she replies her husband's too strict with her. It's always the same when there's only one, isn't it?"

"We will promise not to upset your sister in any way," Ian said. "We will just go and see her and explain to her, as we have explained to you, that the plant is needed for the Flower Show."

Mrs. Stewart's face brightened.

"You'll go and see her, will you?" she said. "Oh, that would be nicer. I was thinking of your writing or sending a telegram—terrible things, telegrams. Always make you think of the war, doesn't it? 'Here's bad news coming in at the front gate' my mother used to say to me; and as sure as I'm standing here, if she saw the telegraph boy coming, down she'd go in a dead faint."

"No, we won't telegraph," Ian said, "and what is your sister's name?"

"Mrs. Tuckett," Mrs. Stewart replied. "Delia's what she was christened. There were eight of us in our family, all born within the sound of Bow Bells! Funny when you think two of us married Scots. Me and Delia. She's the youngest."

"Well, thank you very much, Mrs. Stewart, for all your help. We are exceedingly grateful to you. I do hope you will come to the Flower Show and see the Duke win the prize."

"Indeed, I hope so," Mrs. Stewart said, "and it's sorry I am I haven't got the heather here at the moment, Your Grace."

"Thank you, thank you," the Duke said perfunctorily and led the way back to the car.

Mrs. Stewart watched them go, so they waited until they were a little way down the road before they all let out a sigh of relief.

"We've found it!" Ian exclaimed. "Now then, children, all together, hip, hip, hooray!"

Some of the more respectable citizens of Inverness, passing by on the pavement, stared in astonishment at a car-load of people cheering for no apparent reason. Then Ian turned the car and they drove back into the main street.

"Ices!" he said. "And I could do with a drink myself."

"Out of hours," the Duke said gloomily.

They parked the car outside the Station and having bought the children choc-ices, which they immediately started to suck with much evidence of enjoyment, they went into the hotel and ordered tea, which the Duke refused with the air of being a martyr to the law.

Moida was smiling happily as she sank down in one of the big comfortable chairs in the lounge.

"I was certain that Stewart was the right name," she said, and for the first time Ian realised how anxious she had been in case she might have been mistaken.

"All's well that ends well," he said.

"Damn it. Haven't got heather yet," the Duke exclaimed.

"No, of course you haven't," Ian said. "I was thinking it was all settled."

"Supposing Mrs. Tuckett does what Mrs. Stewart intended to do, until you persuaded her differently, and denies all knowledge of it?" Moida asked.

"Force it out," the Duke answered excitedly. "Can't deny truth if sister giving evidence."

"Now wait a minute, Archie. We've got to be careful over this. If you antagonise Mrs. Tuckett, she may say not only that she has not got the heather, but if she had it, it has been destroyed."

"Destroyed!" The Duke stammered over the word.

It was obviously the first time the idea had occurred to him.

"I am only warning you," Ian went on, "and now I

169

think about it, the sooner we go to Glasgow the better."

"We can't all go like this!" Moida expostulated.

"Why not?" Ian enquired. "It would be a terrible waste of time to go back to Skaig just to get a few clothes. Let me see, Glasgow is about one hundred and thirty miles from here. We ought to be able to do it easily in four hours. I'll telegraph my mother and tell her where we are going, and you hop out and buy anything you need for the night."

"But I can't . . . I mean . . ."

"We can't afford to worry about anything but Archie's beastly heather. Quite seriously, there is every chance the child will get tired of it and throw it away or break the pot."

"Water!" the Duke exclaimed.

They both turned to look at him.

"Heather has to be watered," he explained.

"Yes, of course," Ian said. "I thought for a minute you were fainting or taking the pledge. Well, that makes it even more urgent. We must hurry to Glasgow, whatever the inconvenience to ourselves."

He pulled some notes out of his pocket.

"Here you are, Moida, get yourself and the children whatever you need for the night."

"But I can't take your money," Moida said quickly.

"For an enlightened young woman you are being exceedingly foolish and you know it," Ian retorted firmly. "There is no point in your wasting money you've earned from the newspapers, by abusing me, on this wild goose chase into which you have been inveigled by Archie. We pay or we take the children and leave you behind."

He spoke lightly, but Moida sensed determination behind his joking. For a moment she still hesitated.

It went against the grain for her to accept money even for Hamish and Cathy from a man whom she had declared to be her enemy and whose birthright she was trying to wrest from him.

"You must come, too," Ian said. "How shall we know it is the woman and the child who visited Skaig if you are not there to identify them?"

"Very well," Moida said, reluctantly picking up the notes, "but this is far too much. I'll give you back the change."

"With an account of what you've spent, and of course bills attached, so I shall see that you are not cheating," Ian teased.

There was a flush on Moida's cheeks even while she smiled, and the thought occurred to her that, if Lynette had been in her place, she would not have demurred, but would have accepted it as her right that a man should pay for her.

"How gauche he must think me," Moida thought and then was ashamed that she should worry as to what Ian thought one way or another.

"Are we going to Glasgow?" Hamish asked suddenly.

His choc-ice was finished and, though there remained much evidence of it round his mouth and on the tip of his nose, he was now at liberty to ask questions again.

"Yes, that's where we are going," Ian answered. "Have you ever been there before?"

"No," Hamish replied, "but Mr. Mackay says that's where the poachers take the deer when they kill them. They cut them up for the greyhounds."

"What is all this?" Ian asked, looking at Moida.

"Stick at nothing," the Duke replied before Moida could speak. "Not content with salmon nowadays. After the deer. Damn' shame!"

"Can't you catch them?" Ian asked.

"Not touched any of mine yet," the Duke answered, "but heard they'd been busy on your moor."

"Did you know about this?" Ian asked Moida.

"Nobody's been able to prove anything," she replied, "except that several deer were found wounded one morning and a lorry had been seen going up the

171

strath the night before. They think the poachers used a tommy gun."

"But that's butchery!" Ian exclaimed. "It would be easy to kill dozens when the deer came down to the road at night."

"That's what Willy Mackay was saying," Moida answered. "But who is to stop them? There hasn't been a keeper at Skaig, you must remember, for the last six months."

"All right, it's my fault!" Ian cried, "but it has got to be stopped, and I'll shoot the poachers myself if I catch them at it."

"So will I," Hamish said stoutly. "If I had a gun, I would shoot them. Mr. Mackay says one should aim for their legs and then they can't run away."

"I see you know all about it," Ian said solemnly, "and here's another problem for us to deal with, but let us cope with one at a time. I'll go and telegraph my mother and you do your shopping, Moida. How long will you be?"

"Ten minutes," she answered. "There's a shop round the corner where I can get everything I need."

"Good!" Ian approved.

Actually it was half an hour later before they were back in the car, nosing their way through the traffic.

"Will Mrs. McCraggan mind our going, do you think?" Moida asked as they left Inverness behind and took the road south.

"Mother won't mind," Ian replied cheerfully. "She will be far too occupied with the castle to worry about us. But I'm afraid Lynette will be disappointed not to be with us."

Moida said nothing. She was offering up a little prayer of thankfulness that Lynette was not accompanying them. There was no disguising the English girl's hostility and the idea of being cooped up in a car with her for hours on end was unendurable.

"Pretty girl," the Duke ejaculated suddenly. "When's the wedding?"

"First thing we've got to do is to announce the engagement," Ian answered. "Only the family know so far."

"Will think of present."

"Thanks," Ian said. "Anything you like, but not a pot of blue heather."

Hamish and Cathy were jumping up and down on the back seat, exclaiming at everything they saw, talking and laughing and begging for stories during the first part of the journey.

But after an hour or so they grew tired, and long before they reached Glasgow they were both fast asleep, cuddled up against Moida, her arms holding them close.

When finally they stopped outside the Central Hotel where Ian had suggested they stay the night, Moida was too stiff to move, and for a moment he stood in the doorway looking at her, thinking what an attractive picture she made, as he switched on the light in the roof.

"Wake up, Cathy! Wake up, Hamish! We're here," Moida cried.

Yawning, with their eyes half-closed, the children allowed themselves to be led upstairs and hurriedly put to bed.

Ian had engaged a suite for them with a private sitting-room which opened out of Moida's room, and beyond again was the children's room.

"I've ordered dinner but you've time for a bath first," he told her from the doorway as she shut up the sleeping children.

She thought, as he spoke, how informal it all was and how easily he adjusted himself to every possible circumstance.

It was with a sense of excitement that twenty minutes later she went into the sitting-room to find both Ian and the Duke waiting for her.

It was years since she had stayed in a luxury hotel, and the big rooms with their high ceilings and modern fittings made her feel as if she were taking part in a play.

Everything was so unexpected and so unlike anything that had ever happened to her before. It was also a long time since she had enjoyed herself so much or laughed so easily as she had today.

She liked the Duke—no one could dislike him, she felt. But it was Ian who had kept their spirits high, who had never allowed the journey to seem boring.

Moida began to wonder how she had ever thought of him as a monster of injustice.

He was not responsible for the faults of his forbears, and if, in her opinion, he was misguided in his public life, he was but carrying out the instructions of the Government, and it was at them she should point her criticism rather than at Ian himself.

As he rose from the chair in which he was sitting when she entered the room, she thought that he was almost too attractive to be safe, and the sooner her business with him was finished and she went back to work the better.

"I've got a cocktail all ready for you," Ian told her with his beguiling smile. "You must be tired out. Archie and I ought to have come and helped you put the children to bed."

"There was hardly any putting to be done," Moida answered. "They were asleep as I undressed them."

"It's been a long day for them," Ian said, "and they were awfully good."

"No trouble at all," the Duke approved. "Like children if not a nuisance."

"Pity you don't know more about them," Ian said. "It's time you had an heir or two. I've told you so a dozen times."

"Thought of it often," the Duke replied; "no money for wife at moment."

"Wait till the blue heather is on sale," Ian suggested. "I suppose you've got the formula all right for pollenising some more, or whatever you do with it?"

"Locked up in safe," the Duke replied. "Could grow plenty for next year if this all right. Must be really blue."

"We're back where we started," Ian sighed. "If Mrs. Tuckett doesn't hand over the blue heather I shall be tempted to cosh her!"

"When are we going to beard her?" Moida asked.

"After dinner, of course. Oh, but I forgot the children! We can't take them."

"They won't really be necessary, will they?" Moida asked.

"Not if we are certain Mrs. Tuckett is the right woman."

"I don't think there can be any mistake about that."

"No, and I suppose we've been rather selfish to drag you along all this way with us," Ian said, "but I'm very glad you came."

Moida felt suddenly a little catch in her breath. Why would he say things like that to her, she wondered. It wasn't fair that he could be so good-looking or should have such charm. No wonder he was sent on complicated diplomatic missions.

"I should have been miserable if I hadn't been in at the kill," she said lightly.

"We'll all go and beard Mrs. Tuckett as soon as we have finished dinner. Can you leave the children?"

"They won't move until the morning," Moida said, "but I'll ask the chambermaid to look at them every hour or so. I don't expect we shall be long."

"I hope not," Ian replied. "If they have given away the heather to a friend of a friend to take to Bunga-Bo, I shall burst into tears."

The Duke sat up suddenly.

"Given away?" he asked. "What makes you think . . . ?"

"Calm down, Archie; I was only joking."

"Not funny," the Duke muttered to himself. "What about dinner?"

"It's arriving now," Ian answered.

There was a rattle outside the door. He looked across at Moida and raised his glass.

"To all we are looking for in life," he toasted.

Moida smiled and lifted her glass in response; but she thought as she did so that they were all of them looking and hoping for something which was aptly symbolised by a pot of blue heather.

10

Mrs. Tuckett lived a long way from the centre of the town; and as they sped through streets congested with trams, Moida found herself wishing they could go on driving for ever.

She had never been so happy before, she thought. She had found herself laughing helplessly during the excellent dinner they had all three just enjoyed, and when she was not laughing she was feeling stimulated and excited by her arguments with Ian.

The Duke had taken little part in the conversation except to ejaculate occasionally in his own inimitable way and to insist that they had a bottle of champagne.

"Give us courage," he muttered.

Moida knew that he was terrified lest once again their search should prove fruitless.

Perhaps it was the champagne, she thought now, that had made her feel so gay and so absurdly happy. And yet she knew it was something deeper than that, something which she dared not express even to herself.

She was acutely conscious of Ian sitting beside her as he drove with an ease and dexterity as if he had not been driving for long hours before dinner.

There was a faint fragrance from his tweed coat, the rich smell of cigar smoke and with it all an aura of masculinity which affected her in a way she had never expected to be affected by any man, were he friend or foe.

But Ian McCraggan was different from all the men she had ever known; in fact, she had never before met anyone in the least like him.

Not since her father died had she known the thrill of feeling the tempo rise as she entered into a discussion or a fierce argument in which both she and her opponent fought each other with words and a strange sense of exhilaration. That was the right expression, she thought, exhilaration.

For that was what she felt as she talked with Ian— exhilaration—or was it indeed something else? With a sudden sense of panic she turned her head to speak to the Duke who was sitting in the back seat of the car.

"Only a few more minutes," she said, "and then we shall see your blue heather."

"Hope so," the Duke answered on a note of gloom.

"It will be there, I'm sure of it," Moida cried, adding as if to convince herself: "It must be."

"This is the street," Ian remarked, turning to the left. "Now look for No. 292."

They found the number and got out of the car with a sense of urgency which made Ian rap noisily and imperiously on the front door. It was opened by Mrs. Tuckett—Moida recognised her at once, even though in retrospect it had been impossible to describe the woman she had shown round the castle.

Small, with a white, pinched face and nondescript features, Mrs. Tuckett might have posed for a picture of nonentity. There was nothing about her to evoke comment, nothing to remember.

"Good evening, Mrs. Tuckett. . . . ." Ian was employing his most charming smile and what Moida already thought of as his diplomatic voice.

She wondered if everything he did, all his charm, all his persuasiveness could be turned on and off like a tap; and suddenly, for no reason she could explain to herself, she hated him.

Ian explained their difficulties to Mrs. Tuckett in exactly the same tactful manner in which he had described them to Mrs. Stewart.

"Any other pot of heather would not have been of the least consequence," he said; "but this was a very special kind which the Duke wished to show at the Inverness Flower Show."

As he was speaking, Mrs. Tuckett seemed to get smaller and even more significant. Long before he had finished she was ejaculating helplessly:

"I'm sorry, Sir; ever so sorry. Enid ought never to 'ave taken it, indeed she oughtn't."

"You're not to upset yourself, Mrs. Tuckett," Ian commanded her, "nor Enid either. If you will just let us have the heather, we will send your daughter a present to make up for it—a doll or something she really wants."

"No, indeed she will be wanting nothing!" Mrs. Tuckett replied in an agitated voice. "She shouldn't 'ave taken it, indeed she shouldn't. I can't think what I was thinking of to let her."

"No, please, Mrs. Tuckett, you are not to reproach yourself," Ian said reassuringly. "If the heather is here, that's all we are concerned about."

"But . . . it isn't!" The words seemed to burst from Mrs. Tuckett's lips.

Suddenly they were all very still, silenced as if by a blow.

"Not here?" It was the Duke who spoke first, and the words coming from his lips were not a cry but a wail.

"Not here?" Ian echoed. "You mean you have destroyed it?"

"No, no, not destroyed," Mrs. Tuckett replied. "It's like this, you see, Sir. It was ever such a pretty plant. The flowers came out when we got home . . ."

"What colour?" the Duke interrupted, and once again there was a breathless silence as they waited for Mrs. Tuckett's reply.

"Little blue flowers," she said. "My husband said it wasn't heather that Enid had got, after all, but something else."

"Blue! Blue!" the Duke shouted. "Where? Got have it. What have you done with it?"

"I'm sorry, Sir, indeed I'm really sorry," Mrs. Tuckett apologised, wringing her hands.

"Where is it?" the Duke cried.

"Wait a minute, Archie," Ian said quietly, realising that Mrs. Tuckett was becoming really agitated.

"My cousin is very excited," he explained. "You see he has tried for so long to produce a blue heather."

"Blue heather?" Mrs. Tuckett repeated. "I've never seen such a thing."

"But you have. You are the only person who has seen it," Ian told her, "and now you understand why it is so important for us to have the heather back."

"Yes, I see," the woman's tone was dull, her hands were shaking. Suddenly Moida realised that she must take charge.

This woman was frightened of both the Duke and Ian. If they were to get any sense out of her, they must calm her fears. She moved forward and put her hand on Mrs. Tuckett's arm.

"Listen, Mrs. Tuckett," she said. "It's awfully cold standing here with the door open. Couldn't we come into your sitting-room by the fire?"

"Of course, Miss. I should've asked you before. What am I thinking of?" said Mrs. Tuckett in a fluster. "There's a nice fire in the kitchen and perhaps you'd fancy a cup of tea?"

"We won't worry about that," Moida smiled, "unless you're having one yourself."

"The kettle's boiling."

"In that case, thank you very much," Moida said.

It was only a question of minutes before they were all in the kitchen sitting round the fire; and by the time Moida was given a cup of tea, thick, black and well laced with sugar, Mrs. Tuckett was looking far less agitated and her hands were no longer shaking.

It was difficult to control the Duke's agitation. He was pulling at his moustache and muttering under his breath. But an admiring glance from Ian had told Moida that he approved of what she was doing and she knew that, even though it delayed matters, they would have to let Mrs. Tuckett tell her story in her own way.

At last, with a cup of tea in her hand and sitting on the extreme edge of her chair, she began:

"It's like this, you see. When we got home, the plant came into flower—ever so pretty it was. Blue as a forget-me-not, as I says to Mr. Tuckett. 'That's the right idea,' he said. 'Blue as a forget-me-not. That'll make her laugh, all right.' 'Make who laugh?' I asked. 'She's coming to the Emp. this week,' he said. That's just his joking way of talking. Saves time, he says. We calls the Empire where he works the Emp. It always makes us laugh, but he always was one for a joke."

"Go on! Go on!" the Duke muttered impatiently, but Moida and Ian ignored him.

"The Empire's a Music Hall, isn't it?"

"That's right, the biggest in the whole of Glasgow. Mr. Tuckett's a scene shifter there; has been for over ten years. Always says they can't get on without him, but that's another of his jokes."

"So he has given the heather to someone at the Empire?" Moida asked.

"That's right," Mrs. Tuckett said in a surprised voice, as if she wondered how Moida could have guessed. "But there, 'e gets fond of some of the regulars. You know how it is—they're pally with 'im. Sometimes they stand him a drink and give 'im a tip if he's done something for them. And his Dot— well, she's very special. He always looks forward to her being on the Bill, and what's more, she always gives 'im tickets for us all to go and see her.

" 'Here you are, Fred," she says, "bring the missus and the kid—there ought to be more." That's her way, she always says we ought to have a dozen to be as useful to her as Fred is."

"So the lady who had received the heather is appearing at the Empire this week?" Ian said in the voice of someone who has solved a really difficult clue in the crossword puzzle.

"That's right," Mrs. Tuckett said, "and real pleased with it she was, too. Fred told 'er it'd bring her luck, and she laughed and said she could always do with a bit more."

"The Empire!" the Duke slowly but surely had come to the same conclusion as Ian, and he started to his feet.

"We'll go along and explain," Moida said rising. "I'm sure your friend will let us give her another sort of flower."

"And the lady's name, you say, is Dot?" Ian asked.

Mrs. Tuckett gave a little giggle.

"There, I didn't tell you her name, did I? Only told you what Fred calls her. Dot is just another of his jokes. Doesn't say it to her face, of course. Miss Durham to him, though everyone else in the theatre calls her Dolly."

Moida drew in a deep breath. She might have known, she thought, that somehow, in some fantastic way, by the long arm of coincidence she would be involved in this. First Hamish, and now her mother!

She was not quite certain what was said or what happened after that.

For a moment her brain seemed to be whirling and she was hardly aware how they said goodbye; but somehow or other she found herself in the car beside Ian and he was driving them swiftly back the way they had come.

"Dolly Durham!" he said aloud. "I seem to remember the name. What does she do?"

"Who cares?" the Duke ejaculated from the back. "Heather is what matters."

"Let's hope to goodness she hasn't given it to a friend going to East Africa, or let the conjurer's performing rabbits eat it!" Ian ejaculated. "I'm getting heartily sick of your blue heather, Archie."

"Blue! Said it was blue," the Duke replied in almost a crooning tone of satisfaction.

Still Moida was silent and even when they turned into Sauchiehall Street and saw the brilliant, garish lights of the Empire shining before them, she could not shake herself free of the sense of unreality and of moving in a dream.

That was what it must be—a dream—she thought.

Rory and Janet's death, the misery and horror of being turned out of the little house in Skaig, the sense of desperation which had driven her to the castle, the arrival of Ian, and the sense of being whisked away with him and the Duke all seemed a wild and unpredictable adventure. And now not only were she and Hamish involved, but her mother too.

She could see the name "Wee Dolly Durham" written up in twinkling lights and read it again and again on the posters outside the theatre.

"Stage door," Ian said, taking her by the arm to urge her along.

As they entered the narrow door at the back of the building the years rolled back and Moida felt the same breathless excitement she had felt as a child when going to see her mother at the theatre.

There was the same smell of grease-paint and dust, the same stone floors, narrow stairs and draughty passages, the same distant roar of applause and of music heard so indistinctly that it was a throb rather than a sound.

"Miss Durham's on now," the doorkeeper was saying. "Is she expecting you, Sir?"

"No, but our business is very urgent," Ian replied.

"This is the Duke of Arkrae and I am Brigadier McCraggan."

The man glanced sharply at them both and seemed satisfied by what he saw.

"Miss Durham will be off in a few minutes," he said. "If you will go along to her dressing-room, I'll tell her that you're there."

"Thanks very much," Ian replied and slipped a generous tip into the man's hand.

They moved along the passage in the direction that he indicated. And now they could hear burst upon burst of laughter, then a high note, clear and unexpectedly beautiful.

Her mother could still sing well if she wanted to, Moida thought; and in that moment she knew with a sense of guilt that she was ashamed of Dolly.

Ashamed of the vulgarisms and the buffoonery which had made her the idol of the masses, but which had destroyed the real artiste in her.

She had thought this often before, but never with such a sense of poignancy; and then, even as the applause broke in wave after wave, she knew the truth—she loved Ian!

She could hardly believe what her throbbing senses told her. Suddenly, as she stood there feeling her heart beat wildly, suffocatingly against her breast, she wondered if she could run away.

She could not go with him to see the amused contempt in his face as he viewed Dolly's huge bulk, to watch the scorn in his eyes as he listened to her chatter in the broad North Country dialect which she used on the stage.

Moida could remember when her mother had been a gentle person who spoke in a quiet, educated voice; a mother who bathed her, put her to bed, heard her prayers and then had sat sewing quietly in front of the fire while her father strode up and down the room proclaiming his convictions or arguing fiercely aloud some point on which he wished to convince himself.

That had been her mother as she was meant to be, her true self. "Wee Dolly Durham" was just a travesty, a grotesque caricature of Dorothy MacDonald, who had been brought up in a strict, puritanical household and had married, against her father's wishes, the fiery and brilliant Murdoe MacDonald.

"I must go," Moida thought to herself. "I must go before she comes off the stage. I can't call her Mother, I can't, I can't!"

"Here is Miss Durham's dressing-room," Ian said from behind her. "Perhaps we'd better wait in the passage."

He glanced at the Duke as he spoke and Moida knew that they could not be found rummaging round the flowers to see if the blue heather was there.

"It won't be long now," he added, and as he spoke he put out his hand and took Moida by the arm.

"Are you tired?" he asked, and his voice, it seemed to her, was tender and considerate.

She had an impulse to wrench herself free of him, to run away down the passage and out of the theatre. She knew there was no possible reason she could give for such an action, and the habit of self-control which she had practised all her life stood her now in good stead.

She must face what was coming. She felt herself thrill and tremble as Ian touched her and felt something like fire run through her veins.

She wanted to press herself close to him and while she fought against a thousand strange, enchanting, magical emotions which she had never known before, she heard her mother coming along the passage from the stage.

The applause in the auditorium died away, the next turn had been flashed up in electric lights, the music had started and the curtain was rising once again.

Dolly's act was finished and in her usual inimitable way she was laughing and joking with the stage hands and any of those who were waiting in the wings.

"It's champion tonight, lad, and no mistake!"

Moida heard her voice now as she spoke to some actor going down to the stage from the dressing-rooms.

"Always is for you, Dolly."

"Well, good luck, ducks."

"Thanks."

She came sweeping along. Her dress of flame-coloured satin, deliberately designed to accentuate the overexuberance of her figure, was spangled with glittering sequins, and there were diamonds, expensive enough to appear real at a distance, sparkling in her ears, round her neck and at her wrists.

She was overwhelming, overpowering and terrific as she descended upon them. She seemed to fill the whole passage so that Moida wished she could sink through the floor.

"Friends to see me—that's the stuff," she called as soon as she was within earshot; and then as she automatically smiled a toothy welcome, she saw Moida.

"Well, if this isn't a real surprise, Moida luv! Why didn't you let me know you were coming?"

There was not time for Moida to say anything, no time for her to look at Ian and see what he was thinking or even to guess his surprise. Her mother's arms were round her and she was enveloped by the sheer exuberance of Dolly's welcome.

There were warm, hearty kisses on her cheeks, the smell of grease-paint and expensive perfume, the rustle and flutter of satin and the bedazzlement of so much sparkling jewellery.

And then the door of the dressing-room was open and they were all following her in.

There were flowers everywhere, baskets and vases of them, some expensive, some cheap, some a mere handful plucked from a garden by one of her admirers, who would have trekked into the city specially to see her.

"Tell me what you are doing here. I thought you were up at Skaig. Not that you write much, you naughty girl! But I'll forgive you; I'm that pleased to see you I don't know where to begin."

Dolly sank down on a chair that creaked beneath her weight.

Then, still holding Moida by the hand, she held out her other hand with a huge gesture of friendliness towards Ian and the Duke.

"And these are your friends, luv? Very nice, too, if I may say so."

"This is Brigadier McCraggan, Mother, and the Duke of Arkrae."

"I'm pleased to meet you," Dolly said. "Sit down if you can find a pew and tell me what you are doing with my little Moida. Looking after her, I hope?"

The question was addressed to Ian and it was arch.

Yes, there was no doubt about it, Dolly was being arch and Moida felt that in one more moment she would assume that they were interested in each other.

"We've come to see you about a very serious matter," she interrupted quickly. "The Duke has lost a pot of heather, and we understand that it has been given to you by a man who works here—a scene shifter called Tuckett!"

"Fred! Do you know Fred?" Dolly asked. "He's a very old friend of mine, is Fred. I'm sure the Empire wouldn't seem the same place if he weren't here to greet me when I arrive!"

"That isn't the point," Moida went on. "Fred's little girl took a pot of heather from the Duke's greenhouse when they visited Arkrae a few days ago and we've been looking for it ever since. It is vitally important that it should be found and Fred Tuckett gave it to you."

Dolly threw back her head and laughed the deep, infectious laugh which made audiences all over the country want to laugh with her.

"Fancy old Fred's child getting away with that one," she giggled, "and you looking so serious about it."

"Is it here?" the Duke asked hoarsely.

"It'll be here right enough," Dolly replied. "Ought to be in a place of honour if Fred gave it to me, but goodness knows where Florrie puts everything. Here, Florrie!"

She raised her voice to shout for her dresser. Hastily a thin little woman who looked rather like Mrs. Tiggy-winkle in the Beatrice Potter books, came running into the room.

"Here I am! here I am! Thought you wouldn't be wanting me for a minute, seeing you 'ad company."

"What did you do with the pot Fred gave me?"

"Ain't seen sign nor sight of it."

"What?" the Duke almost jumped into the air.

"Now, Florrie, that's what you always say," Dolly rebuked her. "You remember it well enough—the pot he gave me the night we arrived, saying it was like forget-me-nots and he didn't forget me. You know, we laughed about it at the time. Quite a speech it was for Fred."

"Oh! I remember now," Florrie said.

"Not destroyed it?"

There was agony in the Duke's voice this time, but he looked so fierce as he spoke that Florrie backed away from him.

"Destroy something Fred had given me?" Dolly cried. "Not b——likely!"

She laughed again and then looked at Moida.

"Don't look shocked, ducks, I'd forgotten you were here. 'Never swear in front of your own children' is what I've said often enough. Other people's don't matter."

She roared with laughter again, paying no attention to Florrie who was snuffling around like a terrier looking for a bone amongst the flowers grouped on the table.

The Duke had followed her and was bending over

her shoulder muttering to himself almost hysterically. Only Ian appeared to be listening to Dolly or keeping his attention fixed on her.

It was the first time Moida had dared to look at him. He was smiling and his eyes were twinkling as if he found Dolly really amusing.

Moida had a sudden vision of Lynette, cool and beautiful, calm and well-bred, and squirmed with a sudden misery as Dolly's laugh broke out again.

Then with a sudden revulsion of feeling, which was almost as if she had douched herself with cold water, she forced aside her sense of embarrassment.

This was her mother; however strange or different Dolly might be from the mother she had known as a child, she was still part of her flesh and blood, still her parent.

What did it matter what Ian thought? She might love him, she might feel her whole being yearn towards him, but she would not pursue even an acquaintance with him under false pretences.

He should know her for what she was, the daughter of Murdoe MacDonald and the daughter of Dolly Durham.

They had created her, they had brought her into the world and made her, to all intents and purposes, what she was today.

If he despised her, well, it would not matter one way or the other. Already she had defied him about their position at the castle, already she had antagonised him by refusing to leave, by insisting on pursuing Hamish's claim to the Chieftainship and to the Estate.

Yet, weakly, her heart cried out that he liked her as a person; and in their discussions and their conversations together he had forgotten they were enemies and had remembered only that they were interested in the same things.

Then she thrust this weakness from her, too. She loved Ian, but she must still be honest with him, as

189

with herself; there was nothing to hide, nothing she need be ashamed of in owning Dolly as her mother.

Impulsively, because of the feelings of loyalty welling up inside her, Moida deliberately bent towards her mother and kissed her on the cheek—this time a real kiss of welcome, not just a movement of the lips.

"Mother, I am glad to see you!"

It was sincere, spoken in the same way as she might have spoken ten years ago when she and Janet waited breathlessly in Holyrood Palace for their mother's taxi to come from the station.

"And I'm glad to see you, darling."

For a moment Dolly was serious; out of the great mounds of fat on her face her eyes looked at her daughter with an expression Moida had never seen there before.

Was she lonely? Did her arms sometimes ache for the children who had grown up and grown away from her? Did her theatrical life entirely compensate her for the loss of a home, for the separation from those who once belonged and were part of her?

Then there was a cry from Florrie and yet another from the Duke.

" 'Ere it is now!"

"Blue! Blue!"

They all turned. The Duke, almost transfigured in his excitement, was holding the precious plant in his hand. And it was blue!

There was no doubt about it—the bright vivid blue of the sky in summer, a blue that had never been seen before growing on the deep green branches of Scottish heather.

"He was right then!" Ian spoke to Moida. "I can hardly believe it is real, even now. Can you?"

"Thank goodness we've found it," Moida answered.

"And we must thank your mother, too,"

Ian was smiling at Dolly who seemed at last to realise that there was some reason for the excitement for she rose and stared at the plant in astonishment.

"Never struck me it was heather," she said. "Fred said it was, but I thought he was joking. I just looked on it as a plant and wouldn't have thought of it again if Florrie and I hadn't laughed over his forget-me-not speech. He's always so gallant to me."

"And who wouldn't be?" Ian asked.

"Flatterer! Get along with you," she smiled up at him and gave him a playful slap on the arm, and then turned to Moida. "I'm glad your friends have got what they came for, luv. Are you happy, too?"

There was something in her tone which told Moida that her mother had penetrated her defences and had guessed a little of the feelings and emotions coursing through her.

"Yes, I'm happy," she answered, and was not certain whether it was the truth or a lie.

"Shall I see you tomorrow?"

Moida shook her head.

"The children are here. The Duke and Brigadier McCraggan will be wanting to get back to Skaig."

"I understand, dearie."

Just for a moment there was a note of wistfulness in her voice, as if she would like to keep her daughter and grandchildren with her. But their lives lay apart, and, come to think of it, she had a lot to do tomorrow.

"Thank you so very much for ending our search," Ian said.

"Always glad to be of any service to friends of Moida's," Dolly said lightly.

"She's helped us more than we can possibly tell you," Ian continued. "And if it hadn't been for Hamish we should never have known where to come."

"Give my grandson a kiss from me," Dolly commanded him.

"I don't think he would appreciate it," Ian replied with a smile. "Moida must do that for you."

"She'll make a fuss of him all right," Dolly replied. "She's mad about those children; but, as I've told her often enough, she should have some of her own. But there, like most girls, she's waiting for Mr. Right to come along."

"Of course she is," Ian agreed, and Moida found herself blushing.

There was a flurry of good-byes, kisses and "God bless you, luv" from Dolly, and then they were out in the street again, the Duke clutching his precious pot and muttering over and over again to himself:

"Blue! Really blue! No mistake!"

"We ought to celebrate this," Ian exclaimed.

"I must get back to the children," Moida answered hastily. "We've been away longer than I expected already."

"I was afraid you'd say that," Ian said, "or I would have asked your mother to come out to supper with us."

"I expect she was engaged already," Moida answered. "She's . . . she's very popular."

"And deservedly so," Ian said. "I remembered as soon as I saw her that I had heard her sing during the war. She came out to North Africa when we were there, and again when we were in Italy. She was stupendous. The men adored her and she did a tremendous lot for the morale of the troops. You must be very proud of her."

There was no doubt about the sincerity in his voice. For a moment Moida felt the very relief of what he was saying drawing her strength away from her so that she sat limp, yet absurdly happy and silent.

Then, because her conscience pricked her, because only by being truthful could she make reparation, she replied:

"Sometimes I have been ashamed of her and hated myself for it."

The words made her lips tremble and yet she said them.

"I can understand that," Ian said quietly. "It is the contrast, isn't it, between your father, your mother and

192

yourself? It is always difficult to be set between two extremes, two strong forces pulling in opposite directions.

"You've managed to be strong and sensible and very, very sane between two people who were, each in their own way, a little fanatical—I'm not being rude to them. As you know, I admire them both tremendously. Your father was a genius, your mother in her own way is equally brilliant, and you were suspended between them.

"Yet you have managed to be you. Sane, as I have already said, and of course . . . very lovely."

Moida sat very still; then instinctively she put up her hands to her breast to quell the tumult which raged there.

He had said those words to her, words she had never expected to hear, even in her wildest dreams. "You are very lovely."

The air seemed to vibrate on them; but, before she could answer, before she could even think what to say, they had arrived at the Central Hotel.

"Going to put your blue heather in the hotel safe, Archie?" Ian asked jokingly as the Duke stepped out on to the pavement.

"Sleep beside it," the Duke answered. "Murder anyone tries to take it."

Moida and Ian laughed, but they both knew he was in deadly earnest. He had got back what he had lost and never again should it escape him. Ian drove the car to the garage and Moida and the Duke went upstairs to the sitting-room.

"Good night, and I'm so glad you've found it," she said. "It's beautiful, absolutely beautiful. I never thought that heather could be so pretty."

The Duke's face lit up at her words of praise.

"Beaten then," he said. "Give 'em something think about when they see it."

At that moment the telephone in the sitting-room rang and Moida, who was already turning towards her bedroom, answered it. It was a reporter from the *Glasgow Clarion*. It was a long time afterwards that she learned how the Press had found out so quickly.

At the time she was too astonished to do anything but ask the reporter to hold on.

What had happened was that a reporter chatting with the stage door-keeper was told that the Duke of Arkrae had called on Dolly Durham that evening. Sensing there might be a story in it, the man had gone to Dolly's dressing-room a few seconds after Moida and her party had left.

Garrulous and always glad to talk to a newspaper man, Dolly had told how the precious pot of blue heather had been run to earth in her dressing-room.

Absolutely incredulous of the idea that there really was a blue heather, the reporter had telephoned to his paper, to learn from the night editor that there had been rumours for some time that the Duke and several other people were engaged in trying to pollinate such a thing.

From then onwards, it was just a race for every newspaper in the north and south of the country to get an exclusive story.

The *Glasgow Clarion* carried headlines in its first edition; and from six o'clock next morning the telephone was ringing like a mad thing and reporters and photographers were waiting in dozens in the corridors of the hotel.

Fortunately that evening neither the Duke nor Moida could see into the future and know what tomorrow was going to bring forth.

The Duke merely confirmed the story that he had found the pot of heather he had been seeking for several days and which had inadvertently been taken from the castle greenhouse.

"Yes, it was blue, a definite blue," and that was all he had to say.

He put down the receiver, said "Good night" to Moida and went to his own room. She picked up an evening paper and hurried through her own bedroom to where the children were sleeping. She didn't switch on the light.

She could hear their soft breathing and knew that all was well. She was just beginning to undress when there came a knock at her own door. She opened it and Ian stood there.

"I was afraid you had gone to bed," he said. "I wanted to say good night."

"I think we are all tired," Moida answered. "It has been a long day."

"Come and have a drink with me," Ian said. "There is something I want to say to you."

She hesitated for a moment.

This was unwise, she knew; it would only make her suffering worse. To be alone with Ian, to talk to him was madness, yet a delicious madness such as she had never known before and which was too enticing a temptation to be resisted.

"I must only stay for a moment or two," she murmured; "the Duke has already gone to bed."

"Archie needs his beauty sleep," Ian replied. "I don't think we need worry about ours, do you?"

He walked to the side table and she saw that since she had left the room a bottle of champagne had been opened. Ian poured out two glasses and gave her one, then raised his own.

"To the heroine of a most successful adventure," he said.

Moida laughed and shook her head.

"We should drink to the hero," she said. "The Duke!"

"On the contrary, Hamish deserves that title," Ian replied. "And it is about Hamish I want to talk to you. Sit down."

Moida obeyed him, suddenly serious. If this was a trick, she thought, to deprive Hamish of his rights, whatever her feelings for Ian, she must be shrewd enough to recognise it for what it was.

"I have been thinking about Hamish," Ian began,

"and I have realised that, as you are determined to fight his claim for the Chieftainship and to the ownership of Skaig, we must make plans for the children in the meantime. It will take years before the title can be determined, and it will cost a great deal of money.

"I don't want you to think I am interfering in any way with what is entirely your business; but, while this is going on, Hamish must be properly educated. He is now eight, I think?"

"Eight and a half," Moida said.

"I thought so," Ian nodded, "and it is, of course, the right age for him to go to a preparatory school. Have you thought about one?"

"No," Moida answered, "I haven't. I have been teaching him myself since his father died."

"Well, I'm sure you do that beautifully, but it is not the same thing for a boy as being taught the right curriculum which he will need later at a public school."

"And supposing Hamish isn't able . . .?" Moida began.

"I want to make this very clear," Ian interrupted. "If you succeed in your claim, Hamish will automatically be able to go to any public school you choose and will be able to pay for it himself; but if he fails, I should still like to be responsible for his education.

"All these years my family have considered themselves under some obligation to the Holms inasmuch as they have paid them a thousand a year.

"This shall continue, and because I think I have had a little more experience and have perhaps a little more influence than you where schools are concerned, I would deem it a great favour if you would allow me to choose Hamish's schools for him and also to pay for them."

Moida clenched her hands together. She was trying to think clearly, trying desperately to see if this involved her in any way, trying to decide whether she would have refused such an offer twenty-four hours ago.

Her brain seemed muddled and confused with the beating of her heart, the pulsating of her veins.

Ian was near her, he was looking at her, he was speaking to her, and he was thinking of her and Hamish and being so gentle, so kind, so considerate, that she felt, quite unreasonably and perhaps quite ridiculously, that she dared not listen to him.

"I know that I said the other morning, 'Beware of the enemy when he brings gifts'," Ian said; "but just over this, if over nothing else, I don't want you to think of me as the enemy. Whatever happens, whatever ultimately proves to be justice, the children must not suffer.

"They have done no wrong. They have only been buffeted about by fate and they are too young to encounter the misfortune and the heartbreak which the world brings to all of us."

Moida looked at Ian sharply.

"What do you know about heartbreak?" she asked.

"That is a personal question," he parried, "and I am trying so hard in this not to be personal."

"Why?"

"Because I don't want you to think that it is only because of you I want to help the children. I want you to believe it is for their sakes as well."

"And is it?"

"That is another question that is best left unanswered," he said. "In fact it is almost impossible to answer. If I had only heard about their plight—penniless, turned out of their home, claimants to Skaig—perhaps I should not have been so concerned with them as I am now, knowing them as I do and knowing you. You are a very brave person, Moida, and a very unforgettable one."

His voice was low as he spoke and suddenly Moida could bear no more.

"I must go to bed," she said. "I am tired. I can't decide anything tonight."

"No, of course not," Ian said; "and I am a brute to worry you after a day like today."

He put out his hands as he spoke and, almost without her conscious volition, she placed her own in them.

She felt the hard strength of his fingers, felt the sudden vibration which seemed to run through her like fire because he was touching her, and then her eyes were looking up into his and they were both standing seemingly spellbound by what they saw.

"Moida!"

He spoke her name hardly above a whisper as, desperately, with a terror she could not define, Moida snatched her hands away from him and, running across the room, opened the door of her bedroom.

She shut it behind her and stood against it panting.

She could hear what happened in the sitting-room. She knew that Ian did not move for a long time; then she heard his footsteps; a door closed; and she knew that he had gone.

With her back against the door, she was shaking all over.

Slowly she seemed to crumple up and, as she reached the floor, the tears came coursing down her cheeks, shaking her tempestuously as she crouched there like some forlorn child locked out from happiness.

11

Lynette came down the Castle steps just as a small black car came speeding round the corner to draw up with a screech of the brakes.

The driver was obviously in a hurry, for he jumped out quickly and, walking across to Lynette, pulled a battered felt hat from his head.

"Good morning," he said. "I represent the *Glasgow Clarion*. May we have permission to take photographs of the ruined part of the Castle?"

With the realisation that the man addressing her was Press, Lynette smiled at him in her most entrancing manner.

"I will ask Mrs. McCraggan," she said, "but I feel sure it will be all right."

"I would be very much obliged," he said; "and also can you tell me the exact spot where the stall was?"

"Stall?" Lynette asked, puzzled.

"Where a little boy—Hamish Holm—sold white heather," he said.

Lynette looked puzzled. She was trying to guess what all this was about.

She was too used to being the cynosure of the photographers' cameras not to realise that, when newspapers send special representatives to photograph a place or a person, there is a news story afoot.

"Do tell me why you are so interested," she asked sweetly.

"Haven't you seen our paper this morning?"

"I don't think so," Lynette answered. "You said the *Glasgow Clarion,* didn't you?"

"That's right. We beat the rest to it this time, but they're on to it now like a swarm of hornets. That's why I'd be grateful if I could have permission to photograph the ruins right away."

"Do tell me what it is all about," Lynette pleaded.

"Blue heather of course!" the reporter replied. "The Duke of Arkrae has certainly got something there."

"Then he's found it!"

"You didn't know?" the reporter asked.

Lynette shook her head.

"We haven't heard anything since yesterday when Brigadier McCraggan wired that they had traced it to Glasgow."

"That's right. They found it in the dressing-room of Dolly Durham, and it's her grandson who put them on the right scent. What a coincidence! It's made a grand story."

"Oh, I am glad the Duke has found his blue heather!" Lynette exclaimed. "He will be delighted, and so are we all."

There was something in her voice and the affected way in which she clasped her hands together which made the reporter look at her closely.

"Excuse my asking," he said, "but haven't I seen you somewhere before?"

Lynette dropped her eyelashes very prettily.

"I shall be very disappointed if you haven't," she said.

The reporter stared at her.

"Lynette Trent!" he ejaculated suddenly.

Lynette's smile was radiant.

"How clever of you to guess!"

"Not really," he replied modestly. "I ought to have known at once. I was at the Caledonian Ball last year and we got some tip-top photographs of you there, but somehow I wasn't expecting to find you up here."

"It's not really surprising because Brigadier Mc-Craggan is . . ."

She checked herself suddenly, realising that she was just about to announce her own important bit of news; but a true sense of publicity made her stop. It would be stupid, she thought, to let her news take second place to the Duke's blue heather.

She had not yet heard from her mother, but that would not have stopped Lynette had she made up her mind to give the story to the newspapers. But when she did, she had every intention of it being front-page news.

This, she thought shrewdly, was the Duke's glorious hour and she would do nothing to side-track attention from him.

". . . is a very old friend," she finished, "and so is the Duke of Arkrae. They are cousins, as I expect you know."

"Yes, we got all the dope about that," the reporter said. "It's the children who interest us. It seems a bit of a mystery why they should have been selling things at the Castle before the Brigadier got here."

Lynette only hesitated for a second. Here, she thought, was a chance to play off some scores against Moida and Ian.

She was, in fact, seething with anger that they should have gone to Glasgow yesterday without her; and it was even more infuriating now that the heather had been found and the Press were already on to it.

Fool that she had been, she thought, not to realise the potentiality of such a story if the Duke's heather turned out blue. She should have been there.

In her mind's eye she could see the photographs clearly—"The beautiful Miss Trent holding the first blue heather ever known!"

She had missed that because never for a moment had she imagined that the Duke would let the Press know that the blue heather had bloomed before he got back to Arkrae.

It was idiotic of her not to have anticipated such a development; at the same time, both Ian and the Duke had seemed the type of people to dislike and avoid the Press.

In Lynette's opinion there were two groups of people in the world, those who liked publicity and those who didn't; and she thought that she was a pretty good judge of which was which.

Well, in this instance, she had been mistaken; and yet fate was playing into her hands, for here was her opportunity to make things as unpleasant as she could for Moida MacDonald.

She gave a little laugh, knowing that the reporter was listening to her with admiration in his eyes and that his photographer, who had by now got his camera and all his photographic paraphernalia out of the car, was also standing staring.

"Didn't they tell you who the children really are?" she asked.

"Holm, I understood was the name."

"I didn't mean their names," Lynette said, "but the fact that they are squatters in the Castle—they and their aunt, Miss MacDonald, who went with them to Glasgow."

"Squatters!"

For the moment even the reporter was surprised, hardened though he was to shocks of all descriptions; then his pencil was out and he was scribbling busily. What a break! If this didn't get him a rise on the paper, nothing would.

Answering the barrage of questions which were shot at her, Lynette walked with the two men towards the ruined part of the Castle. She had no intention of asking Beatrice for her permission to photograph the ruins.

She wanted the men to include her in the picture and, needless to say, they were only too ready to oblige.

"Miss Lynette Trent shows the actual spot where the children—squatters in Skaig Castle—sold the produce they had taken from the Estate."

The only thing that Lynette did not tell them was that Hamish was a claimant to the Chieftainship and the title. She kept quiet about that because she thought it might react on the excitement and glamour which would surround the announcement of her engagement to Ian.

But she told how Moida had moved into the Castle and, when Ian arrived, had announced that she would only leave if they provided her with a house equal to the one which had been sold over their heads by the dishonest factor.

"What a story!" the reporter ejaculated once or twice; and when the photographer had finished taking photographs of Lynette, he was profuse in his gratitude.

"You've been very kind, Miss Trent," he said.

"I'm so happy to have been of help," Lynette replied.

"You will forgive us now if we rush, but you have no telephone in the Castle and I've got to 'phone this through to catch the evening edition."

"Well, good-bye."

Lynette held out her hand to have it wrung with such fervour that it was almost painful; then she waved good-bye prettily from the Castle steps as the black car turned and rushed away down the drive.

She smiled to herself as she went back into the house. She hoped that she had made the MacDonald girl look a fool, if nothing else.

Then the expression on her face darkened. How dare Ian go off like this, taking that ridiculous girl with him and those tiresome children.

It had been bad enough thinking of their rushing about from house to house in Inverness the day before; but she had agreed with Beatrice that there was no point in her getting up early and tiring herself in what might be a fruitless search.

She had not expected them to be away all night or, for that matter, to be so successful that the newspapers were interested. She hurried into the library

203

where, as she expected, the morning papers were laid out on a side table.

There was never a shortage of newspapers and magazines where Beatrice was. In fact, it was an understood thing that each guest should be called with six newspapers.

This, however, was not possible in Scotland, for the papers did not arrive until the afternoon mail train, and Lynette, looked at them now, realised that they were all dated the day before.

She wished she had asked the reporters to show her a copy of their paper. They would doubtless have had one with them. Nevertheless there was consolation in knowing that she would be first with the news to Beatrice.

She came out of the library and was just going upstairs to Beatrice's room when she heard the wheels of another car outside and, looking through the open hall door, recognised Ian's car. So they were back!

For a moment a number of emotions warred with each other within Lynette's heart—the joy of knowing that Ian was back and the resentment of seeing that Moida was with him.

She waited for a moment while they began to get out of the car, then the actress within her decided the role she should take.

With a little cry she ran down the steps, knowing what an entrancing picture she made with her hair glinting in the sunshine and her eyes alight with apparent pleasure.

"I have heard already that you have found it," she cried. "Oh! how glad I am."

She ran towards the Duke who was holding the precious pot carefully with both hands.

"I am glad, so very glad for your sake," Lynette said looking up at him, and then she bent forward and pressed her lips against his pale face.

"That's for luck," she said, "and may your heather

be more lucky to you than any white heather could possibly be."

"Thanks," the Duke remarked, obviously somewhat surprised by Lynette's greeting and at the same time flattered.

"And how clever you've been, Ian darling," she said, turning towards Ian and holding her cheek towards him so that he might kiss it.

But though her words were effusively spoken, there was an edge to her voice which it was impossible not to notice.

"We're home," Cathy exclaimed wonderingly as if, after all that had happened to them, she had half-expected to find herself landed on Mars.

"Yes, we're home," Moida said, and she wondered if the flatness in her tone was apparent to anyone except herself.

The adventure had come to an end, she thought. They were back at Skaig and the joy and happiness that she had known for the past twenty-four hours was over.

She had only to look at Lynette to know her place again and to realise that there could be no comparison between herself and this radiant, beautifully-dressed young woman who seemed to have taken all initiative from them so that they stood grouped around her, dumb and looking slightly foolish.

Ian particularly seemed to have lost his voice.

"You must tell me everything from the beginning," Lynette was saying, looking towards the Duke. "I want to hear exactly what happened. It's all too thrilling for words. The papers are full of it, I hear."

"Who told you that?" Ian enquired, speaking for the first time.

"A reporter was here just now," Lynette answered. "He wanted to take a photograph of the ruins."

"Why?" Ian enquired.

"To show where the children had a stall," Lynette replied.

205

"Oh! I see. You didn't say too much, I hope," Ian said. "They kept questioning us as to why the Castle was open to the public; and while it was no use lying, we didn't want to make a story of it."

"I had no idea there was anything secret about Miss MacDonald's activities," Lynette replied sweetly.

There was a hardness underlying her tone and a look which told both Ian and Moida all too clearly what she thought.

Ian glanced quickly at Moida. He sensed that she was feeling embarrassed and he had a sudden impulse to protect her from Lynette's careless and irresponsible tongue.

"You didn't say why Miss MacDonald was here, did you?"

"Why not?" Lynette enquired.

There was a moment's silence, broken only by a mutter from the Duke who was walking up the Castle steps holding the heather in front of him as if it were a holy relic.

"Water!" he remarked to nobody in particular. "Should have water."

"Am I to understand that you told the reporter that Moida and the children were squatters in the Castle?" Ian asked in the tone of a cross-examining counsel.

Lynette's chin went up.

"Suppose you wait until tomorrow and see what I really did say!" she replied and then turned and ran after the Duke.

A second later they heard her voice, high and honeyed, extolling the beauties of the heather.

"I'm sorry," Ian said to Moida.

"I am not ashamed of anything I have done," Moida replied sharply.

"I know that," he replied; "but at the same time there was no reason for you to be involved in what is essentially the Duke's story. It will mean reporters buzzing round you, asking questions and wanting to

206

take photographs of the children. Archie and I were both careful to make no mention of why you were here, save to say that you were staying at Skaig."

"I realise that," Moida said. "It was kind of you."

"Actually, I was thinking of you, and not of myself," Ian went on, "although I suppose you could say that I didn't want to appear foolish."

He looked towards the Castle. Lynette and the Duke had disappeared through the door.

"Of course Lynette could not have known we wanted to keep quiet about it. I should have sent a telegram this morning, telling them to say nothing until we returned. I never anticipated that the reporters would get ahead of us."

Moida laughed suddenly.

"We never anticipated having to fight our way out of the hotel."

"Heavens, no! And I never guessed for a moment that Archie would enjoy it so much. I believe he must have been starved of attention all his life. There was no doubt that he was enjoying every moment of it. I haven't seen him look so happy for years."

"It is his heather he is thinking of, not himself," Moida said. "He believes it will be of great value to Scotland. He is genuine about that, you know."

"I wasn't running him down," Ian explained quickly, and added, looking at her quizzically: "Do you always find extenuating circumstances for everyone's actions except mine?"

She flushed a little at that and answered in all seriousness.

"I haven't written a word against you since we met, but I am afraid that an article I wrote about a week ago is in the *Telegraph* this morning."

"Damn it, why didn't you tell me?" Ian asked.

"I only saw it just as we were leaving and then there didn't seem time to explain anything. I have it here." She held out a copy of the *Telegraph* to him.

207

He took it from her, and, as she tried to move away, he put out his hand and caught her arm.

"No, you don't," he said. "You're not going to run off like that. I'm going to read your article now. You are going to hear my comments, and by George! you will have to justify anything you've said."

"But I can't stay," Moida cried in a fluster. "I have to see the children. They seem to have vanished, anyway."

"They won't come to any harm," Ian replied. "They know their way about by now."

"But I must go," she repeated, trying to pull her arm away from his restraining hand.

"I won't let you," he said.

She gave another tug and looked up at him rebelliously.

"Let me go!"

"I refuse," he retorted. "You've got to take the consequences of your action. If you have flayed me alive, as you did the last time, I think I shall beat you."

He was laughing; but suddenly their eyes met and Moida no longer struggled. They stood looking at each other.

The sunshine around them seemed to close in upon them so that they were in a golden, enchanted place of their own. Everything seemed very still—the world they knew had vanished and they were just man and woman facing each other across eternity.

Then, with a little sound that was suspiciously like a sob, Moida broke the spell that bound them.

She was free of Ian before he could prevent her and she ran, without looking back, round the corner of the Castle which led to the garden door, and was gone.

Ian stood looking after her, the *Daily Telegraph* in his hand, a strange expression on his face, before he turned and walked slowly down towards the loch.

As Moida hurried from the garden entrance up the side stairs of the Castle she could hear Archie and Lynette talking in the hall, and the sound of their voices seemed to echo in her ears long after she reached the sanctuary of the nursery and closed the door behind her.

At the moment she didn't worry what had happened to the children or even notice that the room was dusty and untidy and that the closed windows made it hot and airless.

She sank down in a chair by the empty fireplace and put her face into her hands.

What was happening to her, she wondered? All the control and commonsense which had seemed such an essential part of her character—in fact, the whole foundation of it—was crumbling and leaving her defenceless and frighteningly vulnerable.

She was ashamed of her tears the night before, ashamed now of the chaotic feelings within her breast.

Was it impossible for her to talk to Ian, to be near him without feeling herself a-quiver with love and distraught by his power to thrill her?

She was ashamed and elated, miserable and happy, proud and humiliated all at the same time. She did not know what she thought or what she felt.

She only knew that she loved him and that every barrier that she had ever had or that had stood between herself and the world had been swept away as if by a flood.

"I love him! I love him!" she said, and then rose to walk restlessly about the room, her clenched hands pressed to her temples. "I love him!" They seemed to be the only words that made sense.

She thought of her writing, of the strong, critical article which was published that morning in the *Telegraph,* and wondered how she could ever have penned such words.

She could not even think of such things now. She knew nothing, but was simply engulfed by her own feelings, the feeling of love which had turned the whole world upside down and made it a place of incredible contrasts.

She wanted to laugh and cry, she wanted to sing a paean of praise to the sky because she had met Ian, she wanted to throw herself into the nethermost depths of hell because she must lose him.

It was all so absurd, so ridiculous and she would have laughed at herself if the trembling of her lips had not prevented her from doing so. What could she do? She must get away, she thought.

It was impossible to stay here. It was a bitter-sweet happiness to be under the same roof as Ian; was an agony and a torture beyond words to know that he was with Lynette and that he loved her.

The words seemed to stab her a mortal wound. He loved Lynette Trent! She had got to face facts, she had to force this madness from her heart.

Was it surprising that someone like Ian should seek for a wife a girl from his own social world? And Lynette was lovely.

Moida forced herself to face the truth. It was no use pretending that Lynette was not good enough for Ian and that he was making a mistake. He was doing the right thing.

Moida walked across the room and flung open the window as if it was impossible for her to breathe. She stood there drawing in deep breaths, and after a little while she grew calmer.

She looked at the loch, reflecting the blue sky above it; looked at the clumps of fir trees on the north side of it, growing almost down to the water, dark green, mysteriously shadowed in their depths; and then her eyes went to the white peaks of the far-off mountains.

Suddenly she felt a little less distraught and a little calmer. As ever, beauty could give her the healing touch as nothing else could do.

For one moment she was back again in the Palace of Holyroodhouse. She put out her hand to touch a piece of exquisite needlework done by the unhappy Queen of Scots.

"It is very beautiful, Grandfather." She could hear

her own voice, the clear high voice of a child, as it echoed round the room.

"And so was the woman who worked it," came the reply. "A beautiful woman whom Scotland will never forget. Beauty lives, Moida. Always remember that. Beauty lives when ugliness and evil are forgotten."

"Beauty lives!" Moida repeated the words to herself now and knew that they had brought comfort to her aching heart.

It was the beautiful part of her love that would remain long after the torture and misery had gone, and she knew then that her love was a beautiful thing.

She had tried to hate Ian and failed. All the bad things she had attributed to him had been untrue and in meeting him she had known them to be false.

He was genuine and honest, a man with a mission, a man fired by a desire to give himself to the service of others.

She saw now how stupidly she had misinterpreted his motives. His Government's policy might sometimes have been misguided, but always he had brought to every situation, every problem, a fresh mind, a character untainted by graft or greed.

And because he had been trustworthy and straightforward, he had succeeded where so many had failed.

But she had not given him the credit for all that; she had been absurdly and unjustly biassed.

"Beauty lives"—the words seemed to repeat themselves in her mind over and over again; and now they were driving away every remnant of the resentment and defiance which had coloured Moida's whole outlook for so many months.

Where she had hated there was no more hatred in her heart, only a new understanding which had never been there before.

"I must go away," she thought, "while I can still fight for Hamish's inheritance. I will work for him."

There had seemed nothing wrong at the time, only everything that was laudable in moving into the castle, in facing Ian with anger and defiance because he was one of the unjust McCraggans who, in her opinion, had behaved so treacherously to Hamish's grandfather.

But Ian could not be held accountable for the shortcomings of his forbears. She saw that now as she had not seen it before.

It was the hot-headed Scottish blood in her, she thought, which had made her so headstrong. With a faint smile she remembered the legend of the first Donald, who founded the Clan.

He joined forces with the King of Norway when they were striving to wrest the Isles—Kintyre, Isla and others—from Godred, son of Olave—the Red.

On one occasion when the galleys of the invading force lay in the surf, their leader, eager for battle and anxious to encourage his followers, swore that the warrior whose hand first touched the land should be owner of it for ever.

No sooner had he spoken than Donald sprang to the prow of his galley, with one bold stroke of his dirk he severed his wrist and cast his bleeding hand still holding the sword far over the waves on to the shore beyond, and thus he obtained for himself and his descendants indisputable possession of the coveted land.

A bleeding hand was still the crest of the MacDonalds and the same blood which had inspired Donald made Moida ready to fight, determined to get her own way.

Yes, while she would not admit herself vanquished by a McCraggan, she knew it would be impossible to go on fighting as long as she remained in close proximity to Ian.

She would take the children to Edinburgh. If she was unable to make enough to keep them, then she would go to her mother and beg for help. The reluctance she had felt to do this before had now gone.

It was Ian who had dispelled that, she thought, for his appreciation of Dolly had made Moida see her mother in a very different light.

It was decided then, Moida thought. They would go away. Yet part of her cried out against the decision. At least so long as she remained here she could see him.

She could watch him from the window, she could see him in the house and in the garden, she could speak with him, she could hear his voice call her name.

She felt herself begin to tremble again at the thought of it, his eyes looking down into hers, the sudden turn of his head, the way his hair grew at the back of his neck.

She loved every aspect of him, every moment, the breadth of his shoulders, the strength of his fingers, the easy, natural grace with which he walked, and the sudden look of seriousness in his eyes as they talked of world affairs.

"I love him," she said the words aloud and knew that, if she stayed where she could see him, her weakness would betray her.

He must never know, never! She must remain proud and aloof, worthy of the name she bore, of the clan to which she belonged.

He was proud, so was she, and rightly for the finest Scottish blood ran in their veins and they bowed their heads to no one save to a Stuart king. Moida sighed and then with a start realised that she was neglecting her duty.

She must find the children. She leaned out of the window. They must be somewhere near at hand, perhaps playing in the ruins or playing hide and seek in the garden.

She could see no sign of them; and then, just as she was deciding that she must go and search for them, she saw them, and with a sudden leap of her heart, realised whom they were with.

They were down by the loch and Ian was with them. They were throwing stones and making them skim across the water as she had loved to do as a child and as Ian must often have done here at Skaig.

She could see all three of them absorbed first finding the right flat stone and then in counting the times it touched the water, and doubtless, though she could not hear their voices, counting boastfully how many leaps each stone made.

How happy they looked she thought, and wished she was with them. The temptation was too great to be ignored. She had the excuse that it was nearly tea time and the children must come in.

With a little flush in her cheeks and a light in her eyes, she ran towards the door.

She had reached it and even turned the handle when it was opened from without and only by moving quickly to one side did Moida avoid collision with someone coming into the room. It was Lynette.

One look at her face told Moida that she was angry. There was a tightness about her lips which revealed itself even before she spoke in a sharp, aggressively condescending tone.

"I wish to speak to you, Miss MacDonald."

"Yes?"

"I have come to tell you that I will not tolerate your behaviour any longer, nor will Mrs. McCraggan when she hears about it."

"I don't know what you are talking about," Moida answered.

"I think you do," Lynette said. "The Duke has told me how you dined with them last night and that you and Brigadier McCraggan drank champagne after the blue heather was found. I think you forget your position, Miss MacDonald.

"You have forced yourself upon the Brigadier. He has no acquaintance with you and though you may be able to deceive a mere man, I am not such a fool. I realise that you are trying to trap him and I warn you that you will not succeed, however clever you may think you are."

Lynette was speaking in the white heat of anger and

214

when she was angry she seemed to lose all her radiant beauty and become actually plain.

Her voice was strident and her narrowed eyes and compressed lips would have told any observer how much her loveliness depended on youth and her exquisite colouring.

For a moment Moida was too astonished to reply to the onslaught and then, quietly and with a dignity which seemed to come from some far-off ancestor, she said:

"You forget yourself, Miss Trent. Whatever you may think, it does not entitle you to address me in such a manner."

"It's no use trying to pull the wool over my eyes," Lynette answered rudely. "I can see that you are just a shameless adventuress and that you have taken the opportunity to worm your way in here."

"That may be your opinion," Moida said, "but other people think differently."

"Your friends can hardly be qualified to judge," Lynette replied, "and if you want the truth, I believe you engineered the whole thing from beginning to end."

"Engineered what?" Moida asked.

"The stealing of the Duke's blue heather," Lynette replied. "You may get Brigadier McCraggan to believe it was all coincidence, but who else would be so credulous? Your friends stole it, you put the children up to saying where it had gone and then your mother restores it. A pretty story, isn't it?—very cleverly done, but don't imagine for a moment that you will get away with it, because I shall see that you don't."

"It's a lie!" Moida said.

She did not raise her voice, but the words were spoken forcibly.

"It's the truth," Lynette retorted. "It has been a nice family hand-out all round, hasn't it? Your mother's got the publicity she wanted. I wonder how much she is paying you to act as her Press Agent?"

"How dare you speak to me like this?" Moida took an almost menacing step towards Lynette.

Perhaps it was her words, or perhaps the fact that she looked so pretty in her anger which made Lynette lose her head.

With a sudden exclamation of fury she slapped Moida in the face with all the force she could muster. The sound of her hand meeting Moida's cheek was almost like a pistol shot and perhaps it was that more than anything else which brought Lynette to her senses.

She stared at the Scottish girl and for a moment the blood seemed to drain away from her face. Moida stood looking at her for a long second. Neither of them moved, neither of them spoke.

Then Moida's voice came calmly from her lips:

"No one shall hit a MacDonald and get away with it. You have struck me in anger, and I shall strike you in return. Not because I have no control over myself, but merely because I intend to insult you as you have insulted me."

She raised her hand as she spoke and slapped Lynette hard and painfully first on the right side of her face, then on the left.

As the English girl gave a little cry and put her hands up to her cheeks, Moida spoke again.

"You have the manners of a gutter-snipe, and I'm sorry for the man who ever marries you."

She walked past Lynette as she spoke and went slowly and with immense dignity down the stairs. She was out of sight before Lynette moved.

She stood there, with her hands to her burning cheeks, shaking with a rage such as she had not experienced since she was a child and had been put to bed for one of her "tantrums" as they were called.

Then she stamped her foot.

"I would like to kill you," she cried; but whether from fear or discretion, her voice was very low and no one save herself heard it.

12

"What's the matter, Ian?" Lynette asked, looking at him across the dining-room table.

"Nothing," Ian replied.

It was an irritating answer and he was conscious of the fact. At the same time he noted how pretty Lynette was looking in the soft candlelight, and wondered why that in itself did not soothe his feeling of irritation.

"You are very silent."

Lynette made the statement a reproach.

"There's no rule that says I must be a gay little chatter-box all the time, is there?" Ian enquired and knew as he spoke that he was being rude.

"Ian! Really!" Beatrice ejaculated. "What is the matter with you? You've been snapping at us the whole evening."

"I'm sorry, Mother. Forgive me, Lynette."

Ian was sincerely contrite now and he held out a hand to each of them. Lynette laid her fingers delicately in the palm of the hand extended to her, but Beatrice gave him a little slap.

"He's always been the same," she said to Lynette; "if something upsets him, we all have to suffer."

"Nothing has upset me, really nothing," Ian replied. "I am just being horrid for no reason at all. Perhaps it is the Press or too much of Archie and his blue heather."

He knew it was none of these things, but something

which he dared not face even to himself, something which had been worrying him all day until now it seemed to overshadow him like a dark cloud which could not be brushed aside.

"I agree with you there. I never want to hear of blue heather again," Beatrice said with a little sigh. "But we shall—it will be with us night and day for a long time, I can see that."

"The Duke will make money out of it, won't he?" Lynette asked.

"Millions," Ian said briefly, "so long as he can keep the formula to himself. By tomorrow morning I should imagine that orders will be pouring in from all over the world, and how Archie will enjoy the excitement. I believe he is already secretly preparing his speech for the Horticultural Society!"

"Can he? Speak, I mean," Lynette enquired.

"He will manage it somehow, even if it is only in monosyllables. I've never met anyone who enjoyed publicity more. Did you see him with the photographers this afternoon? He was still ready to go on posing after they had got quite enough pictures."

"It's his mother's fault," Beatrice said. "She always ignored him and took all the limelight for herself, and his father was a selfish old man. He never once let Archie take his proper place. He was brought up on the theory that children should be seen and not heard, and look at the result."

"You are right as usual," Ian said. "This will do Archie the world of good and I for one am delighted about it."

He tried to speak heartily, but somehow the effort was a failure. He was pleased about the Duke, more pleased than he could possibly put into words, and yet at the moment he was finding it difficult to be enthusiastic about anything.

He wanted to be alone; he wanted to think; he wanted to admit to himself that he was tired and depressed and many other things besides, and not to be forced to keep up a façade of being pleasant either to his mother or to Lynette.

Instead, he knew that he must sit taking part in polite conversation and making a pretence of eating the delicious dinner that was being served with almost regal state.

Beatrice's staff had arrived, Alphonse was in the kitchen, protesting, it appeared, against everything and everybody in this strange northern land that he disliked so much, but turning out meals which would make even an epicure think he was in heaven.

"The bedrooms will be passably habitable by next Wednesday," Beatrice said suddenly. "I have wired the Halfords and Glamorgans to say we expect them, and I thought we might ask those two friends of yours who are such good shots, Ian—you know who I mean—Lord Blackmore and Colonel Huggins."

"All right, Mother. Just as you like," Ian replied.

"Archie will expect to be asked to shoot, and I suppose we'd better invite Mr. Struther over one day."

"Of course."

Ian's tone of indifference made his mother glance at him quickly, but she said nothing, finished her coffee and rose to her feet.

"I have some letters that I must finish, but I don't suppose you two will miss me!"

Lynette had risen too, but now she looked back uncertainly at Ian.

"I'm coming with you," he said. "I don't want to sit alone with my glass of port like Great-Uncle Duncan used to do."

"Where he was concerned the word "glass" was in the plural," Beatrice said tartly.

"Are you going to write in the drawing-room?" Ian enquired.

"Yes," Beatrice replied. "You two go and sit in the library. I'll join you as soon as I have finished."

They walked down the passage in silence and separated in the hall. As Ian opened the door of the library for Lynette, he said:

"I ought to be writing letters, too. There is an enormous pile of correspondence which came by the afternoon mail and I haven't even looked at it yet."

"I want to talk to you," Lynette said quickly.

Ian shut the door behind him and followed her across the room to stand in front of the big log fire burning in the fireplace.

"I had a letter from my mother this afternoon," Lynette announced as Ian reached her side.

"Did you?" he asked, his thoughts obviously preoccupied; then he gave a start, "Oh! yes, of course—you mean a reply to yours!"

"That's right. She has not answered before because she was on safari. She is delighted about our engagement—absolutely delighted."

"I'm glad about that," Ian's voice was very quiet.

"Are you? You don't sound very enthusiastic."

"I'm sorry. Must you keep on finding fault?"

"I don't see why not, if it is necessary," Lynette retorted rather loudly. "You appear to be upset about something, but you don't seem to consider my feelings. I have been alone here while you have been gallivanting about with Miss MacDonald and those two precious children."

Ian said nothing, but drew his cigarette case from his pocket and stood looking down at it as if he had never seen it before.

"Now, listen to me, Ian," Lynette went on. "I've got something to say and it is important for you to attend to it. Quite simply it is this—either that MacDonald woman leaves this Castle at once, or I do. She was rude to me this afternoon—incredibly, impertinently, rude. I am not going to tell you what she said—I should be ashamed to repeat it—but she has got to go.

"I told your mother so before dinner and she agrees with me. But it is for you to turn her out—after all, it is your house. And it has got to be at once or I shan't stay another night at Skaig."

Ian shut his cigarette case with a snap and returned it to his pocket.

"Now, what is all this about? What have you been saying to Miss MacDonald?"

"What have I been saying to her? The question is what has she been saying to me! The girl is unbearable, besides being nothing but a common adventuress, or worse, I shouldn't wonder!"

"It is utterly ridiculous to talk like that and you know it," Ian said angrily. "Miss MacDonald is a very nice girl. She has been forced into this²most unfortunate position by undeniable crockery on the part of my great-uncle's factor. Personally I think she did the only thing possible in the circumstances, coming here and hoping we would treat her justly, which is exactly what I intend to do."

"So now you are taking her part, are you?" Lynette asked. "She must have been very clever on the trip to Glasgow to get you round to her way of thinking so quickly."

"I don't know what you are talking about," Ian replied.

"Oh, yes, you do!" Lynette replied. "The girl's tricked you into believing she is a suffering little angel. My dear Ian, how can you be such a fool and fall for the scheming of a common little slut like that?"

"I don't think those expressions are very becoming, Lynette," Ian answered quietly, "nor are they true. She is not common and what is more, she has a brilliant brain. I have the greatest admiration for her."

"That is very obvious," Lynette said bitterly.

She turned her back on Ian and stood looking down at the fire. She was trembling with the rage which had been burning within her ever since her scene with Moida earlier in the afternoon.

Yet she had enough control over herself now to

realise that she was making a great mistake in speaking as she had to Ian.

Men were all the same, she thought; a woman could always twist them into believing anything she wanted them to believe; and she already knew Ian well enough to realise that nothing she could say would ever alter his opinion of anybody about whom he once made up his mind.

With a superhuman effort and at the cost of sacrificing her pride, for the moment at any rate, Lynette turned round with a smile on her face.

"Darling, we're quarrelling!" she said. "Our very first quarrel, and it's much too soon. I take back all I said. I love you—that is all that matters, isn't it?"

"Yes, of course."

Lynette waited for Ian to take her in his arms, to kiss her tenderly and soothingly as he had done before when she was in any way upset or distressed. But instead, to her surprise, he took his cigarette case out of his pocket.

"Forgive me," he said, "I must go and find some cigarettes."

The case was full, Lynette knew that, for she had seen him open it a few minutes before; but she was wise enough to say nothing as he walked away from her.

He opened the library door and, passing through it, shut it quietly behind him.

For a moment she stared blindly in front of her and then she put up her hands to her face. It was still burning from where Moida had slapped her, and now she asked herself how she could have been such a fool ever to become involved in a row or to have mentioned it to Ian.

With a little sigh of exasperation she walked to the table where the newspapers were placed in orderly array. She picked up *The Tatler* and opening it found a photograph of herself.

It was only an informal picture taken at Goodwood

222

Races, but she was looking very lovely in a beautifully-cut dress of flowered silk and a big straw hat. It was captioned,

"Miss Lynette Trent, who was the most beautiful debutante of her year, picks a winner."

As always, the sight of her much-photographed face gave Lynette a satisfaction which nothing else could do. Her feeling of anger and exasperation with Ian began to disappear.

A few seconds later she was smiling, a soft smile which deepened on her lips as she glanced towards the door a little impatiently, anxious for Ian to come back to her.

He was not far away. In fact, when he left the library, he had walked straight through the open front door, down the steps and out on to the terrace. It was not completely dark.

Although the stars were beginning to glitter in the sky and there was a pale ghost of a moon rising over the hills, there was also a faint glow in the west left from the dying sunset.

The moors were shadowed but the loch seemed still to shine beneath the sable of the sky. It was very still and very peaceful, yet Ian felt that there was no stillness and peace within himself.

He knew he was facing something he had never faced before—a personal crisis and one which seemed to tear him to pieces, so that for the moment he could neither think nor feel coherently.

"What am I to do?" He asked the question of the night and the only answer was the faint touch of the sea breeze against his cheeks.

He walked to the edge of the terrace. Below, the ground slipped away to where he had gone before tea to the loch, to be joined by the children.

He had known then, he thought, known it in that moment when he walked away from the Castle carrying the *Telegraph* Moida had just given him.

223

He had been surprised at his own reluctance to open the paper and read what she had said.

He had not understood for the moment why he should mind what she wrote about him; and then, as he reached the loch and saw it in all its breathtaking beauty, the thought had come to him that he wanted Moida to be there.

Three geese had risen from a small island and with a great flutter of wings had skimmed across the water, rising higher and higher until, pointed like an arrow against the sky, they had flown off towards the sea.

As he watched them go, they reminded Ian of Moida with her strong, free mind, soaring into heights attempted by few other people. Yes, he had known then, he thought to himself now as he stood on the terrace, known that he loved her as he had never loved anyone else before.

He was old and experienced enough to realise that love could have many sides and many facets.

He had loved Lynette for her beauty, for the sheer joy of looking at her and for knowing that she could quicken his senses and make his blood rise in his veins simply because she was desirable.

But all the time some inner voice had warned him that it might not last. His love—if that was the right word for it—could fade or alter as easily as Lynette could change her dress or style of hairdressing.

It was not a spiritual love, but the love of a connoisseur for something that was exquisitely beautiful.

His love for Moida was very different. He knew that now and was afraid—afraid not that he might lose his love, but that he would not be worthy of it.

This was something he had been looking for all his life; something he had sought unknowingly, yet persistently; which had made every other woman he had met fall short of the standard which had lain secret and hidden within his heart and which only now stood revealed.

It was Moida's mind which had first delighted him—as shrewd and sharp as a tempered sword, as swift and unerring as a dagger.

He might have admired her for that and still not have loved her if he had not seen the tenderness and sweetness in her eyes when she looked at the children.

She seemed to him then like the Italian paintings of the young Madonna—dark hair growing so beautifully back from her white forehead, her eyebrows winged over her downcast eyes and her mouth full and soft and red—all woman, although her mind could be utterly and confoundingly masculine.

All woman—he had thought that about her as he had watched her come from the doorway of the room at the hotel when she had been putting the children to bed.

She had been tired, a little dusty and dishevelled after the long hours they had spent in the car. She was dressed in her familiar green sweater and tartan skirt, and her hair was rumpled because the children had thrown their arms round her in an affectionate, if sleepy good night.

But Ian had known at that moment that that was how he wanted a woman to look—with tenderness in her face and a sweetness in her eyes and a gentleness on her lips which were ready to kiss and be kissed, not in passion, but in love.

All woman Moida had seemed to him, the slim, curved lines of her body showing as she moved and he called out to her that he had ordered dinner and that she had time for a bath before it.

Then he had shut the door on himself with the feeling that he was losing something that was desperately important, although at that moment he could not think why.

He knew now. He dared not, he could not lose her. This was what he wanted. This was the uttermost and ultimate desire of his heart, of his body, of his very soul. How strange, he thought, that he should think of that!

His soul had meant nothing to him for a great many years; yet now he remembered it was there, a part of him, a very intrinsic part, and he was sure that it was his soul rather than his heart that had recognised Moida and known her for what she was.

He loved her, but what could he do about it? He walked across the terrace, his feet noisy on the rough gravel. He loved her, but he was honour-bound to Lynette.

He was not quixotic or old fashioned enough to believe that an engagement was irrevocable or that an unhappy marriage was preferable to a broken engagement. He was only sensible enough to admit the difficulties.

Lynette had not kept their engagement secret from her intimate friends and relations. It was only surprising that the Press, with its ear to every keyhole, had not learned before now that one of their most favoured social pets was engaged. It was a news story all right, for Lynette was news and so was he.

Mercifully it had not been headlined as yet, but Ian knew it was only a question of time.

Lynette would, he thought, mind a broken engagement more from a publicity point of view than from losing him.

Yet even as he thought it, he wondered if he was being fair. Lynette did love him in her own way. At least he attracted her and he had known at times that he could arouse a response to his kisses almost equal to the desire he felt within himself.

She had done nothing to deserve this, he thought. He had asked her to marry him and she had accepted; they had both been old enough to know their own minds, and both at the time had been very much in love. That was the truth.

Ian could remember moments when they had sat looking at each other across the pink-shaded table, moments when their hands had sought and found each other's, moments when it had been sheer excitement to seek her lips and know that they sought his.

He must be honest, he must be straightforward with himself. He had been in love with Lynette until he met Moida.

With Moida there were no moments of excitement to remember, no pressing of hands or lips, no beating of hearts or whirling of senses. Instead, it was as if a great light had seared its way into his mind and heart and shown him the truth.

This was the woman he wanted for ever and for all time as his wife, as the mother of his children.

Somehow he had never thought of children in connection with Lynette. He had assumed automatically that they would have them one day.

With Moida it was an aching need—it was a desire almost as great as his desire to possess her and make her his—their children who would be part of him and part of her.

Children who would grow up here at Skaig and belong, even as he had always known, from the time he could think at all, that he belonged.

Moida! He wanted to cry her name aloud, and then he knew there was no need.

She was as much a part of Skaig as he was, part of the moor, the sky, the loch and the river, part of the breeze blowing from the sea, part of the cry of the grouse echoing over the hill.

Moida! He wondered to himself how he had ever lived without her, how the world had ever seemed complete or satisfying until she was in it.

This was love—not one which gave or withheld, but a love which was all-powerful, a love from which there was no escape, no appeal.

With a sudden start Ian found himself on the river bank about two miles from the Castle. He had not been conscious of walking or moving, but only of thinking and feeling intensely.

The light of the moon was on the river, the sky was alight with stars and because of them it was not dark. He could see his way clearly, but he had walked without looking.

He glanced at his watch. It was long after midnight. For the first time since he left the library he remembered that he had left Lynette alone and without explanation.

She would be angry, he thought; and yet somehow it did not matter—nothing mattered save Moida and all that he felt for her.

He turned his face towards home. From where he stood the Castle was black and gaunt, its ruins darkly silhouetted against the stars. There was nothing welcoming about it, and yet he felt as if it beckoned him.

Moida was at Skaig and the ancient building held her safely and securely. At that moment there was nothing more that he would ask of life, save that the two should be together—Moida and Skaig.

He would work for them, he would be ambitious for them, and he would, if necessary, die for them, the two things he loved and the two which mattered most in his life and would do so for ever.

He walked back slowly, taking the long path by the river bank. For the moment he was at peace within himself.

For hours he had suffered and thought and concentrated to the exclusion of all else; and, though he had come to no conclusion, what he had experienced had somehow purged his mind and heart so that now he had reached quintessence—he was at peace!

The future would right itself and he would find a way, an honourable and decent way, so that he could kneel at Moida's feet.

For the moment he could only think of her as a goal, wonderful and shining, the woman he had been seeking, the woman he had found.

He reached the terrace and stood looking at the Castle. The upper floors were in darkness, everyone would have gone to bed and only the lights in the hall were left burning for his return.

He climbed the steps, opened the door and found, as he expected, that there was no one about.

He went into the library, managed to pick up a newspaper and his unopened letters by the light of the dying fire; then, carrying the candle in his hand, he went upstairs to his own bedroom.

When he reached it, with the usual perversity of the human body when it experiences new emotions he no longer felt tired. He felt exhilaratingly and excitingly alive.

His mail looked at him reproachfully, but he threw it down on the table and, drawing back the curtains, stood looking out into the night.

For a moment he contemplated going back the way he had come, tramping over the heather, or even taking a boat and rowing across the loch; and then, as he stood there, there came a rap on his bedroom door.

For a moment he did not answer—a number of thoughts chased themselves through his mind.

Then the knock came again and the handle of the door turned. He swung round and saw, by the light of the candle, who stood there.

It was Moida. For a moment he could only stand staring at her, vaguely taking in the fact that she was wearing a dressing gown of some soft green material.

"Ian! Thank God you are here!"

It was the first time she had used his Christian name, but neither of them was aware of it.

She came hurriedly into the room and now he could see the bareness of her neck and that her eyes were dark and frightened in a very white face.

Instinctively he went towards her, his arms outstretched without any conscious volition of his own.

"What is it?"

She could hardly gasp the words.

"Hamish! Hamish has gone!"

She seemed almost to stumble then, and now his

229

arms were actually around her, holding her close, feeling her body tremble beneath the thin silk.

Her head dropped forward and for a moment she laid it against his shoulder as if she clung to his very strength.

"Tell me all about it," he said quietly.

She moved and began to speak, still supported by his encircling arms.

"I was late going to bed," she said; "and when I was undressed, I went in to have a last look at the children, as I always do; but when I went into Hamish's room, it was empty. . . . His clothes had gone, too, and his gun which came today—the one your mother gave him. I thought he was playing some prank, although he is usually very good, so I woke Cathy.

"She told me that he had come into her room some time before—she wasn't certain how long because she had been to sleep since—and had told her that he had heard a lorry going up the strath.

'They're after the deer,' he told her. 'If the Laird's in his room, I'll tell him to tackle them. If not, I'll shoot them myself.'

"Cathy wanted to go with him, but he wouldn't let her. 'It's a man's work,' he said, and then he went."

Moida's voice seemed to strangle in her throat, and desperately she held on to Ian.

"They won't hurt him, will they? They won't hurt him?"

"You are upsetting yourself needlessly," Ian said soothingly. "For one thing, it may not be poachers; and for another, why should they hurt a little boy like Hamish? He can't do them any harm. Go back to bed. I'll find him. I'll bring him back to you."

His words made Moida pull herself together. For the first time since she had entered the room she spoke calmly:

"I'm being silly, I know, but I'm frightened."

"But you're not to be. This isn't like you."

"No, I know it isn't. But the poachers have been here
230

before and Mackay has told us things about them, how cruel and ruthless they are. It is only hearsay, of course, but I'm afraid for Hamish."

"Go back to bed, please," Ian pleaded.

"Let me come with you."

He shook his head.

"No, as Hamish said, this is man's work. I'm going to wake Hull and Mackay—Mackay will know where they are most likely to be."

He looked down at Moida for an instant and his arm tightened about her.

"Don't worry," he said, "I'll bring him back."

And then he kissed her.

He didn't mean to do so, but instinctively, as if he had the right, he bent forward and laid his lips against hers. It was a gentle kiss, a kiss that a man might give to a dearly-loved wife whom he leaves for but a short time.

And then, before Moida could speak, before, it seemed to her, she could even breathe, he was gone and she could hear only his footsteps receding down the passage.

It took Ian only a short time to rouse the men-servants and get the car out of the garage. By the time Hull and Willy Mackay were dressed, he was waiting for them in the drive.

Willy clambered in beside him, a gun under his arm. He saw Ian glance at it and said:

"Ye dinna ken what ye're oop against, Master Ian. These poachers'll stick at nathing. We ken 'em weel around here. They're no the type they used to be—a mon who wants a cheap meal for his bairns. They're men o' business; they kill for money an' they dinna care how much the poor animals suffer sae lang as they git the cash for themsel'."

"How many times do you suspect them of having been here before?" Ian asked as he started the car up the strath.

"Twa or three times. Maybe mair. Some folks say as

231

mony as a dozen, but 'tis hard tae tell. When the deer are doon on the road at nicht, 'tis easy enough to kill 'em."

"Butchers!" Ian ejaculated briefly.

They drove on, peering from side to side as they went, hoping for the sight of a small figure in a kilt crouching amongst the heather or waving to them from some stone cairn. But the road was deserted.

It was when they were about a mile and a half from the Castle that Willy Mackay ejaculated:

"Steady, Sir."

Though he was old, his eyes were sharper than either Ian's or Hull's when it came to strange marks on the road. Ian stopped the car; and now that it was pointed out to him he could see on the faint dust, on which no rain had fallen for a week, the marks of a lorry.

They all got out. About a dozen yards from where they were a rough quarry at the side of the road made a passing place. It was here the lorry had turned—that was obvious.

Hull had brought a torch with him and was flashing it around.

"Look here, Sir."

Ian and Willy Mackay went to his side. There was blood in the dust and the marks of heavy animals having been dragged along. They found the place where the deer had been killed a little further down the road. There was the mess of the gralloch and several empty cartridge cases.

Ian said nothing. Willy Mackay, moving from place to place, was swearing under his breath.

"The bloody murderers!" he muttered. "May they rot for this deed."

"No doubt as to what they've done, Sir," Hull said at length.

Ian nodded.

"Parked the lorry and waited here," he said. "perhaps for an hour, until the deer came down to the road. Then one burst from the gun would get five or

232

six of them, perhaps more, before the rest galloped away. Then they loaded them up and drove off. What we want to know is what happened to the child."

The three men looked at each other.

"He may be back at the Castle now, Sir," Hull suggested.

"Let us hope so," Ian answered. "We will drive a little way up the road first before we go back, in case he has seen the tracks as we have and followed them."

They drove for two or three miles, but there was no sign of anyone. They turned and went back.

As they reached the Castle, they saw someone standing by the gate and for one second Ian thought it might be Hamish; but as they drew nearer, he saw it was Moida waiting for them.

Her face was white against the darkness as he stopped the car and climbed out.

"Have you found him?"

It was obvious by the tone of her voice that she knew the answer even while she asked the question.

Ian shook his head.

"You are quite certain he has not come back to the Castle?"

"He hadn't when I left about twenty minutes ago." There was a sudden gleam of hope in her expression. "Let us go back and see."

She climbed into the car and they drove up to the front door. Ian helped her out.

"Wait here," he said to Mackay and Hull; "I shall want you to come with me if the boy isn't upstairs."

Without a word Moida ran up the broad staircase. Ian waited. There was a little pause and then he heard her coming down again and knew by her hurrying footsteps that Hamish was not there.

"What are we going to do?"

She barely breathed the words as she reached his side.

"We are going to the Police," Ian said quietly. "We'll get him back, don't worry."

"You will, won't you."

It was a statement more than a question and for a moment her eyes looked up into his. There was only one oil lamp in the hall, but he could see her very clearly—her little face with its lovely lines, the gold-flecked eyes, and the softly-parted lips.

"I'll find Hamish for you, my darling," Ian said.

It was as if he vowed himself to her service for all eternity.

13

Hamish had been sitting up in bed playing with his torch when he heard a lorry going up the strath.

Playing after the lights were out was forbidden, but his torch was a new toy and he could not resist the temptation of trying it in the darkness of his room.

When he went to bed it was not completely dark even with the curtains drawn; but now the circle of yellow light could be seen in all its beauty and he sat for a long time pointing the torch first this way and then that until he heard the wheels of a lorry.

He held his breath and listened. He had no idea of the time, for he had fallen asleep as soon as he got into bed and then had awakened slowly and drowsily.

But he knew only too well that it was a very unusual occurrence for a truck or lorry to come up the strath after dark.

A car was different; but even that would cause comment, for after the Castle there was only the open moorland stretching empty and uninhabited until one came to the west coast and the sea again.

In the day time there were lorries working on the roads, collecting the peat, trundling through to Betty-hill or taking the twisting, steep road which turned south eventually to end up at Lairg. But these were working lorries and their day ended at five o'clock.

All this Hamish remembered and therefore a lorry going up at night could mean only one thing—poachers. He sprang out of bed, went to the window and looked out.

There was nothing to be seen but the star-strewn sky; and although he thought he could still hear the rumble of wheels, he guessed that in reality the lorry would already be out of ear-shot.

He began to dress himself quickly, pulling on his shirt, fastening his kilt, and slipping into his rough tweed jacket which, among a great assortment of other necessities in the pockets, held his beloved catapult.

Stockings and shoes took him a little longer for the laces were hard to tie, but he managed them; then almost reverently he turned towards his bed and picked up his gun.

It had lain there on the foot of the bed all night— the gun which Beatrice had promised him and which had arrived that very afternoon.

It was double-barrelled, just as she said, and though it shot corks instead of bullets, it looked, in Hamish's eyes, exactly like the real thing.

He opened the door of his bedroom quietly and went into Cathy's room. She was fast asleep.

He could hear her gentle breathing before his torch picked her out, her red hair vivid against the pillow, her face very young and vulnerable in repose.

Hamish, however, was not interested in his sister's appearance. He shook her shoulder and, when she awoke with a little cry, put his finger to her lips.

"Shush!" he whispered. "Don't wake Aunt Moida!"

"What is it? What's the matter?" Cathy asked sleepily.

"The poachers have gone up the strath after the deer," Hamish answered. "I heard the lorry, I'm going to wake the Laird and we'll go after them."

"Let me come," Cathy said, wide awake now, her eyes shining.

Hamish shook his head.

"No, this is man's work," he answered, "but I thought I'd tell you."

They smiled at each other with the confidence and trust of children who have grown up together and who have had no secrets from each other.

"Please let me come too, Hamish," Cathy pleaded.

"No, it might be dangerous," he answered. "Besides, I can't wait."

He was moving away from her as he spoke. She heard the door close behind him and put out her hands in the darkness in a pathetic little gesture.

"Hamish—wait! Take me," she pleaded: but instinctively she kept her voice low and knew he would not hear her

Two big tears welled into her eyes and ran down her cheeks and, sobbing a little from self-pity because she must be left behind, Cathy snuggled down in her pillows and in a few moments was fast asleep again.

Hamish ran down the front stairs. They were in darkness, but he knew his way to Ian's room on the first floor. For a moment he hesitated outside the door.

Had he really forgiven the enemy so completely as to concede him authority on such an adventure as this? For a moment his old enmity warred with his new friendship; friendship won, and Hamish knocked on the door.

There was no answer and, thinking that Ian might be asleep, he turned the handle and went into the room. After a few seconds of listening he switched on his torch. The bed was empty!

Hamish wasted no further time. He hurried down the next flight of stairs into the hall. Here the lights were on, but the library was in darkness and Hamish decided that Ian had gone out.

There was nothing then he could do but go and look for the poachers himself. It never occurred to him to seek the help of any of the other men in the house.

His experience with the Mackays was that they treated him as a child and he guessed that, if he told them what he was about, they would send him back to bed or worse still, wake his Aunt.

He knew that Moida would not approve of his getting up after he had been put to bed; but this, he told himself resolutely, was something that had to be done, and done quickly.

Without wasting any more time thinking and worrying, he let himself out through the front door and, taking a quick cut across the gardens, reached the road within a few minutes.

Once there, he set out to walk briskly and with a speed which many men might have envied in the direction in which the lorry had gone.

Hamish had lived all his life in Scotland and was used to long distances and to keeping up with men. Another boy might have felt apprehensive at setting off on a long walk alone in the middle of the night, but Hamish was not afraid of the dark.

The strath was as familiar to him as his own bedroom had been at home. He knew every landmark, every curve and rise of the moor ahead of him.

A little way below him and on his left he could see the river winding silver in the moonlight. He stepped out, but at the same time he was wise enough not to run. He knew that running exhausts a person very easily.

After a short way he began to feel hungry and felt in his pockets hopefully. But there was not even a piece of chocolate or a biscuit to relieve the emptiness of his stomach.

He must have been walking for nearly half an hour before he heard shots—a burst of them following quickly one upon the other. They seemed to shatter the silence with almost horrifying intensity, and then there was silence again.

"Not far away," he thought.

For the first time since he left the Castle he began to run, an easy jog-trot which his father had taught him was very much less exhausting than an all-out effort.

Instinctively, too, he moved from the centre of the

road to the soft sand on the side, where his footsteps made no noise.

On and on he went until suddenly round the corner he saw ahead of him two or three men bending over the heather. He paused then and, crouching down, began to stalk them.

Now crawling, now moving forward with his body bent low, he came nearer and nearer.

The men were gralloching the deer they had shot. There were three of them. They were working quickly and with experienced hands. It was a question of shooting and getting away quickly on jobs like this. But the deer must be gralloched, then camouflaged in case the police stopped them.

There was straw in the lorry and each deer, as it was ready, was thrust under the straw.

"Is that the lot?" one of the men asked, wiping his hands which were stained with blood and turning towards the other two who were still working in the heather.

"Two more," another answered.

It was at that moment that the small figure rose to its full height and, pointing a gun, said:

"Hands up, you poachers!"

There was a moment of silence when the three men seemed suddenly frozen into immobility; then at last one of them spoke:

"Ga'an, it's only a kid!"

"I've got a gun," Hamish said, "and I'll shoot you."

One of the men felt in his pocket; the next second a torch was flashed full in Hamish's face. For a moment he blinked, dazed by the light; then the men began to laugh.

"A hold-up with a pop-gun," one of them said with a Cockney accent. "Blimey! for the moment he had me scared."

"You've no right to come here," Hamish stormed. "It's wrong and wicked what you are doing and many of the other deer will die, too, because you have

239

wounded them. It is cruel and you're beasts. Do you hear me—you are beasts!"

"Now, laddie, there's no need to git yoursel' worked oop like that," another of the men answered.

He wiped his knife as he spoke and handed the carcass to a big, red-headed man to throw into the lorry.

"Ye are only thinking of the deer, that's what ye are doing. There are ither animals as weel. We're thinking of a lot of paure wee doggies that are hungry. Ye wouldna like to think of that, would ye?—paure, wee doggies, who wouldna git a square meal in weeks if it wasna for chaps like us!"

"Aw, stow it, Ben!" the red-headed man exclaimed.

"Then it's true that you poach the deer for the greyhounds," Hamish said.

"That's reet," Ben answered him. "How did you ken? Ye're a smart laddie, ye are."

"Bit too smart, if you ask me," the red-headed man said.

The Cockney carried his sack across the intervening space to the lorry.

"That's what I'm thinking, Fergus," he said. "Too sharp by half. What are we going to do with him, I'd like to know?"

"Leave him here, of course," Fergus replied.

"What? And have him running back to Skaig and telling on us? They could telephone and stop us at Lairg—you know that as well as I do."

"Coo, now I never thought of that!" Fergus remarked, scratching his red head. "What do you say, Ben? Is Ted right?"

"It's a question, richt enough," Ben replied slowly.

It was now easy for Hamish to see him by the light of the moon. He was a small, wrinkled old man with a quickness of movement which bespoke strength and a heavily lined face. His eyes were not unkind as he looked at Hamish.

"Ye're a brave laddie," he said, "but ye have got yersel' into a fix the noo and nae mistake."

"You and your talk of doggies—haven't got the brains of a louse, either of you!" Ted sneered, "but I'm sharp, I am. If I hadn't been, I should have been behind bars before now. Cut the little perisher's throat and dump him in the river, I say."

For the first time Hamish felt frightened. Instinctively he wanted to turn and run; then he knew that he would rather die than show these men that he was afraid.

"I'm not afraid of you," he said stoutly, "and if you do murder me, you will hang for it—hang by your necks unto you are dead—and you won't like that."

"Nor will you, you cheeky little blighter," Ted snarled at him. "I'll slit your guts for you."

He walked towards Hamish; but with a swiftness that seemed incredible at his age Ben was between them.

"The laddie's richt, Ted," he said. "Ye'd never get awa' wi' murder, and what is mair, I'll have nun of it. Killing beasties ane thing, but bairns is anither. He'll have to came along wi' us."

"What?"

It was Fergus who spoke now, and the exclamation came out like a roar.

"Ye heard what I said," Ben replied. "We canna leave him here, sa there is only ane thing to be done—he comes wi' us!"

"Then, for Gawd Almighty's sake, let's get on with it," Ted said. "Or are you waiting for someone to come and ask who's been doing a spot of shooting?"

As if his question galvanised them into action, Fergus hurried to the front of the lorry and started the engine with a swing of the handle.

Almost before Hamish realised what was happening, he found himself bundled roughly, if not unkindly, up into the front seat. He tried to expostulate, he tried to argue, but his voice was drowned by the noise of the lorry and he knew that to struggle would be hopeless.

Squashed between Fergus who was driving and Ben

on the other side, he found himself for a moment almost asphyxiated by the smell of oil, grease and stale tobacco; and then they were off, rattling and crashing along the road at what was nearly a breakneck speed.

"Where are you taking me?" Hamish asked at length when he had grown used to the noise of the engine.

"Them as asks no questions don't get told no lies," Ted snapped.

"If you know what's good for you, Sonny, you'll keep quiet," Fergus added as he steered the heavy lorry along the twisty, narrow road with a skill which bespoke long practice.

The heat and the atmosphere and perhaps the reaction from the excitement, made Hamish sleepy. It was very warm, squeezed between the two men.

After a time his head fell forward and he slept. He awoke a long time later and found it was still night. The men had stopped to buy sandwiches and a cup of tea.

They gave him a sandwich, but he was too tired to eat it and after a few bites fell asleep again with his head against Ben's shoulder.

It was morning when he awoke again with a dry, choking feeling in his throat, a stiff neck and cramp in his legs.

It took him a few seconds to realise where he was and what was happening to him; then, as he stared around him, the lorry came to a standstill.

"Put him out," he heard Fergus say, and the next minute he had been passed along the front of the lorry from Ben to Ted, lowered through the door and thrown into the heather with a sudden hard and decisive push of Ted's hand.

He sprawled head first, his face and hands scratched, his knees grazed a little by the fall; and when he picked himself up, the lorry had gone.

He was on a desolate, empty road. There was no sign of human habitation, but the road itself was wide and tarmaced. Hamish looked around him.

He had never before seen the place where he was—there were moors stretching away to the horizon, there were trees, too—it had not the desolate, empty beauty of Skaig.

"I don't suppose I'm far from Glasgow," Hamish thought.

It was morning, but very early morning, he decided, perhaps not later than five o'clock. He tried to reckon how long it would take the lorry to get to Glasgow, and failed. He only knew it was a long way.

It was then he realised that his gun was missing. For the first time since he had set off from the Castle the night before on his perilous adventure he felt like crying. His gun—his precious gun, which he had only had for a very short time!

Then with a philosophical optimism he guessed that someone, either Beatrice or Ian, would give him another one. He had done his best to save the deer. It was not his fault that he had failed.

More important than the loss of his gun was the fact that he was hungry and that he must get home.

He rubbed his eyes, noting as he did so that his hands were extremely dirty, and recalling with something akin to pleasure that he could not wash them and there was no one to tell him to do so.

Then he did up his shoe laces and set off down the road in the direction from which he had come.

It was just about this time that Moida and Ian, with Willy Mackay and Hull in the back of the car, returned to the Castle.

They had spent a weary night finding the police and galvanising them into action; then searching the strath road over and over again for a sign of Hamish.

Too late Ian realised that he should not have turned back after finding the tracks of the lorry—he should have gone on. He might have caught up with it had he done so.

Instead of which, he had wasted precious time in

243

going back to the Castle and then taking Moida to the nearest police station.

This was at Brora, but even then there was delay. The Constable-in-charge had to await an Inspector; the Inspector had to hear all the facts before he took any action.

By this time they all realised that the lorry would have passed through Lairg, if that was the way it was going, and would be safely on to the Inverness road, heading for Glasgow or Aberdeen.

It was suspected that deer were being taken to both places, the Inspector told them. Moida, white-faced, listened to the consultations. Ian knew that she was almost distraught with anxiety as to Hamish's safety. He himself was very nearly as anxious.

Men who would shoot deer with a Tommy gun were not likely to be particularly gentle with a child, especially a boy who was trying to interfere with them.

It was the longest night Moida had ever known. When she got back to the Castle to find it was only five o'clock she could hardly believe that only four hours had passed since they had left it.

The Inspector promised to let them know at the first possible moment when anything was discovered or any trace of the lorry found. Ian also said that he would go down to the village every hour and ring the police station.

In the meantime, there was nothing they could do except go home. Tearing about the roads was going to help no one. If Hamish was found, it would only complicate matters if they were missing.

As they walked wearily up the steps and in at the Castle door, Hull slipped ahead of them.

"I'll light the library fire, Sir," he said, "and bring you some breakfast in there."

"Thank you, Hull; I think we could all do with something to eat," Ian replied.

"I don't want anything," Moida protested. But Ian, taking her arm, answered:

244

"Nonsense! If you don't look after yourself, you will be ill and quite useless to anyone."

Moida knew he implied that Hamish on his return might need nursing, and instantly she pulled herself together.

"A cup of tea, then, and some bread and butter, if it's no trouble," she said. "I don't think I could eat anything else."

"Eggs and bacon for me, Hull," Ian said firmly.

The ashes in the library fireplace were still smouldering and it was only a question of seconds before they had kindled some dry wood and the fire was burning brightly.

"I won't be long, Sir," Hull promised as he left the room.

"Sit down and relax," Ian said to Moida. "I'm going upstairs to change."

"Don't leave me!" The words came to Moida's lips before she could prevent them.

"Only for a short while," Ian said. "I can't spend the day in a dinner jacket."

"I'm sorry," she replied, putting her hands to her eyes; "I'm being ridiculous, but somehow I can't think of anything but Hamish—Hamish in the hands of those devils!"

"I know. As soon as we have had something to eat we will make plans as to what to do next," Ian said soothingly. "In the meantime, remember they haven't had him for very long."

"He will be cold and hungry."

"Stop imagining things," Ian answered. "I know it's hard, but in moments like this one has to acknowledge only facts. If one's imagination runs away into fantasy and speculation, then sanity becomes almost impossible."

There was a ring of truth in his voice which told Moida that he had suffered at some time exactly as she was suffering now. Perhaps, too, he had been afraid.

With a little gesture of helplessness, which somehow contrived at the same time to be completely and overwhelmingly feminine, she surrendered herself to his strength and wisdom.

"I won't think," she promised. "Go and wash. I ought to do the same."

"Stay where you are," Ian commanded. "If we all go rushing round the house, we might wake someone; and that is the last thing we want."

Moida looked at him gratefully. How well he understood!

The reason she refrained from going upstairs the moment she entered the Castle was because Beatrice or Lynette might hear them and wonder what was happening.

She knew that for the moment she could not tolerate their questions and curiosity. Cathy would be asleep— there was no need to worry about her. She seldom woke before seven in the morning and often slept on long after Moida and Hamish were up and dressed.

Alone, Moida rose to go nearer to the fire. She was shivering despite the warmth of her coat; and when she had warmed her hands, she automatically looked in the mirror over the mantelpiece to smooth her hair and powder her nose. It was an effort which made her feel better and more like herself.

"I'm behaving like a coward," she thought; and yet she knew that her dependence was in part due to the fact that Ian was there.

Had she been alone, she would have taken command, she would have forced herself to do what he had done, though not with such calmness and authority. It was very nice to feel dependent.

With a sudden rush of emotion she knew that it was dependence on Ian that mattered and she could never have felt the same about anyone else.

How kind, how wonderful he had been to her! She closed her eyes and felt as if his strength encompassed her as his arms had done when she clung to him that

246

first moment in his bedroom when the terror of finding that Hamish was missing had made her almost incoherent.

And then, even as she thought of it, the blood rose in Moida's cheeks.

Only now, for the first time, did she begin to wonder what Ian must have thought of her, coming to his room like that, running into his arms as if for protection, letting her head rest for one helpless moment against his shoulder.

Her hands flew to her cheeks.

She must have been crazy. It was, in fact, the truth—she had been crazed with fear. But had he understood? She knew in her heart of hearts that he had; and yet another part of her kept asking the question.

She was ashamed of her own weakness and at the same time she gloried in it because Ian had been so kind to her. And he had kissed her! She must not think about that. This was not the moment.

Later, later perhaps, when she had gone away and Ian was no longer at her side, she would dare to remember it; but not now!

She must think of something else, anything rather than herself and Ian, or of Hamish—little Hamish, tackling a crowd of poachers by himself.

With a little sob Moida walked across the room blindly. She put her hand out to the book shelves and selected a book at random.

It was leather bound; and after a moment, when she had fought back the mist from before her eyes, she saw that it was written in Latin.

She put the book back in its place and took down another. This was printed with the long "s" and, after turning over a few pages, she replaced it, too.

Fiercely she tried to concentrate on what she was doing. A large, heavily-bound Bible caught her eye. She had a sudden desire to read it, to find some comfort in the beautiful words of the Gospels which she had known almost by heart when she was a child.

She could remember her grandfather reading to them on Sunday afternoons in Holyrood Palace. His room had been lined with books, even as this room was—books that he loved as much as he loved his grandchildren, if not more, books that he handled with the care that a miser might expend on his gold.

"The Lord is my Shepherd . . ."

Moida could remember him reading his favourite psalm and then turning to the Gospel of St. John and letting the beauty of the opening chapter hold her and Janet spellbound so that, although it was beyond their comprehension, they knew that some mystery was being expounded to them.

She took down the Bible now. Perhaps if she opened it at random, she might find a message for herself—a message to tell her that Hamish was safe!

The book was heavier than she thought and, staggering a little under its weight, she set it down carefully on the arm of a chair and then opened it at the fly leaf.

"Duncan McCraggan, born 1871" was written there. It was Ian's great-uncle's Bible, Moida thought, and she saw that on the other side of the page was a roughly-drawn family tree.

She looked at it with interest. It went back to 1400, but she saw that only the eldest son was included each time.

Family names occurred over and over again—Duncan, Euan, Ian and Angus. All down the centuries she found them, father to son, father to son. And then there was Duncan, almost at the end, born 1871. Beside his there appeared another name, Angus, born 1872.

That would have been Ian's grandfather, she thought; and with a sense of excitement, she looked lower.

"Euan, born 1898," she read, and beneath his name, Ian's. Moida's lips curled a little disdainfully. So even in the family Bible Ian's grandfather had been prepared to lie. He had known about Malcolm, the elder son, born in 1896, but his name was not included here.

She shut the Bible with a decisive snap and lifted it to put it back in the bookcase. It slipped a little in her hands and would have fallen off the arm of the chair if she had not prevented it.

As she did so, something fell from the Bible, something which had lain hidden between the pages.

It was a letter in a crumbling, faded envelope and as Moida went to pick it up, she gave a little gasp, for she recognised the handwriting.

She stared at it for some seconds before, resolutely and with an air of one who is determined, whatever the cost, to know the truth, she drew out the sheets of closely written paper from the envelope. . . .

When Ian came back to the library about ten minutes later, Hull had already laid a table in front of the fire and set down a silver dish of eggs and bacon.

"I'm hungry, I must admit," Ian said. "Moida, you must try to eat. We have a lot more to do and we can't have you fainting from starvation."

"I'll try," Moida answered.

There was colour in her cheeks now and Ian thought, as he looked across at her, how pretty she was looking.

There were dark lines under her eyes and the same fear in her eyes which had been there all night; but she was no longer pale and trembling, and he knew that her vitality would carry her through whatever ordeals lay ahead.

At the same time he was well aware that she was suffering.

It was always the clever, imaginative people who suffered the worse in crises like this; and although he talked glibly about training oneself to face facts, he knew only too well how difficult it was and how easily terror could override common sense.

He was relieved to see that Moida was drinking her

tea and although she ate very little, she did manage a few mouthfuls.

He longed at that moment, as he had never longed before, to tell her how much he loved her and that whatever happened he would protect and keep her from all danger.

And yet he must bite back the words on his lips. He dared not say them. He was not free to do so and he would not offer Moida, whom he loved, anything but the very best, the very truest and the very highest of himself.

He finished his eggs and bacon and rose to his feet.

"I am going down to the village to telephone," he said. "I shall be as quick as I can."

"Thank you."

She rose, too and it seemed that they looked at each other for the first time since the night was passed and the daylight had come.

"I haven't said 'Thank you' have I?" she asked in a voice that trembled a little.

"There is not need to thank me yet," he said, and his tone was rough.

He dared not look at her. She was standing within arms' length, her mouth trembling, her eyes troubled, and yet with a faint colour on her tired little face.

He wanted to sweep her into his arms, he wanted to kiss away her fears; and because for the moment he did not trust himself, he turned abruptly towards the door and, hurrying through the hall, ran down the steps and got into the car outside.

He had already started the engine when a policeman on a motor bicycle came speeding round the corner. Ian knew before the man dismounted that it must be good news, and Moida, who had heard him arrive, came running down the steps.

"You've found him?" She hardly breathed the words, and yet the policeman heard them.

"It's a' richt, Miss," he said smiling. "One of our police cars has picked the bairn oop near Dunkeld.

They telephoned us and he'll be on his way hame the now."

"And he's safe?" Moida could hardly say the words through her tears—tears of relief which were flooding her eyes and running unchecked down her cheeks.

"Quite unhurt and not even frightened," was the report; "but he's hungry and I was to tell you he had lost his gun."

"This is wonderful news, Constable," Ian said, but he was looking not at the policeman but at Moida.

She was crying unashamedly, while her eyes shone like stars through her tears.

"I'll buy him a dozen guns," she cried. "Oh, thank God! Thank God!"

She turned to Ian as she spoke and he put his arm round her as if to steady her.

"It's all right now," he said.

"I know, that's why I'm crying."

She laughed as she spoke and turned again to the policeman.

"Thank you, thank you very much indeed for coming," she said, and, turning, ran back into the Castle and up the stairs to the nursery.

It was a dirty, untidy, but very over-excited Hamish who arrived at the Castle just before luncheon.

He jumped out of the police car and flung his arms round Moida who was waiting in the drive with Cathy, and having given her a quick kiss, disentangled himself from her embrace and ran to Ian.

"I couldn't catch them all by myself, Laird," he said, "but the policemen are going to catch them. They've asked me lots of questions and what I told them will make it easy to find the poachers, they are sure of it."

Ian looked over Hamish's head to the Inspector.

"Is this true?" he asked.

"I think so, Sir," the Inspector replied. "We've only got the Christian names of the men, of course; but the

251

description of the lorry is a help and the fact that the boy told us they stopped for a sandwich and a drink in the middle of the night. There aren't many cafés open and it should not be hard to get his description of them confirmed. Besides, we have a shrewd idea which butcher in Glasgow is dealing with poached venison."

"They are going to catch them for you, Laird," Hamish exclaimed, "and I did help, didn't I?"

"You've been an extremely brave and clever boy," Ian said, "and we are all very proud of you."

Cathy had been silent till now, but her natural feelings could be restrained no longer.

"You might have taken me with you, Hamish," she cried resentfully. "It was mean and horrid of you and I'll never forgive you, so there!"

"It was a jolly good thing you didn't come," Hamish said; "you'd have been frightened."

"I shouldn't!"

"Yes, you would. The men were rough. When they threw me out of the lorry, they scraped my knees—look!" He showed his grazed knees and Cathy's tender heart melted immediately.

"Poor Hamish! I am sorry. Does it hurt?" she asked.

"No, of course not!" Hamish replied. "Nothing hurts me, but it would have hurt you."

"Come upstairs and let me wash you," Moida said.

"Oh, no, Aunt Moida!" Hamish protested resentfully.

He was no longer a tough resisting pain, but only a little boy who didn't want to be washed, and Moida carried him away protestingly. She wondered, as she went, how Ian had contrived to be so tactful as to get both Beatrice and Lynette out of the way this morning.

It was almost as if he understood that she could not bear any more difficulties. Beatrice and Lynette had driven over to Arkrae Castle just before noon and Moida had seen neither of them.

"Tell us all about it, Hamish," Cathy was asking as

they climbed the stairs, "everything from the very beginning."

"I've told it lots and lots of times already," Hamish answered, "but I'll tell it again to you and Aunt Moida."

"I should hope so, indeed!" Moida exclaimed as they reached the nursery. "You have given us all a terrible fright, you know, Hamish."

"Were you frightened about me?" Hamish enquired. "I was quite all right, I had my gun." A spasm of pain crossed his face. "But I've lost it," he added.

"Yes, I know," Moida replied, "and I'll get you another one."

"Today?" Hamish asked.

"Not today, but tomorrow," Moida promised.

They had reached the nursery by now and Moida, crossing the room, led Hamish towards the bedroom.

"You must change your clothes," she said. "I've put a clean shirt out ready for you."

Cathy gave a sudden cry.

"Why, Aunt Moida, you've been packing," she said. "Are we going away?"

Moida turned hastily and looked over her shoulder to the nursery door—it was closed.

"Yes, Cathy," she answered. "We are going away this afternoon, but it's a big secret and you must tell nobody—do you promise?"

"Yes, I promise," Cathy said, "but why is it a secret?"

"I can't tell you now," Moida replied, "but you promise that you won't say a word about it, either of you?"

"I promise," Cathy repeated.

"All right," Hamish agreed.

Moida gave a little sigh; but the children, intent on their own interests, had no idea that it came from a misery and despair almost beyond words.

14

Ian awoke with a start to the sound of voices and realised that he had been asleep for some time.

He had sat down after luncheon in an armchair in front of the library fire and must have fallen into a deep sleep, dreamless and completely relaxing.

Now it took him a few seconds to remember what had happened or why he was here.

"I must be getting old," he thought to himself with a grimace. One night without sleep and here he was drowsing in front of the fire like an old man.

He got to his feet hastily, smoothing back his hair as the library door opened and Lynette came into the room followed by the Duke. Ian had not seen Lynette since the morning when she had informed him rather coldly that she and Beatrice were going over to Arkrae Castle for lunch.

It had been with a feeling of relief that he had heard the news. He had wanted to be with Moida when Hamish was brought back by the police, and he felt that Lynette, as a disinterested, if not a hostile spectator, would be only an embarrassment.

As he looked at her moving across the room towards him, her beauty struck him afresh, as if he were seeing her for the first time; and although he must admire it, for her sheer perfection of feature and colouring demanded it, he knew that personally it meant nothing to him any more.

How truly his old nurse had always remarked, when people praised his looks as a child, that beauty was only skin deep. He could remember the tartness in her voice as she said it.

Now he was prepared to admit what he would never have acknowledged in his childhood, that Nannie was right—for Lynette's beauty was only skin deep.

But he could only blame himself for not having discovered it sooner. Like any stage-struck youth of nineteen, he had been carried away by her loveliness into believing that he wished to spend the rest of his life in her company, listening to her platitudes, being appalled by the emptiness of her brain.

It was because he felt guilty and uncomfortable and ashamed of his own stupidity that Ian greeted Lynette with an effusiveness which was actually very far from an expression of his true feelings.

"I've been wondering when you would get back," he said. "I've missed you. What have you been doing? Have you enjoyed yourself?"

Lynette had reached his side by this time, but instead of looking at him she turned to the Duke and with a gesture that managed to be both dramatic and graceful at the same time, said.

"Tell him, Archie!"

Ian looked at his cousin expectantly, but the Duke was for the moment tongue-tied. If it were possible, he appeared more deprecating and insignificant than usual.

He seemed somehow to have shrunk; his bare knees beneath his kilt were pressed close against each other; he was pulling at his moustache; and his eyes, blue and watery, protruded as usual when he was agitated.

"What is it?" Ian asked after a pause.

Lynette gave a little cry.

"Archie! you promised!"

With an effort the Duke found his voice.

"Difficult thing to say," he muttered.

"What is?" Ian asked.

He glanced from Lynette to the Duke and back again.

"What has happened?" he asked apprehensively. "You haven't lost the heather again?"

The mere words seemed to galvanise the Duke into speech.

"Heather all right," he said hastily. "Success! No doubt. Castle's besieged by photographers. Lynette and I left by back door."

"Whatever for?" Ian enquired. "I thought you were enjoying the excitement."

"Lynette said . . ." the Duke began, and then was interrupted by Lynette herself.

"Archie! tell Ian!" she said impatiently.

The Duke's elation, which had been very obvious when he spoke of the blue heather, seemed to ebb away from him again. He shuffled from one foot to the other and then, almost pulling his moustache out by the roots, he said:

"Like this, old chap. Sorry, all that sort of thing. . . ." He came to a full stop.

"I must be peculiarly dense . . ." Ian began as Lynette turned to face him.

"Well, if Archie won't tell you," she said, "I must. We are going to be married. I'm sorry, Ian; but really I don't think you and I would be very happy together."

For a moment it was Ian's turn to be speechless. Any words which came to his lips seemed somehow inadequate to express his feelings or his surprise.

Then he saw what he fancied was an expression almost of spite in Lynette's beautiful eyes and knew that she was hoping that he was hurt and unhappy, wounded and distressed.

He had hurt her, he had damaged her pride and she would never forgive him for that. This was her revenge because he had neglected her for Moida and the children.

But he knew, too, that Lynette would not have been standing here telling him of her engagement if they had not restored that precious pot of blue heather to the Duke.

It was the publicity, the excitement, the thought that the blue heather was going to bring a great deal of money to its owner which, combined with the Ducal title, had been too much for the socially ambitious Lynette. And yet she was so beautiful that it was hard to think of her being mated with Archie—Duke though he might be.

For one moment Ian contemplated forbidding the marriage. He remembered how Lynette's lips had quivered beneath his kisses, how she had clung to him, how her breath had come quickly.

She loved him in her own way, he was sure of that, but love was not enough for her. She wanted so very much more than he could offer her.

"No, don't do it! You can't sell yourself that way!" he contemplated saying.

But he knew how ridiculous his words would sound and how little effect they would have. Lynette had made up her mind to become a duchess; she would doubtless make a success of it, and would be an outstandingly beautiful one.

"Look fine in the tiara," the Duke announced suddenly.

It was almost as if he had been able to read Ian's thoughts.

"You're right—she will," Ian agreed.

"I've treated you badly, I know," Lynette said softly, "but you must forgive me. We must still be great friends, and promise me that you will always go on helping and caring for Archie as you have in the past."

Ian had an impulse to applaud. Lynette was saying and doing the right thing like a good Girl Guide. And she did it very well, too, he thought.

She would be excellent at opening and closing

bazaars in just the same delightful manner, and would captivate everyone by her apparently deeply felt sincerity.

In spite of the fact that he knew she was playing to the gallery, Ian wanted to make things easy for her.

"Of course we will always be friends," he said, "and I hope you and Archie will be very happy together."

With the traditional gesture, Lynette slipped her engagement ring—a big blue-white diamond—from the third finger of her right hand, where she had been wearing it until the public announcement should allow her to put it on the correct finger.

"I'm sorry to give this back to you, Ian," she murmured, and there was no doubt that she was sincere in this.

"Keep it," he replied hastily; "let it be my first present to you on your engagement."

Lynette's eyes were alight with relief.

"Do you really mean that?" she asked. "Thank you, darling, you are always so generous."

She raised herself on tiptoe and kissed his cheek. Ian felt her lips soft and warm against his skin and knew it meant no more to him than if he had been kissed by old Mrs. Mackay.

"You mustn't mind my kissing Ian, Archie," Lynette said coyly to the Duke. "It's just a thank-you kiss for all his kindness to me and to you—to us, in fact."

"Glad everything all right," the Duke ejaculated.

The nervousness he obviously felt on entering the room was leaving him and now he seemed taller and more sure of himself.

"I think we ought to have a drink to celebrate this," Ian said, "and by the way, where's Mother?"

"We left her in the village. The car's going back for her. She wanted to telephone. . . ." Lynette hesitated.

". . . To the family to tell them the latest news," Ian finished with a grin.

"That's right; how did you guess?" Lynette asked.

258

"I have known my mother quite a long time," he answered.

The door opened and the butler stood there waiting for instructions.

"A bottle of champagne, please," Ian said.

"Very good, Sir."

The door closed again and Lynette put out her hands to the Duke.

"As Ian has been so kind and sweet, Archie dear, we can announce our engagement right away—tomorrow if you like. What is more, I've thought of the most wonderful idea. I shall have my bridesmaids all dressed in blue, the colour of your blue heather, and they can carry bunches of white orchids and white heather for luck. Don't you think that will be sensational?"

"Good idea," the Duke approved. "Keep people talking."

"That's what I thought," Lynette said. "Not that they won't be talking about the blue heather, and us, of course, for a very, very long time; but where the Press is concerned, every little helps to keep the ball rolling."

"Important chaps," the Duke commented.

Ian suppressed a desire to laugh out loud. How eminently suited to each other these two were. Both were supreme egotists, both were able to concentrate fiercely on themselves to the exclusion of everything else . . . and he was free!

The full importance of what this meant to him seared its way into his brain like a brilliant light, shining where before there had been only darkness.

He was free—free to tell Moida that he loved her; free to seek the one woman who he knew meant more to him than anyone else he had ever met in the whole of his life.

Moida! He wanted to go to her now, to waste no further time before he demolished the barriers which stood between them; but he knew he must do the conventional thing, he must drink Lynette's and Archie's health.

Impatiently he glanced at the door. It was taking a long time to bring a bottle of champagne.

He frowned unconsciously as he did so, and now he realised that Lynette had seen his expression and interpreted it in her own way. She laid a gentle hand on his arm.

"I know what you are thinking," she said in a low voice, "and believe me, I hate myself for having to hurt you. If only I could marry you both—I would be the happiest woman on earth."

"Don't think about it," Ian told her, and knew that she believed he was keeping a stiff upper lip and making light of his wounds.

He was excused from saying more because the champagne arrived. The cork was drawn with a gratifying bang, glasses were filled and handed to them on a silver salver.

"Thank you, that will be all," Ian said to the butler.

"Excuse me, Sir, but did you see the note on your desk?" he asked. "I brought it in earlier in the afternoon, but you were asleep."

"Note?" Ian enquired. "From whom?"

"Miss MacDonald, Sir."

"She gave you a note for me?" Ian enquired.

"Yes, Sir. Before she left. I brought it in right away, but I didn't like to wake you."

"Has Miss MacDonald gone?" Lynette asked, "and the children, too?"

"Yes, Miss. They left to catch the afternoon train from Brora."

"Well, that's really wonderful news," Lynette said with a little cry, "and, now the rooms are free, we can have the Featherstonehaughs after all. Your mother was longing to ask them, but didn't know where to put them."

She was speaking to Ian, but he had not heard one

word of what she said since the butler told him that Moida had left.

In two strides he crossed the room to the big, flat-topped writing-desk standing in the window. There was the note lying on top of the various other letters and papers.

He had never seen Moida's writing before; but he felt he would have known it because it was so individual, so unlike everyone else's.

Oblivious of Lynette's high chattering voice he tore open the envelope. There was a sheet of writing paper inside and enclosed with it another letter in a faded envelope, yellow and crumbling with age.

With a sense of apprehension such as he had never known before, Ian read what Moida had written.

I am going away today and taking the children with me. You will see from the enclosed how wrong I was in all I thought and believed. I found the letter in your great-uncle's Bible in the library.

For all I have said and for all I have done I can only ask you to forgive me and if possible to forget.

Thank you for all your kindness last night. Hamish is none the worse for his adventures.

> *Yours sincerely,*
> *Moida MacDonald.*

Ian read the letter through twice; then he looked at the aged envelope and drew out the letter it contained. He looked first at the date.

It was written in 1890 by his grandfather, Angus McCraggan, to his brother, Duncan. It spoke first of all of his engagement to Elizabeth, daughter of the Duke of Arkrae, and it went on to say that before he married he wanted to tell his brother something he had never breathed to any other member of the family, but in which he asked Duncan's help in case anything happened to him.

Angus McCraggan then wrote of his love for Ula

Holm. He told how he had met her quite by chance and then by intention, how he had pleaded with her to run away with him, and how finally she had consented.

He had asked her to marry him not once but a dozen times. He had loved her as he had not believed it possible to love anyone in the whole of his life, and she would hold first place in his heart until he died.

Had she lived, he believed he would have persuaded her to marry him; but even when she was about to have a child she had refused.

She was acutely conscious of the difference in their stations in life and though he had done everything to make her change her mind, she was adamant.

She was prepared to bear his son, but she would not take his name or ask him to introduce her to his friends and relations.

We were happy beyond words, Angus McCraggan wrote; *and because I loved her so deeply, I find it impossible to live alone with only my memories.*

He spoke then of the arrangements he had made for his son Malcolm. The people who were bringing him up would be kind to him and everything possible would be done to see that he was happy and properly educated.

If anything should happen to me, I look to you, Duncan, to carry on this sacred trust. Malcolm must be provided for; but it was Ula's wish that he should not know who his father is, and I must command you to respect her wishes, as I myself will carry out all those she laid upon me.

It was a long letter. Ian read it slowly, and when he had finished, he put it back in its envelope and took up Moida's letter again. No wonder it had been a shock to her, he thought.

This at least was conclusive evidence that he was the rightful heir to the Chieftainship and to Skaig, and yet he wished that he had found it himself so as to prepare her for the breakdown of all her ideas regarding injustice and treachery.

He wondered why Great-Uncle Duncan had never spoken to him of the matter and thought that perhaps the old man had waited his opportunity, believing that when the war was ended he must come again to Skaig.

It was like him, he thought, to have laid the paper in the family Bible rather than with the family papers.

But what was more important at the moment was not to worry about the letter, but to find Moida. With almost a sense of being disturbed he realised that Lynette and the Duke were in the room.

"I have to go out now," he said. "Tell Mother when she returns that, if I am not back to dinner or even for the night, she is not to worry."

"But where are you going?" Lynette enquired in astonishment.

Ian looked at her and suddenly a gay and irresponsible smile flashed across his face.

"The gentleman at the booking office is going to tell me that!" he replied.

Before Lynette could express her astonishment further, he had hurried from the room. It took him but a few minutes to have some things packed in a suitcase and his own car brought round to the front door.

There had been a faint mist blowing in from the sea earlier, but now, as he drove away from the Castle, the sun came out and the shifting lights on the hills were lovelier than he had ever known them.

Perhaps that was because his heart was singing, he thought, singing with joy and happiness because he was free to go and find Moida, to tell her of his love.

As he hoped, the booking clerk at Brora remembered a pretty girl with dark hair taking a single ticket for herself and two halves for the afternoon train.

"Edinburgh, Sir. That's where they were going."

"That's what I expected. Thank you very much."

"They would have to change at Inverness of course," the booking clerk called after him.

But Ian was already hurrying out of the station and back into his car, and now he settled down to drive faster than he had ever driven before, yet steadily and with a skill which never allowed him to take unnecessary risks.

He thought, as he went, that he should have anticipated that, even without finding the letter which had been written by his grandfather, Moida might have decided to leave the Castle.

He knew that her antagonism and hostility had gone, and he guessed that she would have found it impossible to remain there once she could no longer feel herself a crusader.

He cursed himself now for letting her out of his sight; but when the butler told him that luncheon was ready, he sent up a message to suggest that Moida and the children should eat with him, only to receive the reply that they had already finished their meal and were resting.

He had wanted to see Moida then, to talk with her, to suggest they did something together during the afternoon; but he thought it would have been selfish on his part to disturb her.

He imagined she would take the opportunity of catching up on the sleep she had lost during the night and the rest that she sorely needed after so much anxiety.

Instead, he had slept while Moida and the children had gone from the Castle, slipping away without his having the least idea of their intention. Now he felt fresh and alert as he travelled on and on, the big, swift car eating up the miles.

He stopped once to fill up with petrol and he bought a sandwich and a glass of beer at the local pub while the car was being attended to. It was eight o'clock when he stopped at a call box and rang up Dolly Durham at the Empire Theatre, Glasgow.

264

He gauged the time exactly right. She was in the theatre in her dressing-room.

"Hello. Who is it?" she asked and her voice came rich and warm down the telephone so that even at this distance Ian was conscious of her vital personality.

"It is Ian McCraggan," he said. "Do you remember me?"

"It would be difficult to forget you with the papers linking our names together," Dolly laughed. "How is Moida?"

"It is because of Moida that I am telephoning you," Ian replied. "She left my house today for Edinburgh, taking the children with her and I don't know where she's gone."

"Left, has she?" Dolly asked and Ian heard the curiosity in her tone.

"Listen, Miss Durham—or should I call you Mrs. MacDonald—I love Moida and I want to ask her to marry me."

"Good boy!" the words came promptly.

Then, quietly, in a voice that was very different from her theatrical one, Moida's mother said,

"I'm glad. Very, very glad. I liked you and I had the feeling when she was here that Moida had changed in some way. It wasn't anything I could put my finger on, but I know now that it was because she is in love. Take care of her and make her happy. She's worth it."

"I know that," Ian answered, "and I promise you that all I ask of life is that I may have the opportunity of looking after Moida."

There was a little pause; then he added,

"But I've lost her. Where shall I find her?"

"I'll give you the address of her rooms in Edinburgh," Dolly Durham said. "93 King George Street, but if she's got the children with her she won't go there. They are students' quarters—a kind of hostel—and they wouldn't take in children."

"Then would she go to a hotel?" Ian enquired, his

heart sinking. There were a great number of hotels in Edinburgh.

"Personally, I think she would go to the Palace," Dolly Durham said. "She's great friends with the house-keeper there. If Moida was worried or in trouble, she would go to see Mrs. Campbell. At any rate, that is the person who would be likely to know where she is."

"Thank you," Ian said. "Thank you a thousand times, and wish me luck!"

"Sure, luv. I wishes you everything you wishes your-self," Dolly said,

Now she was back to being her stage self again; but somehow Ian knew that she meant it and that her heart was pure gold through and through.

He hurried back to the car. Holyrood Palace—per-haps that, after all, was a fitting setting in which they should meet and plight their troth.

There was, it seemed to Ian, as he drove on, no incongruity in the thought of Murdoe MacDonald's daughter being brought up in the Palace of Holy-roodhouse.

All through the ages, the Palace had typified the spirit of Scotland. It had moved with the times, until, ancient and steeped in tradition, it was today a Palace, fit for a young and lovely Queen.

Ghostly with memories, it could still serve as a standard and symbol for the youth of the country. A Palace that had known love and beauty down the centuries, a Palace which had echoed with laughter as well as tears, with happiness as well as sorrow, a Palace ready for tomorrow, alive to the future even as it cradled the past.

Ian felt his spirits rising as he crossed the Firth of Forth by the ferry.

Through the mists he could see in mid-channel the little islet of Inchgarire, where one of his ancestors had assisted its owner, John Dundas, to build a fortress against the plundering of English pirates.

Prince Charles had visited the island and inspected

its fortifications during the Dunbar Campaign, but later it fell into ruins and eventually the debris was used to make concrete ballast for the Forth Bridge, the engineering wonder of a new age.

A mile or two down the road Ian saw the roofs and spires of Edinburgh and high above them the battlements of the Castle, bathed in moonlight.

There was something so beautiful, so awe-inspiring about the city under the star-strewn sky that Ian felt a sudden rush of pride that he was a Scot, here in the capital of his own land.

Then he was driving through the Old Town to the Palace. He passed through the great wrought iron gates at Canongate and came at length to a side door.

As he got out of the car, he was conscious of feeling not tired, as might be expected, or even a little dazed after the speed at which he had been travelling, but instead he was exhilarated and tense with an excitement which had something very youthful about it.

He was no longer sophisticated or experienced. He was no longer a diplomat, a Brigadier or a man who had headed a dozen international missions.

He was just a man in love, a man seeking the one woman in the world whom he wished to make his wife.

Mrs. Campbell was fat, smiling and white-haired.

"Yes, Moida MacDonald is here," she said, in answer to Ian's question. "She told me what a terrible time you had last night looking for young Hamish. The children are in bed this very instant and asleep I hope, and Moida's gone up to the State Rooms."

"She is all right?" Ian could not prevent the quick question slipping from his lips.

Mrs. Campbell nodded her head wisely.

"She was looking awfu' sad and white-faced when she arrived here, and was sair distressed about where she was to go with the children so late at night. 'We'll do all the looking that's necessary on the morrow,' I told her. 'In the meantime you'll stay with me. It may be a bit cramped, but there's a roof over your head and a warm hearth for your toes.' "

"Thank you for your kindness," Ian smiled.

"I'll go and tell her you're here," Mrs. Campbell said, and he knew by the look in her eyes that she guessed why he had come.

"One minute," he cried impulsively as she would have left the room. "Will you let me find her myself?"

Mrs. Campbell looked surprised.

"You'll not be after upsetting the poor bairn? It's my belief that her heart is aching already."

"I promise you I will not upset her. It's just that I wish to see the expression on her face when she first sees me."

He would know from the look in her eyes whether she loved him or not—he would trust Moida's expression rather than any words.

He felt that he could no longer countenance insincerity or be deceived into believing in love simply because a pair of beautiful lips spoke the words. Lynette had told him that she loved him, but it had not been a true or real love.

He had believed her and had forgotten that words are very poor vehicles to express the vacillations and emotions of the heart.

Love—what did it mean? Such a little word or such a tremendous one according to what one meant by it.

"I love you" a young man or a young woman could say nothing more momentous to each other, and yet it could also mean as little as a glass of champagne which would give a fleeting and transitory pleasure.

He must know this time. If Moida did not love him as he loved her, then their happiness was doomed from the very beginning.

For not the first time in his life Ian cursed the money which had embarrassed him as a schoolboy and which had been as often an encumbrance as a benefit all through his life. Money, titles, possessions—what did they mean in reality?

What mattered was if a man and a woman could come together in love and knew that the emotions they felt for each other were part of the Divine pattern of creation.

He must know the truth about himself and Moida. He felt his hands clenching and unclenching in his coat pocket. Mrs. Campbell was smiling at him.

"You will find Moida in Queen Mary's rooms," she said. "Look, I will show you how to get there."

She pointed to an ancient framed plan of the Palace, hanging on the wall. Ian followed her finger as she traced the way.

"Thank you, I feel sure I can find her," he said at length.

"And God bless you both," Mrs. Campbell murmured softly as he hurried from the cosy, well-lit sitting-room into the high passages which led him to the centre of the Royal building.

With but momentary hesitations he found the wrought iron stairway leading to the Historical Apartments.

Passing through the Picture Gallery with its portraits of one hundred and eleven Scottish Kings and the tapestry-hung Staterooms with their gilt and plaster ceilings, he came to the turnpike stair leading to the second floor, which had once housed the exquisite beauty of Scotland's Queen of Hearts.

Here, beneath the diamond-paned windows, torches had blazed as wild northern voices welcomed the nineteen-year-old widow.

And the rooms themselves, gay with painted heraldry and furnished with richly-embroidered chairs, seemed still impregnated with the tumultuous emotions of the past.

Yet violence and murder, treachery and bitterness, were not the only memories that lived in Holyrood. There were gaiety and courage, hope and love.

For Ian, moving swiftly through the empty rooms, some of them lit only by the moonlight streaming through the uncurtained windows, the atmosphere was pregnant with love—the young, ardent love of those who had not yet been disillusioned, the eager, excited love of those who had never been betrayed.

If he had never known it before, he knew now that love is eternal, unquenchable, a part of the Divine. For love in Holyrood had survived the mortal hearts which created it, and is still lived on.

And now at last Ian found whom he sought. Moida was standing in the Queen's Bedroom.

She stood very still and a little forlorn in a window recess beneath an old and tarnished mirror which had once reflected the face of Mary Stuart. But her eyes were closed and her lips moved in prayer.

Because his love gave him an intuition and understanding he had never had before, Ian knew that Moida was asking that she might face an empty and desolate future with the same courage that an unhappy Queen had shown four centuries earlier.

The room was lit and for a moment he stood silent in the doorway, watching her. He saw the sweet sadness of her soft mouth, the intensity of her small fingers clasped together as she prayed.

As if his presence communicated itself without the need of sound, she opened her eyes.

For a moment it seemed to Ian as if the expression in her face did not alter; and then, slowly, the crimson crept from her neck to her chin, to the exquisite curves of her cheek and up her white forehead to her hair.

One small hand crept to her breast, the other stretched out towards a chair as if she would steady herself.

"You!"

She hardly breathed the word; but now her eyes were round and shining, her lips parted in a sudden ecstasy, and he knew, as clearly as if a voice from Heaven itself had told him so, that she loved him.

"Why are . . . you . . . here?"

The question did not matter; it was the happiness flooding over her face which counted and which was as easy to discern as the blush which made her more beautiful than she had ever been before.

"Why did you run away?"

He wanted to catch her up in his arms, to waste no more time in talking, and yet at the same time he was savouring this moment, knowing that it was enchanted, as their eyes met and he saw that she was trembling.

"I had to go." She spoke very quietly. "I was so . . . ashamed, so . . . humiliated. I thought we had a right to move . . . into Skaig, you believe that . . . don't you?"

"Of course," he answered, "and you do have the right to live there, an absolute irrefutable right."

"No! You can't have read the letter, the letter I left behind for you!"

"I have read it," Ian replied, "and I'm glad that you found it. But not for the reasons that you imagine, not because Skaig belongs to me, but because now I can offer it to you, offer you Skaig for yourself, for Hamish and Cathy, too—and for our children, yours and mine, in the future."

His voice was low and deep as he spoke and slowly he went forward to take her hands and raise them to his lips.

"Moida, I love you," he said very gently. "I think you know that already. I love you and I am free to tell you so. And there is nothing to stop our being together. Let us get married quickly, darling, and go back to Skaig and make it our home—a real home—a home where nothing matters except love."

He felt her fingers quivering within his hold, her eyes were raised to his, searching his face, listening to what he said, trying to understand that this was not some amazing, wonderful dream from which she might awake.

"I love you." Ian said the words again and now his arms were round her and he was holding her very close.

"Aren't you going to answer me?" he asked. "Aren't you going to tell me that I am not mistaken, that I have found all that I sought and that you and I were made for each other? Moida? I must know the truth."

Then suddenly the tension which had held her spellbound broke and she gave a little inarticulate cry and hid her head against his shoulder.

"I'm . . . afraid," she whispered, "afraid that I am . . . dreaming. Did you really . . . say that you . . . love me?"

He slipped his fingers under her chin and turned her face to his.

"Shall I say it again?" he asked; but before she could reply, his mouth possessed hers.

It was a long kiss, a kiss that seemed to draw her very soul from between her lips and make it his.

They clung together. It was as if they had come through deep waters to find each other; then his arms tightened around her and her hands crept up against his neck, his lips grew passionate and more demanding.

They were each of them conscious of a flame rising within them, burning, consuming, devouring all their unhappiness, all their humiliations, destroying the dross and letting the golden glory of their happiness shine forth with an almost blinding light.

They were one, joined together for all time, man and woman made perfect for the moment by the Divinity within their own hearts.

After a long time Moida stirred, and moving a little within Ian's arms, looked up at him, her eyes alight, her face transfigured with sheer untrammelled happiness.

"I love . . . you," she whispered, "I love you, . . . darling, with . . . all my heart."

And this time Ian knew it was true and he had found the blue heather which all men seek and so few discover.